Murder be hanged

A secret night meeting at the eerie site of a moorland gibbet between Detective Superintendent George Rogers and an adolescent and unpleasant Willie Sloane, fearful of his stepfather's murderous intentions towards his mother, is coincidental with the firing of a pistol at her from the darkness of her garden.

Sloane's mother, Rachel Horsbrugh, head of the Schenck English Language School and believed to be a tranquillizer for younger deprived men, is interviewed by Rogers. Visibly shaken by the shots fired at her, she discloses that her second husband, Lieutenant-Colonel Henry Horsbrugh, a former officer cashiered from the Gurkha Rifles and suspected of a later disreputable past, had, before the shooting, unaccountably disappeared together with his small-bore pistol. Rogers, against his own wishes and in spite of what he fears to be the onset of a male menopause, feels physically attracted to her.

Involved in his ensuing investigation are Daniel Skinner, a blond way-back Saxon-type teacher with an unobliging girl-friend and a couple of undiscovered affairs with Mrs Horsbrugh and a fellow-teacher; the Colonel's unadvertised intimacy with married Primrose Booker and his earlier association with an elderly Lady Caroline de Vaugh, subsequently found drowned in her fishpond.

Assisted by his elegant second-in-command, Detective Chief Inspector David Lingard, and a much-too-attractive-for-comfort Woman Inspector Millier, Rogers untangles a confusion of guilt and murderousness involving three violent deaths, ending in a moonlit denouement holding within it a lethal menace against Rogers himself.

MURDER BE HANGED

Jonathan Ross

Constable · London

First published in Great Britain 1992
by Constable & Company Ltd
3 The Lanchesters, 162 Fulham Palace Road
London W6 9ER
Copyright © 1992 by Jonathan Ross
The right of Jonathan Ross to be
identified as the author of this work
has been asserted by him in accordance
with the Copyright, Designs and Patents Act 1988
ISBN 0 09 471770 2
Set in Palatino 10pt by
CentraCet Ltd, Cambridge
Printed in Great Britain by
St Edmundsbury Press Ltd
Bury St Edmunds, Suffolk

A CIP catalogue record for this book
is available from the British Library

1

Detective Superintendent George Rogers, refurbishing himself after a sandwich and coffee lunch in his office at County Police Headquarters, was of the opinion that were there such a condition as a male menopause then he was probably suffering its onset. None too sure of its symptoms, he hesitated to look them up in his copy of *Black's Medical Dictionary* in case they existed and were proven true. Were it not a premature menopause, then it must be what the medical bods were calling Yuppies' Flu, even though he could hardly be regarded as a yuppy. In either event, it seemed that he was over the hill and almost ready for the knacker's yard.

Though his forty-two years in the flesh were what he had hitherto regarded as too early for the ageing process to show itself, it had recently dawned on him that his long-standing and quite understandable interest in attractive women with black hair, slender throats and small breasts had uncharacteristically lost ground to a reawakened compulsion for knocking a golf ball around a tiring stretch of expensive real estate. In his work, he thought that he was becoming too easily irritated by the discovered incompetence of a few of his staff. Too, he suffered periods of depression – though with no hot flushes – as a probably delayed after-effect of his wife's divorcing him and his having to subsidize her and the man with whom she was apparently so expensively cohabiting with substantial outgoings from his salary.

Using the absent Assistant Chief Constable's washroom for his refurbishment, he looked hard in the mirror for any of the physically deteriorating changes he expected to descend on him like a blight. He thought that he saw signs of it in his deep brown eyes that had looked too often, too searchingly, at the sadness of the violently dead and the dishonestly dispossessed for him to have any belief in the alleged inner goodness of *Homo sapiens*. His beak-like nose suggested a certain inquisitorial thrustfulness, though with no signs of ageing's wear and tear, his black hair revealing only the beginning of dulling and the mouth showing a paradoxical amiable sternness, though little of the cynicism to which he thought it entitled. The whole face, swarthily skinned, normally showed no more than an impassive reserve; his defence against revealing what he considered to be an unprofessional sympathy and compassion or, otherwise, a withering contempt in the conduct of his investigations. He thought with some small justification that he bared his teeth more often in *bonhomie* than in anger.

His self-esteem was minimal and he was invariably surprised – an imagined 'Who, me?' and a looking behind himself to check that there hadn't been a mistake – when a woman displayed a sexual interest in him. And in his present indisposition, in what he considered to be his emptiness of response to attractive women, he believed with some priggish satisfaction that to fall completely and besottedly in love with one could be the most terrible thing which might happen to a man. Other than his own death of course, and this he qualified. Whether his customary wearing of dark-grey suits with white shirts and plain soft-hued silk ties reflected an aspect of his persona was nothing that had bothered his thinking.

When, generally uncomforted, he returned to his desk that was uncluttered by the papers of any current murder investigation, he pondered on the telephone call he had received earlier that day. The switchboard operator had then reiterated the caller's insistence on speaking to the head of the CID, and Rogers had accepted it.

'You are the chief of the detectives?' the voice had asked. It was an educated youngish voice, rather on the deep side and sounding not too sure of itself.

'Yes, my name is Rogers,' he had replied. 'Could I have yours, please?'

'Is this a confidential telephone line?'

The question had come awkwardly and Rogers said drily, 'It's not hooked on to the *Daily Echo*'s newsdesk if that's what you mean. Your name?'

'I'd rather not. Not yet. It would be risky.'

'It would? Tell me why?'

'Not now, please. When I see you.'

'All right. I take it you've something to tell me? To ask me?'

There had been long moments of humming silence, then, 'There's a man . . . I'm not certain, but I believe he intends harming the lady to whom he's married.'

'Harming her? In what way?'

His caller's swallowing had been audible. 'I believe he intends to kill her.'

'I see. While you needn't give me your reasons for believing it over the phone, it'll be necessary that you do so when I see you. You'll come here? I assume you live locally?'

'Yes, but I can't do that. I might be seen and recognized. And I don't want him to know I've spoken to the police.' There had been apprehension in his voice. 'It is quite important that I'm not identified in this.'

'You want us to meet in the middle of nowhere, I suppose?' Rogers had had experience of the reluctant informer, of the cagey and the downright secretive.

'Yes. You say where. I would prefer this evening after it's dark.'

'You've transport?'

'Yes.'

'You know where the Gibbet is?'

'Yes, of course.'

'Ten o'clock then, and please don't keep me waiting.'

He had replaced the receiver on its cradle, squinting his eyes at the early summer's sun streaming in lateral bars through the venetian blinds, feeling irritable at callers who sounded of dodgy purpose and showed a lack of self-confidence in not identifying themselves.

Now, in the relatively unbusy mean time, he thought he might get in a round of golf before it started to bucket down with rain. As it surely would once he had decided to take a little time off.

7

2

The clump of trees growing on the site of the long-gone gibbet occupied a prominence on the rising slope of Morte Moor. Rogers, having deliberately arrived twenty minutes early, stood waiting in the deeply shadowed fringe of the thick-boled beech trees, his parked car ticking its cooling engine below the clump. It was quiet but for the rustling of leaves in the soft night wind, only just audible small animal and insect noises in the under-growth and the mechanical whining of traffic passing below him.

Rogers, occasionally sensitive to the ambience of particular places, thought that something of what had been the dreadful-ness enacted on the gibbet in the past still lingered there. With the huge cyanosed globe of a risen moon giving the luminous landscape an unsettling eeriness, it was no place for the over-imaginative to dwell on the grisly hideousness of strangled deaths, of pitch-covered bodies hung in chains or iron frames, of the lonely blackened horrors that were warnings of a barbaric justice to passers-by. He tried instead to think of his round of golf which hadn't been all that much of a diversion. It hadn't rained, but it had been swelteringly hot and his calf-muscles had taken a beating from dragging a trolley of heavy ironware in his six thousand or so yards' exhausting pursuit of a tiny white ball. Before the onset of whatever it was wrong with his mating instincts, he knew that he would have been employing his mind more pleasurably in thinking about attractive women.

At eleven minutes before the time of his appointment, he heard the whinnying tinny sound of a car's engine being used in fits and starts somewhere adjacent to the entrance to the track below him, then being switched off to silence. This hadn't surprised Rogers, for he had anticipated it. The nature of the telephone call from the anonymous informant had smelled strongly of the wary secrecy that made natural the precaution of leaving his car concealed and walking to the Gibbet to check that the detective would be on his own at their meeting.

Rogers heard the approaching footfalls first, then saw clearly in the moonlight a tall well-built figure with an odd thick-necked loutishness about it climbing the slope of the track. When within a few feet of where the shadowed detective stood motionless, the youth – plainly an as yet immature male – paused and looked around him. Dressed in a linen jacket and dark trousers with an open-neck coloured shirt, he wore peculiarly a panama-style hat that appeared to come down to his eyebrows. Below them, the lenses of his tinted spectacles reflected the moonshine that gave his partly shadowed features a livid cast. What he could see of the face – it had in it a suggestion of not-yet-gone puppy fat – made him guess his age to be about eighteen years.

'I'm here,' Rogers called softly, smiling inwardly at the youth's startled reaction to his voice. He moved out from the shadows to meet him.

The not quite composed youth narrowed his eyes as if focusing at him from behind the spectacles. 'You are Mr Rogers?' he asked in his remembered voice. In the flesh he sounded a could-be truculent character with his voice pitched lower than it might naturally be. 'You're on your own?'

'Manifestly,' Rogers said drily. 'Now you are here, perhaps you'll introduce yourself?'

'My name's Sloane. Willie Sloane.'

'Just that?'

'Yes. What's wrong with it?'

'Nothing. Your address, please.'

'The Lodge, Tower House, Kingfisher Avenue.'

'At Spaniard's Rise?' Rogers asked. That, he knew, was in an up-market area giving way grudgingly to the ingress of the more respectable and profession businesses. 'Good,' he said when the youth had agreed. 'May we now get down to considering the details of the complaint you made to me this afternoon? Who do you believe intends to kill whom, and why and how?'

'Do I have your promise of confidentiality?' Sloane looked anxious.

9

'No, you do not.' Rogers was necessarily uncompromising. 'You've made a very serious allegation against another person which I'm bound to investigate and which may have a conclusion requiring you to give evidence in a court. *May*, I said. I don't know enough yet to advise you either way. Even if it mattered.'

'You mean that I now have to tell you? Despite the possibility that I may be identified?' There had been an indication of irresolution in his voice and he turned his face away from Rogers, though not enough to wholly conceal the anxiety it was showing. 'In this particular case it would make my life unbearable, I couldn't stay here.'

Rogers put sternness in his words. 'You've told me that you believe a woman is in danger of being killed. You said it, I assume, of your own volition and not because you were forced to. Now you've to carry it through. If you're right in your belief or suspicion, time's being wasted which might be fatal for her.'

Sloane held fingers over his chin, staring at the ground in thought. 'I'm sorry,' he said. 'Of course it is.' He hesitated as if searching for words. 'If I tell you that I'm talking about my own mother and her husband who calls himself my stepfather I hope that you'll understand my need for confidentiality. At least, until he's caught.'

'Ah!' Rogers stared at him curiously. 'I do understand, naturally I do.' Nevertheless, he prepared himself for the probable exaggerations and misconceived conclusions that seemed inevitable when *Homo sapiens* chose to complain of, or make accusations against, close relatives. 'I make no promises, but should the information you give me prove ill-founded or mistaken, it'll go no further. In that event, you will not be involved or identified unless you yourself are a party to an illegality.' He made his voice persuasive against the doubts showing in the youth's face. 'Look at it like this. You've committed yourself now and you've explanations to make to me of one sort or another. So tell me in sufficient detail for me to take whatever action I may consider is necessary.'

Waiting for him to start – he was silent, apparently putting his thoughts in order – Rogers stuffed tobacco into the decidedly expensive meerschaum pipe he had persuaded himself was a

10

good and necessary buy and lit it, studying intently the worried-looking face as he did so.

He started with his arms folded across his chest, appearing to aim his words at Rogers's tie. 'First of all, I do apologize for not giving my name when I called you and I hope you'll now understand why.' He rather overemphasized it, making it sound as though he had committed the biblical abominable crime, blinking his eyes afte removing his spectacles and putting them in the breast pocket of his jacket. Then he made a token gesture in lifting his hat and returning it to his head, having exposed an unruly mop of hair. 'I don't normally wear either of these things,' he said.

'A disguise?' Rogers said, mildly amused. 'Not, I think, a particularly good one if it's your stepfather you wish to decieve.'

'I'm sorry.' He sounded deflated. 'I really didn't know whether I'd be followed.'

'You were about to tell me of your mother being in danger.'

'Yes, I'm sorry,' he apologized again. 'I'm really not used to this sort of thing. My mother married a Lieutenant-Colonel Horsbrugh two years ago. Until her marriage, which I have never understood and thought was a mistake from the begin-ning, I had lived at home – that is, at Tower House which belongs to my mother – though I've been mostly away at school. Just before the marriage it was decided that it was better that I moved into the Lodge which was unoccupied at the time. This was convenient for me, for during Vac it meant that I could remain close to mother in the event that she might need me. I do try and visit her regularly, and more often naturally when I know that Colonel Horsbrugh is not there.'

He lifted his head to meet Rogers's steady gaze, chewing on his bottom lip in noticeable irresolution. 'During the Short Vac in December I noticed that my mother and her husband were quarrelling and that he was making her unhappy.' Sloane's breathing sounded troubled and he repeatedly licked his lips. 'Worse than that, I came in one evening and heard him shouting at her that he had had nothing from her but trouble. He was furious, swearing vilely and threatening her, saying that she had tricked him and had spoiled his life, that he had given her everything he possibly could for no return.'

11

'It put you in an awkward position, I imagine?' Rogers suggested. 'Did you become involved?'

Sloane turned his gaze from him, wincing at some inner unhappiness. 'I wanted to be. I would have too, but I was outside the room when I heard it and I knew it would be a terrible mistake, an unforgivable intrusion, to go in then, though I regretted it later. I have to say that mother sounded quite angry herself, accusing him in turn, I thought, of having an affair with some woman, though whether before their marriage or not I can't say. When I couldn't make up my mind about what to do, I returned to the Lodge without them knowing what I'd heard and tried to forget it.' He paused, looking, Rogers thought, rather bereft for a youth of his size, for his build suggested the well-muscled strength of an athlete.

'Probably for the best,' the more wordly Rogers agreed, knowing of the dangers inherent in taking sides in a domestic dispute. He breathed out aromatic tobacco smoke that drifted like silver floss against the night sky. 'There's more about Colonel Horsbrugh, of course?' he pressed him.

'Yes. When I needed to visit mother, I did it only after making sure that he was out; that way to avoid any unpleasantness. On another occasion a month ago when I thought he'd gone out for the evening, I heard from outside one of the sitting-room windows him and mother fighting again. He said among some quite rotten abuse, 'For Christ's sake get off my back. Don't push me or it'll be the last thing you'll ever do. Just shut up.' That's as near as I can remember it,' he said apologetically, 'and he did sound as if he meant it.' He hesitated for a moment or two. 'I do know that he has a gun in a metal box he keeps in his study.'

'You've seen it?' Roger's back was beginning to ache and, were it not for the imagined possibility of being discovered at night in his parked car with a youthful Sloane, inevitably giving rise to the most horrendous suspicions which didn't bear thinking about, he would have chosen the comfort of the car's interior in which to do his questioning.

Sloane hesitated. 'It sounds sneaky, I know, but I did go there one evening when he and mother were out. It's supposed to be locked up, but isn't. It's a gun with a long barrel and

12

funny-shaped butt – or is it the handle?' He was deeply apologetic again. 'I'm dreadfully sorry, but I'm not familiar with guns . . . I don't like them enough to be interested.'

'You're believing he might use it on your mother?'

'Am I?' He shook his head. 'I don't know. Not for sure, anyway. But he might, and if he did I could never forgive myself . . .' His voice shook. 'Never. Absolutely never.'

'For all that, it isn't much to prompt an investigation into an intent to murder, is it? Offhand, I don't believe that an intent to commit anything but treason is a criminal offence, and nothing of what you've told me amounts to an attempt to further imprecise verbal threats into action.' He didn't know why – for he had so far heard was only a little more than a commonplace domestic discord between seemingly unpleasant people – but something in the manner of Sloane's telling it was causing him a niggle of professional disquiet. 'Is there nothing else?'

'There was an incident long before I knew he was threatening mother. This was at the end of last summer's Long Vac. I heard him go out in his car one evening and decided to call on mother. I entered the house by the kitchen door, which I usually do for convenience, and found that one of the cooker's jets was on and unlit under an empty saucepan, and the kitchen full of gas. I turned it off and did everything that was necessary to get rid of the gas, telling mother, who was in the sitting-room, quite sharply to please be careful with gas because with her being a cigarette smoker it could lead to a disaster. She said that her husband must have left it on because she definitely hadn't, not having been in the kitchen for two hours at least and then not to use the cooker. I believed her – I still do – for she is far from being a forgetful person. It wasn't until recently that I remembered the incident and realized how it could tie in with his threats to mother later on.'

Rogers allowed his doubts to show. 'It's a pretty thin circumstance to pin on anybody. Have you spoken to her about it?'

Sloane's face showed agitation. 'I couldn't. How could I? I mean, one doesn't. It would be too embarrassing, too shaming, for her to know that I'd heard what he said to her . . . what I suspected.'

Rogers, applying a match to his gone-out pipe, examined in

his mind what he knew of the law of intent to commit an arrestable offence, which was nothing, and its attempt if it was supported by nothing at all. He said, 'Considering that you require me to respect your confidences and that there's no positive evidence of an offence having been committed, what do you imagine I can do?' He shook his head, answering his own question. 'Nothing very much. To interview your step-father could result only in my making a bloody idiot of myself with a possible extremely expensive slander suit made against me as a bonus, which you're unlikely to volunteer to pay. Further, in doing it, I would amost certainly inadvertently expose you as the source of my information.'

'Can't you put a watch on him? It's my mother's life that's at risk.' He was an oddly Edwardian-looking figure in the black-shadowed cyanosed-blue quietness, starting a sideways jerking movement of his body, shifting his weight from one foot to the other. '*Please*, Mr Rogers.'

'I can't promise you that either, for it isn't effectively poss-ible,' he said with what he believed to be sweet reasonableness, though feeling that he was being distinctly unhelpful. 'Not with a person in his own home. Even if the gas cooker business has the significance you give it, no police surveillance that didn't involve looking through kitchen windows day and night would have been able to prevent it. And whatever you may believe, continued close surveillance is virtually impossible to maintain undiscovered.'

'I see,' Sloane muttered, his voice lifeless. 'I'm sorry I've wasted your time.'

'You haven't,' Rogers assured him, relighting his pipe which was proving fractious and wasteful of matches. His intuition – wayward and occasionally equally fractious – was telling him that something nasty might be on the simmer in the Horsbrugh household. There had been a degree of conviction in Sloane's manner and in his words and that, in Rogers's opinion, under-lined what he had told him. 'I haven't said I'll do nothing. I shall do what I can within the limits of the information you've given me, and it'll be helpful if you'll answer a question or two. You agree?'

Sloane's prominent larynx jerked and he nodded, though his attitude spelled out wariness.

'Tell me what you know of Colonel Horsbrugh.'

'Being away most of the time and not being too friendly with him anyway, I'm afraid I know very little. It's stupid, isn't it, but my mother met him at the Thurnholme Bay Sailing Club where she occasionally crews a friend's yacht and she told me nothing until she broke it to me by letter that she was to marry him.' For a moment his features tightened in resentment. 'That wasn't too much out of character for mother, for father's been dead for some time and she does have a life to lead of her own. I do know that this man served in the Gurkha Brigade abroad – I believe Hong Kong – and had retired or whatever it is that he did Christ knows how long ago. He's older than mother, much older, and he's managed to persuade her that he's capable of acting as her Director of Studies.' He sounded bitter. 'It's mother's business and thank God she's had enough common sense not to have had him as a partner.'

'Your mother's in business?' Rogers interrupted him.

'Yes.' He clearly thought that the detective would have known that. 'She owns the Schenck English Language School.'

'I've heard of it,' Rogers lied. 'Carry on about Colonel Horsbrugh.'

'I won't make any secret of it, but he doesn't like me and I don't like him. He's a crude and vulgar man who once told me to my face that I was an undisciplined . . . well, that I was undisciplined in my living habits. As if he knew anyway. He resents, I'm positive, my staying in the Lodge and even having frequent contact with mother. Seeing that I'm her son and nothing to do with him, his attitude's completely unreasonable. I don't think he's quite normal.'

'You mean he's mentally unbalanced?' Rogers asked.

Sloane was clearly not going that far. 'I don't know. He's a frightening man if contradicted, even quite reasonably, or when something's done of which he doesn't approve. He gets into the most frightful tizzies; most often when he's been drinking.'

'He was a bachelor? Or married before?'

'I'm sure married before, but whether he divorced his wife or she died, I don't know.'

'You said you didn't like him. Is that partly because he doesn't approve of you?'

Sloane's eyes reflected moonlight as his head turned sharply to the detective. 'I dislike him only for what he's done and is doing to my mother,' he said with no heat in his voice at all.

'Describe him to me,' Rogers demanded. 'His full name, age, build and height, hair colour, type of clothing usually worn and anything unusual by which we can identify him.'

'His name's Henry Fraser Horsbrugh and he's sixty or maybe more. He's five feet five or six inches and a bit on the scrawny side, and his skin looks tanned. His hair's grey and so is his moustache.' He shrugged his shoulders. 'He wears ordinary clothes, nothing very special. Never a hat. He does have a monocle, but apparently only for reading when he's away from home and hasn't his glasses. Is that enough?'

'Has he a car?'

'Yes, a very old grey Rover.' There was a touch of mockery in his words. 'It's in a garage – I don't know which one – being repaired or serviced or something and he's using mother's.'

'Which is?'

'A white Toyota coupé. That isn't important because it's still with mother.' He was showing signs of restlessness. 'May I go now, please? I've told you all I know and I should get back to her.'

'In a moment,' Rogers said. He tapped ashes from his pipe against the heel of his shoe, making Sloane wait for the time it took him. 'You haven't told me anything about yourself.'

Sloane was surprised and he showed irritability. 'Does that matter?'

Rogers raised his eyebrows. 'It might. All I know is that you appear to be a student. Don't you wish to tell me?'

'I've no reason not to and there isn't much anyway. I'm in my second senior year at St Wulfric's School and studying for my A levels.'

'Your age?'

'Nearly eighteen.'

'And your car? The one you came in?'

Sloane was manifestly holding back a show of irritated impatience. 'It's an orange Beetle. Now may I go?'

'Yes, of course you may.' Rogers put on a look of surprise as though that had been Sloane's first intimation that he wished to. 'Just one thing. If you have access to a recent photograph of Colonel Horsbrugh I'd be grateful if you'd post it to me or deliver it at the police station. In the middle of the night if it helps you, and as soon as you possibly can.'

'You are going to do something about this, then?' Sloane asked.

'Or course.' Rogers gave him an encouraging smile. 'Get in touch if you have anything further to tell me. I shall certainly be in touch with you in any case.'

Rogers watched him as he returned down the path, thinking that he had carried his need for secrecy to excess with his spectacles and his no doubt borrowed hat. Had he been expecting his choleric stepfather to be following him? Or somebody else? To anybody knowing him, his disguise would have meant nothing had he driven his own car – and he had, he was sure – to the meeting.

To his own irritation, he wasn't sure how to treat Sloane's allegations. Neither was he wholly happy about the reason for them. In his experience of the breed, retired half-colonels – even the more irascible of them – confined their instincts to violence to the shooting of small birds and rabbits and in barking their concept of personal discipline at non-military incompetents.

3

In Rogers's opinion the apartment to which, following his interview with Sloane, he now returned had been designed for mini-pygmies having a mania for occupying depressing square-shaped rooms sandwiched above and below by identical square-shaped rooms. After his divorce – his ex-wife's capacity for closing the gate to him, yet opening it to others, still giving him something of a so far indefinable complex – circumstances had forced him to rent it, a pro tem arrangement that slid unnoticed by a much too occupied man into a vague kind of permanency.

17

Provided that on earlier occasions he had restricted his female visitors to those of less than hippopotamus size, the smallness of his habitat had ceased to bother him, even less so now in his new-found disinterest.

Whatever there was of it was kept in good order by his thrice-weekly cleaning lady who was elderly, short of breath, smelling nicely of wax polish and being only an ounce or two short of an average hippopotamus's weight. He had long known without any particular rancour that she had regularly interested herself in the papers he kept in his unlockable bureau. Because she was a good cleaner and a woman he liked he put up with it, but he fabricated and planted all manner of improbable and outrageous handwritten letters and carbon copies for her to read, creating a fictitious background somewhat in the manner of a few villainous customers he had investigated in the past.

One series of letters referred to a quite torrid affair he was supposed to be having with a fictitious viscountess whose husband, the owner of a brace of Purdey shotguns, was showing signs of suspecting what was going on in the Long Gallery during his bird-shooting absences on the moors. Another fabrication was the signed number two page of a letter purporting to come from the President of the United States inviting him to join the next NASA Shuttle flight as the Chief Security Officer for Space and its Adjacent Environment. He was not without a sardonic sense of humour and it amused him that, should he happen to be present when she was cleaning, she invariable managed to keep a chair or a table as a barrier between them.

Switching on the telephone answering machine which he hated but which had been installed on the persuasion of his Chief Constable, he began to pour himself a generous undiluted single malt in preparation for a shower and bed. With his tumbler held poised on its way to his mouth he almost disbelievingly heard the duty chief inspector telling him that an emergency call from a woman had been received at Headquarters at 10.14 p.m. to the effect that two gunshots had been fired on the premises of Tower House, the residence of a Mrs Rachel Horsbrugh. There was no report of injuries and Detective Sergeant Tomkin and WDC Witheridge were attending.

Rogers looked at his wrist-watch. It read twenty minutes past eleven and time must now be pushing him. Several unhappinesses entered his mind, the most grinding of them being the recollection of his general unwillingness to accept wholly the seriousness or Sloane's suspicions of murder about to be committed. He would justify or qualify it later, he knew, but at the moment it gave him a reason with which to beat himself.

When he thought about driving his car and the offchance of being required to blow into a breathalyser, he said, 'Sod it!' and put down reluctantly the single malt he had been about to drink. He felt that he was leading a dog's life – a probably neutered one at that – and it was of no comfort to him that the moon had now been obscured by clouds that were already dropping rain on the street outside.

4

The rain rained on Spaniard's Rise, a lush residential area of large houses, as much as it did on the lesser, grimier areas of the town. In particular it drummed heavily on the roof of Rogers's car as he entered Kingfisher Avenue. Its road surface, seen through water streaming down the windscreen, illuminated by his headlights and by the occasional flash of electric-blue lightning, glistened tar black. Thunder reverberated across the heavily clouded sky. Seeing the nondescript CID utility wagon and the area patrol car parked outside a stone-pillared gate, Rogers pulled in behind them, turning up the collar of his trench coat and climbing out into the wetness.

The wrought-iron double gate opening on to a gravelled drive had at its side a small compact stone building in pseudo rococo style, being obviously what Sloane had referred to as the Lodge. It was overshadowed by a large dripping tree and only God would know what Victorian or Edwardian ambition had impelled its building. A cursory glance by the getting wet Rogers as he hastened through the gate suggested that if it contained two rooms they must of necessity be proportionate in size to the narrow door and the tiny roundel windows from which lights shone. It couldn't have a garage, for an orange Volkswagen – presumbly Sloane's – was parked in an opening in the shrubbery at its side.

The building called Tower House loomed blackly above him as he approached the over-elaborate stepped porch. A three-storeyed tower built on one side of the main building showed lights in its lower and uppermost windows. The main building, also of three storeys, its bulk softened by an overlay of creeper that glistened fitfully in whatever faint illumination reached it, had lights burning only in its ground-floor rooms. The unlit porch was no protection against the driving rain, and a wet, impatient and irritable Rogers, having pulled at a large brass knob without an immediate response, pushed down on the handle of the panelled door and walked into a box-shaped lighted hallway. There was a door in front of him and one at his side. Attached to the door at his side was a notice-board stating in gold lettering on a green background that it was the entrance to the Schenck English Language School.

Having waited too long, Rogers was about to bang on the inner door with his fist when it was opened by a uniformed WPC; a large, well-built and self-confident woman who made it plain that she was nobody to worry over-much about a frown from an irritated detective superintendent. 'In there, sir,' she said with a rebuke in her strong voice, indicating an open door near the end of a passage behind her. 'They've been waiting for you.'

Rogers, though no man to be chided by forceful women, especially one who appeared to regard him with distaste, was content to say, 'So be it. It's supposed to be good for the soul.' He now remembered that her name was Doust, that she was an area patrol driver and was married to some presumably unfortunate bugger in the lower ranks of the force. He shrugged himself from his dripping raincoat and said, 'Find somewhere to hang that, please, and when you've done it get on your radio and have Sergeant Magnus report to me here straight away.' One of the names of the game was anticipation, and he knew that he would need Magnus, the finder of the driblet, the snippet, the microscopic speck of evidence that would escape the eye of any less meticulous searcher.

It was a spacious room with a lofty decorated ceiling that he entered. The windows were tall with elderly faded velvet side drapes and semitransparent gauze curtains. The room was made a civilized retreat by its furnishings: a long and plushy tapestry-covered sofa and matching tall-backed wing chairs – one of which had been covered with a blue bedsheet – mahogany sitting-room furniture that gleamed redly in the soft light given out from wall and standard lamps, and comfortable-looking well-trodden carpets over polished wooden flooring. Standing four-legged near the draped chair was a large cube-shaped object which had been similarly covered.

The young Sloane who, on Rogers's entry into the room, had given him an almost imperceptible warning shake of the head, was seated on the sofa with a comforting arm around the shoulders of a woman who could be no other than his mother. At her feet lay a black cocker spaniel, greeting his approach with a wagging tail. Detective Sergeant Tomlin, who had risen from his chair on seeing Rogers, held a notebook and ballpen in his hands.

Rogers gave a damp smile of sorts and said 'Good evening' to the two on the sofa. 'I'm Detective Superintendent Rogers,' he said, 'and I'm sorry if I've kept you waiting.'

Sloane said, 'This is my mother, Mr Rogers. She's had a most frightening experience and I do think that she should go to bed as soon as possible.'

Nodding at Mrs Horsbrugh and smiling in a less formal greeting this time, Rogers studied her. His preconception of her – God only knew how he had arrived at it – had been that of a schoolmistressy sort of woman, possibly wearing a dark suit and a white shirt over an ample behind and a barrel stomach with her hair fashioned in a severe chignon.

He admitted to himself that he couldn't have been more in error. Seated, she was manifestly a tall woman with a lean, almost featureless body dressed in a slip of a white dress of flawless simplicity that exposed a long length of bare tanned legs. Her hair, a glossy Japanese black, was worn short, her tight-fleshed face coffee-brown from exposure to the sun, the over-lipsticked mouth generously sensual. Her mascara'd eyes – he thought he could read a sad cynicism in them – were a bright chocolate brown in her regard of him from below lids shadowed a deep woad-blue. Despite, in his opinion, her not possessing a classic beauty and being overmade-up, despite her present appearance of highly strung tautness, there was palpably an aura of a strong sexual attraction about her. Her appearance reminded him uncomfortably of a less blatantly sexual Liz Gallagher from whose capricious affections he had so recently been parted. It wasn't, he thought, the kind of start to an investigation he needed.

He said, 'While I appreciate that you've probably told Sergeant Tomlin what has happened, Mrs Horsbrugh, it would be helpful if you'd give me the essential details now so that I may consider anything arising from them.'

'Are you able, mother?' Sloane said solicitously, squeezing her with his arm. 'You're sure?'

'Don't fuss, Willie dear,' she answered him with an accent that could only have been cultivated in a top drawer school. 'I'm quite capable.' Her mouth, not her eyes, smiled at Rogers, showing her beautifully kept teeth. 'Of course I will. I'm quite all right now.'

'Thank you,' he said, accepting that her appearance of being highly strung might be a normal expression of her personality. 'I'd prefer that I spoke to you alone. If your son could go to another room with Sergeant Tomlin to make his statement I'd be obliged.' He spoke to Sloane, who had already released his hold on her. 'I'll not upset your mother, I promise you.' To Tomlin, he said, 'Is there anything you wish to say that won't keep for a few minutes, sergeant?'

'Only that Colonel Horsbrugh hasn't returned home yet. And that WDC Witheridge is in the tower interviewing Mr Skinner.'

There was an awkward silence from the sofa that seemed to hang leadenly in the air while Rogers waited for Sloane and Tomlin to leave, though Sloane showed no sign of appreciating that he was being pushed out away from his mother.

With WPC Doust entering the room as the two men left, Rogers pointed a finger at a chair standing against a far wall as an indication that she should sit on it and not butt in without being asked.

He pulled one of the high-back chairs reasonably close to Mrs Horsbrugh and sat in it, smiling amiably at her and thinking it politic to include the spaniel in his smile. He said, 'Will you accept that I know almost nothing – which is true – of what led to your making an emergency call to us this evening, and tell me what led you to do so?'

She was apparently a woman who fixed a person she spoke to with an undeviating stare from the deep-brown eyes and this promised to disconcert the detective. 'There isn't a lot to tell,' she said. Despite her earlier assertion, there seemed to be an underlying shakiness in her voice. 'It was all over in a second and Willie tells me . . . I honestly can't believe it.'

'There were two shots,' he prompted her. 'From where were they fired?'

She turned her head to one of the windows behind her. 'The garden,' she said. 'I'd left the drink I'd poured for myself on the sideboard when I was about to watch the late night news.' She indicated a massive mahogany sideboard in a corner near the window farthest from them. 'While I was getting it, two horrible bangs came from outside, terrifying me. I was so shocked . . . I saw afterwards that the television set had exploded, but when it happened my first reaction was that somebody was trying to kill me. Bessie had been sitting at the side of the chair I use and she had been frightened as well.' She reached down, smoothing the spaniel's head with her thin fingers. 'I waited, hiding behind the table over there, mainly because I was too petrified to do anything else.' She gave a nervously derisive laugh. 'I'm not very brave, am I? After a while, when nothing more happened, I crawled over to the telephone and dialled the emergency number. Then Mr Skinner came in and we stayed here until the policewoman arrived and then the detectives.'

'Was the chair hit as well?' Rogers hadn't somehow been able to visualize the elegant Mrs Horsbrugh crawling on the floor with all dignity fled.

'I didn't know until Mr Tomlin told me. He asked for bedsheets to cover it and the television set.'

23

'Would that be the chair you were about to use?'

She nodded. 'Yes, I was going to.'

'And was its back to the windows?'

She nodded again. 'To the middle one.'

'I see the glass is unbroken. It was open?' Rain was still rattling against the windows and through them came an occasional flash of lightning followed by the rumble of distant thunder.

'Yes. Willie closed it when he came home. It didn't begin raining until afterwards.'

'Does anyone other than yourself use that particular chair?'

She bit at her lower lip before replying. 'Yes. Willie does occasionally, and my husband often.'

'Would there be anybody with a reason for trying to kill you, Mrs Horsbrugh?' he asked gently.

The flesh over her cheekbones tightened, her eyes dropping to narrow hands resting on her thighs. 'No,' she whispered. 'I cannot imagine why. Or who would.'

'But you did say that you believed someone was trying to kill you in particular, not somebody else.'

'I said it because that is the chair I usually sit in.' She shivered. 'The one I would have been in had I not forgotten my drink.'

'And you usually look in on the late night news?'

'Yes. Invariably.'

'And what time does it come on?' He knew, but that wasn't the point.

'At ten.'

Here cometh the awkward part, he thought. He would now have to dissemble somewhat in order not to expose her son. Unless she were abysmally dense she was going to realize that he, Rogers, had arrived at the scene knowing more about her and her ménage than a first visit would explain. He smiled encouragingly and said, 'Sergeant Tomlin mentioned something about your husband not having returned home.' He looked at his wrist-watch. It had passed midnight. 'Are you expecting him?'

There was a sustained silence from her during which he felt free to wonder why she – a woman whose very thinness would in normal circumstances have animated in him, and presumably

24

in some other men who didn't measure attractiveness by weight, a strong sexual attraction – had married a man who would probably be the scrawny exhausted old man of sixty-plus her son had described to him. Unless, of course, his age was outweighed by his money or his social position. Also, and distinctly unfairly, she was wearing a scent which was threatening through his nostrils to stimulate what he thought of as his baser instincts.

When she spoke she turned her head to look briefly at the silent but listening Doust, though not before Rogers had seen pain in her eyes. 'This is an embarrassment,' she said hesitatingly, lowering her voice, 'But I haven't seen or spoken to him since he left the house this morning. And before we go any further, I must tell you that he has been my husband only for the past two years.'

'I see,' Rogers said, his face expressing nothing. 'You're saying that his being absent isn't the norm?'

'It isn't.' There was a pink tinge on her throat. 'Although it is Saturday and he has no class commitments, as our Director of Studies he does have other necessary duties in preparation for next week.' Her voice dropped even lower as though she were intent on excluding Doust from the conversation. 'And our breakfast this morning was not what I can call a happy one. We had disagreements over several matters and he left the house some time during the morning without telling me where he was going, or why. I thought he could have gone to the Rodmaris Arms, but had he, he would have returned long since.' As she had progressed through her account of her husband's absenteeism so there had been a sense of a weak anger rising.

Rogers had noticed that Doust, despite being pointedly excluded from what was passing between Mrs Horsbrugh and himself, had been regarding her with something of the expression of a caring mother hen. He was amused, for it was to him that she was supposed to give her allegiance, her present role being to act as a kind of nanny in protecting him from any later unjustified accusations of sexual familiarities from female interviewees.

'Could you tell me what the matters were that caused your disagreement at breakfast?'

25

She shot him a sharp glance. 'I don't think so. It was over our personal and business relationship. It can have nothing to do with what has happened.'

'Having regard to all that you've told me, would I be justified in believing that in all probability he won't be back?'

'There is something else I feel I must tell you,' she said frowning, appearing to avoid answering his question. 'Would you hand me my bag, please? It's on the coffee table.'

He rose from his chair, retrieved the black leather shoulder-bag she had indicated and handed it to her, receiving a heady inflow of her scent in his nostrils before returning to his seat. Taking a pack of cigarettes from it, she lit one from an enamelled lighter. She said, with sad distaste in a voice that was still kept low, 'My husband is, I am positive, having an affair with a woman who is unknown to me. I hope that you'll not ask me how I know, for I can't tell you, and I do so now only because I believe that you will find out anyway.'

A curious woman, he thought. Though he had noted the contempt, she certainly hadn't sounded or looked as though she gave a damn about his screwing around. And in all this she had given unwittingly a denial to his hasty appraisement of Colonel Horsbrugh as a worn-out exhausted old man. In Rogers's opinion, any man in his sixties who kept advancing decay at arm's length by his association with an active mistress deserved a medal for gallant persistence in the face of odds.

He said, 'Your telling me this suggests that you don't believe that he'll return and that if he does he wouldn't be welcomed.'

'I'm sorry,' she said. 'I hadn't meant to mislead you in any way, but when it's one's husband . . .' She held her cigarette to show him its lengthening ash. 'Would you mind? The ashtray, please?'

It was on the coffee table and he obediently collected it and placed it at her side. This time she looked up at him and her quite beautiful brown eyes added to the impact her scent was making on him. He asked, 'Does your son know about this?'

'No,' she replied, allowing cigarette smoke to trickle from her mouth. 'At least, I hope that he doesn't.'

He thought that he had seen alarm in her eyes, and some resentment. 'Has your husband a car?'

'Yes, but it's being repaired somewhere. At a garage,' she added unhelpfully. 'If necessary, he would take a taxi or use mine in an emergency, though not without telling me. Which Willie tells me he hasn't.'

She was beginning to look pale beneath her summer tan and he decided to bring his questioning to an early close. 'An odd thought,' he said, almost wryly, 'but does there happen to be a gun of any kind in the house?'

With the answer already shown as disquiet in her face, she said, 'I'm afraid there is, though not of my doing.' Her chin came up. 'That doesn't mean . . . it's absurd to even think so. Despite everything, he just isn't that sort of a person.'

'He probably isn't,' Rogers equivocated, 'and it doesn't have to be his gun that was used. Or, if it was, him that used it. What is it? And where is it kept?'

'I haven't actually seen it, but it's in his study locked in a metal box.' She sounded decidedly uneasy. 'Do you wish to see it?'

'Later, if I may.' He looked at one of the wing chairs, indicating it to her and smiling encouragingly as he stood. 'If it won't upset you, would you be obliging enough to sit in that chair for a moment?'

'Yes, of course.' Neither returning his smile nor rejecting it, she held out her hand to be helped from the sofa. Unnecessarily, Rogers considered, but pleased however to take its slim warmth in his own and lift her, finding her standing to be as tall as he had guessed. 'Stay,' she said to the spaniel as she released her hand from Rogers's.

When she was seated in the chair, poised, though with an edge of strain in her face, he moved behind it. Apart from a glimpse of parts of the fabric of her dress on the arm-rests and cigarette smoke drifting upwards, she was wholly concealed from view by the high back of the chair. Deciding not to comment on the implications arising from that, he returned to face her, saying, 'I shall need to examine this room, Mrs Horsbrugh, and to interview Willie before I leave. Have you another room to go to?'

'I shall go to bed,' she said. 'I would have done so before had

27

I not been told you wished to speak to me.' She looked worried. 'Do you wish to be informed should my husband return?'

'I hope it won't be necessary,' he told her, believing that there would be no return of her husband that night, but not sure enough about it to do nothing. 'But I will have a PC making regular calls here once we've finished and left, and for as long as it needs. And before I forget it, who is the Mr Skinner who joined you after the shooting?'

'He is a teacher in my employ and he has a room at the top of the tower,' she said, standing from the chair and being close enough to Rogers to unsettle a little of what he considered to be his present physical insensibility. 'He heard the gun and came down to see what was happening.'

Something in her voice and expression suggested to him that she wasn't too fond of Skinner, though he wasn't intending to ask her about him. Not yet, anyway. He said, 'I'd be grateful if I could use your telephone to make one or two local calls.'

'Of course,' she replied. 'And I'd be glad if you would be careful in what you say to Willie about his stepfather.' With her mouth showing an understandable gravity she held out her hand again, this time in parting, allowing him only a socially formal touching of her flesh. It was enough for him to be made to feel clumsy and gauche against her elegance.

Watching her leave the room, he was cynic enough to believe that for a woman who could, consciously or otherwise, send a normal man's blood surging through his veins, she must have definitely married the absent lieutenant-colonel for something other than love, affection or a sexual need.

5

The departure of Mrs Horsbrugh left, Rogers felt, a curious emptiness in the room, though it still contained WPC Doust and himself. He said to Doust, 'Would you tell Sergeant Tomlin and young Sloane that I'd like them here? When you've done that you can toddle.' He thought that he may have torn a disciplinary strip from her husband in the forgotten past and the resentment resulting from it had continued to be nursed by her.

Lifting the bedsheets from the television set and the chair, he first scrutinized the high back of the chair. A small, difficult to see hole in the mostly dark-green design of the tapestry weave was located two inches below the top edge of the high back, possibly where it would be likely to hit the head of a person occupying the chair. Checking further, he found that the bullet had torn its way through the chair's stuffing and fabric to hit into the wall it was facing. What he could see of it embedded in the plaster convinced him that it was no larger than a .22.

Another bullet, aimed lower down, had missed the chair and hit the screen of the television set, shattering the tube. There was no certain indication which bullet had been fired first, nor did he think that there would be. Seeing by a tiny ruby light in the wall plug that the set was still alive, he switched it off.

Taking a line from the trajectory of the bullet piercing the chair he found himself with his back against the middle of the three windows. Taking advantage of his being alone, he loaded tobacco into his meerschaum and lit it, waving the smoke away from him into the upper reaches of the ceiling. Somewhat comforted, he pulled aside the window's gauze curtain, peering frowning through the streaming water on the glass into a vista of wildly tossing black foliage and the wet shininess of what appeared to be an asphalted path several feet from the side of the house. Summer weather it was not, and he thought that he might defer with some justification an immediate visit to the garden, leaving it to the drenching rain which would have already distorted and rendered valueless any footprints that may have been left by the user of the pistol. There were, however, a couple of apparent facts that needed clarification and, because there was no sudden enlightenment, he was scowling through the window when an unaccompanied Detective Sergeant Tomkin entered the room.

Tomkin – his given name was Nigel – was a squat, broad-chested and muscular man who was prematurely bald. He had, as a younger bachelor DC, astonished his colleagues by asserting several times with an undoubted sincerity that he very much preferred a brisk game of football on a winter's cold afternoon to sharing the warm bed of some affectionately compliant girl. Even when he later married he was never allowed to live down his former aberrant freakishness in masculine sexuality, and the standard greeting to him, remorselessly pushed home by the coarser of his colleagues, was, 'How's the football going then?'

He said to Rogers, 'The boy's gone up to see his mum. He says he's worried about her, but he'll be down soon.'

'Right, sergeant,' Rogers acknowledged. 'I've had words with her and she's told me something of what happened.' He held out his hand. 'You've taken a statement from her?'

'Yes, sir.' Tomkin pushed a hairy paw into a pocket of his raincoat and produced his police notebook.

Taking it, Rogers flipped its pages and read the statement, noting that she had given her forenames as Rachel Isobel and apparently denying the sergeant access to her age. She had said substantially what she had later told Rogers, though holding back on any mention of the disagreement with her husband, or anything about his suspected association with an unknown woman. There was nothing in it that would clarify the two points raised in her later account of the shooting which were giving him a creased forehead.

While he was about it, he also read the statement made by Sloane. It was understandably short and simple, detailing only his return from – he had said – visiting a friend, whom he had circumspectly declined to name, to find his mother badly distressed and trying to recall what had happened in his absence. He had expressed astonishment about the whole episode, did not know where his stepfather was and had not seen him since earlier that day. Rogers didn't wholly approve of his having lied about a so-called friend in an official document.

Both statements had been taken by Tomkin, who had lacked his senior's inside knowledge of the family, and Rogers hadn't expected much from them. Handing back the notebook, he said, 'Thank you, I'm sure that they'll be useful. I'll take over from here, so you get on back to the office and do a check on Horsbrugh. Find out whether he has a firearms certificate and, if he has, for what. Exactly what. His first names are Henry Fraser so, while you're at it, check on what's known about him. Use the NIB, the Army List, the Military Police Investigation Branch, and anywhere and anybody you think I might have thought up if I'd had more time. Before you do go, tell Miss Witheridge to report to me when she's finished with the Skinner chap.'

When Sloane entered the room, Rogers was crouching with his bones creaking and examining a damp patch on the carpet near the table under which Mrs Horsbrugh said she had hidden. The spilled liquid smelled of brandy; an unbroken balloon glass from which it appeared to have come lay beneath the table. He straightened himself upright and said, 'There're things I need to do without delay. First, a few words with you and then I'd want to see Colonel Horsbrugh's study and his gun. That's if it's still where it's supposed to be.'

As he spoke he was, for the first time, able to take in Sloane's appearance, to assess something of his persona, in a good light. The features didn't look so different from when the youth's eyes – surely there was arrogance there? – had been focused mainly on his mother's suffering, though now he could also see in the face a suggestion of shiftiness. Otherwise, it reflected an unlined immaturity not yet blurred by too many of the facts of life he was yet to meet. A shaver had surely yet to touch his chin and jowls and his unruly fair hair affected a thick strand flopping over his forehead. Rogers decided that he wasn't going to particularly like him.

'I've looked,' Sloane said, 'and it's gone. But mother told me that she would like to see you before she goes to bed. She had something to tell you she thinks might be important. And I ask you to not keep her up too long.' He had sounded to the detective to be adopting a shade too much exaggerated proprietorship over his mother.

'I thought she had already gone,' he pointed out.

Sloane shrugged. 'She's waiting for you. I shall show you up.'

Rogers, resigned wryly to more delay, followed him from the room to the stairs in the hall, climbing them to the first floor. There, in a long corridor of white-painted doors and stairs rising to another floor, Sloane knocked on one of the doors. Waiting until his mother's voice called out a subdued 'Come in, Willie,' he opened it and preceded Rogers in.

The room was high-ceilinged with an overall décor of soft-hued pinkness, the bed it contained being richly flounced and prepared for a single occupant. Mrs Horsbrugh, wearing a cream satin robe over her dress, was seated at a mirrored dressing table with her back to her son and Rogers, her hands folded on her lap and turned her head only at their entry. The pink-shaded light over her head was the only one on in the room. Her dog was lying in a basket bed near her.

She said to her son, 'Please go downstairs and wait, Willie,' watching him in the mirror as he left. Keeping her back to the detective – he was already feeling uncomfortable at being in a bedroom with this so very desirable woman without the damp-ening presence of WPC Doust – she said, 'Sit on the bed if you wish, Mr Rogers. I shan't keep you long.' She looked pro-foundly depressed and not, he judged, too far from tears.

'Willie said there was something you thought important,' he answered her, remaining standing. The perfume she was still wearing was reaching out to him, threatening to do things to his *savoir-faire*.

'I'm sorry. I should have told you before.' She was abstract-edly screwing and unscrewing the silver cap of a small blue phial, her eyes liquid and dark and not meeting his. 'It might help to explain that . . . well, what had happened, I mean.'

'Then it would be important,' he told her. He felt intrusively bulky and rooted to where he stood, a pink-hued monolith, yet feeling it too unprofessional and possibly unwise to sit on the bed she had offered in a plainly chairless bedroom. Sod it, he said in words unspoken behind the reassuring smile he gave her.

'I . . . I believe that Henry – my husband, that is – is mentally ill.'

'Because you are now forced to believe that he was the one who shot at you?'

She nodded miserably, back to meeting his stare.

'Apart from that, why do you think he's mentally disturbed?'

'I should have told you . . . he believes I am being unfaithful

32

to him.' She quirked her mouth in a sad grimace. 'That I have a lover here when he is away. He shouts at me like a madman, then makes quite outrageous demands on me . . . demands that he would never make in his right mind . . . how he used to be . . .' She trailed off miserably.

Rogers raised his eyebrows. 'Though, as you suspect, he was having an affair of his own?'

'That is something he would hardly admit, is it?' About that she was oddly passionless.

'None of that necessarily means that he is mentally ill,' he put to her. 'If I may say so, apart from the shooting, it's about par for not a few marriages. Was there nothing else?' He thought he saw resentment in her eyes at what he had said.

'Yes, there was. I often heard him talking to himself in his study and it was occasionally embarrassing with the students here. Often I could hear him in his bedroom, not talking so much as being angry with whoever it was he thought was there. He shouted sometimes in a language that I couldn't understand, though it sounded Asian. He commanded a Gurkha regiment once, so that might have been it.'

'Nepali?'

'I imagine so.' She brushed that aside as if of no importance. 'At first I used to go into wherever he was to see what was the matter, for it could frighten me to hear it. Several times I've seen a quite extraordinary expression on his face as though he was looking at something or somebody I couldn't see. Then it would vanish and he would seem completely normal, often asking me what it was that I wanted.' She shook her head as if trying to convince herself that it had never been thus. 'Poor Henry,' she said sadly. 'I really don't think that he is always aware of what he's been doing.'

Rogers had met female ambivalence often enough not to take it too seriously and he said, careful not to lead her, 'If, as you appear to believe, your husband tried to harm you, would you know why? I mean, if there is anything apart from your imagined, ah, unfaithfulness.' That word seemed terribly dated to Rogers – he was more often used to being told that some-body's husband or wife was screwing around – but she had used it.

33

'I can't honestly believe that he can think there's a reason. Not other than that he thinks I have a lover.'

Acceptance of that was something that Rogers was going to put on hold. He said, 'Accusing you and threatening you are not the same things, Mrs Horsbrugh. Has he actually threatened violence against you?'

'Yes,' she said reluctantly.

'Has he threatened to shoot you? To kill you?'

She moved restlessly on her stool. 'What he said – I cannot recall his exact words – was that he would see me dead if forced to . . . if he found out whatever it was he thought I was doing. He was never specific.' Her eyes were large and distressed, meeting his in the mirror.

'You said earlier that he wasn't the kind of person who would shoot you,' he pressed her. 'You've now changed your mind?'

'I don't know.' She was clearly unhappy at being asked to point a finger, biting at her bottom lip in uncertainty. 'I have and I haven't, if you know what I mean. He *is* my husband, so I think that I need something more certain before being convinced that he is.'

'I must ask you this question,' Rogers said patiently, thinking that so far he had had a bellyful of what was proving to be next door to damn-all and that they had been going round in circles. 'Would you tell me what your husband's outrageous demands on you specifically were?' He smiled encouragingly at her reflection, trying hard to look a man on to whom a woman could safely unload her problems. In the uncomfortable silence that followed he noticed that the rain was no longer beating against the bedroom windows.

Her expression was one of embarrassment as she tightened her lips and broke off her staring at him. It was after some obvious inner conflict that she said, 'We have slept in separate bedrooms for some months now. I feel that that is as much as I can help you. *Please,*' she added pleadingly with distress showing again in her eyes.

'I'm sorry,' Rogers apologized hastily, now wishing he had Doust there to ask the same question in his absence. He scurried through his mind's catalogue of known male sexual perversions, trying without success to fit one or two of them to this rather lost and seemingly tragic woman with her haunted eyes and discriminating taste in perfume. 'I shouldn't have asked you,' he said, shying away from a matter that so obviously embarrassed her. 'About Willie. Does he get on with his stepfather?'

She had been momentarily nonplussed at his change of subject and hesitated. 'What an odd question,' she replied. 'So far as I know he does, though he isn't here very much, being still at school. You knew?'

'That he was still at school,' he said. 'Yes, I did. I asked because it isn't unusual for the relationship between a mother's son and a fairly recently acquired stepfather to be a touch prickly for a while.'

'When Willie is not at school he occupies the Lodge which you passed on your way in. So it's not surprising that they don't meet too often.' There was a shadowed questioning look in her eyes. 'When they do I haven't noticed any friction between them, and there probably isn't.'

'I'm glad,' Rogers said. 'That's how it should be, isn't it?' He was sure that she was covering up something to do with her son. Not by a few millions the first mother to have to do that. 'I take it there isn't anything more about your husband?' He moved as if to leave, hearing the ghost of a movement from behind the closed door. In the partially shaded room with its essentially feminine odours he thought his mind might be responding to the eroticism of the woman, though not, it seemed, his body.

'Only this.' She rose from her stool and turned to him, taking in his exterior with an expression that was suggestive to him of a woman eyeing a horse she might be thinking of buying. He had been the recipient of similar appraisals and this particular one wasn't displeasing him. 'It's possible that you may find him with the woman he visits. But whatever you do, please do not allow him back here.'

He bowed his head and smiled amiably. 'I'll bear it in mind,' he said, turning the handle of the door to remove from the room his often unrestrainable interest in attractive women. Opening it quickly he was able to catch a glimpse of a male figure vanishing around the shadowed corner of the stairs

35

leading to the ground floor. Listening, he heard rapid footfalls muffled by thick carpeting descending and then diminishing to silence.

Making his way down the same stairs, he knew that although he wouldn't swear to it he was convinced that it had been Sloane listening in to what was being said in the bedroom. And why not, he told himself philosophically. There need be no other reason than mere curiosity.

6

Willie Sloane was seated in one of the high-back chairs with one foot propped on his knee when Rogers entered the sitting-room. An open book rested on one thigh and he held a half-emptied glass of red wine in his hand. It looked contrived and the air of insolent nonchalance about him immediately got up Rogers's nose.

'Your mother will probably tell you what that was all about, if you don't know already,' he said to Sloane who had mockingly lifted the glass to him in greeting. 'We'll have words after I've had a look at the garden. Show me how to get out there, will you?'

'It's through the door at the end of the corridor,' Sloane said languidly, a look of amusement on his face as he remained where he was. 'I don't think you can miss it.'

Rogers stared poker-faced at him for a few seconds, then turned and left the room. The door, unlocked and situated a few yards along the passage, opened into a green-glassed porch containing shelves of potted plants. Outside, in a graveyard quietness, the moon shone fitfully through the broken cloud of a still stormy sky. It illuminated a dripping jungle of densely bushy laurels surrounding an immense Cedar of Lebanon whose upper foliage was lost in shadowed darkness. The asphalted path led a few feet outwards, then turned left to finish at a wrought-iron gate. The gate, to which Rogers walked, finding it on the latch and insecure, was set in a high brick wall.

In the darkness, he had to assume that the wall enclosed the whole of the spacious garden.

Taking up a position he judged would have been taken by Colonel Horsbrugh – assuming him to have been the assailant – he found that the path was at least fifteen feet of muddy soil and rose bushes away from the house and not lightly to be walked on. From where he stood, sighting along the supposed trajectory of the two bullets, he could see directly into the illuminated window and obliquely into the windows at either side of it. In imagination he was now the man with the gun. The centre window gave him a diaphanous picture through the gauze netting of two of the high-back chairs; of one – the target chair – facing the shattered television set, of the other – in which he had seen Sloane sitting – sideways on to the window. The window on his right was filled mostly with partly pulled drapes, a segment of shelved books and a parchment-shaded standard lamp. Through the window on his left he could see a perspective of mahogany sideboard with the upper half of Sloane standing at it and apparently recorking a bottle.

Closing his left eye and focusing his stare and intent, he held out his arm, aiming at the target chair with the stem of his pipe simulating the nozzle of a pistol. That he could see nothing of the left-hand window and only indistinctly a yellowish rectangle that was the right-hand window failed to answer wholly the doubts; no, not doubts, but the ambiguities that exercised his mind. On the assumption that Mrs Horsbrugh would be sitting in the chair, though concealed from him as her assailant, his forefinger pulled at the imaginary gun's trigger. Twice, subjectively, it jerked in his hand at the explosive discharging of the bullets before he dropped his arm to his side. Then he thought that perhaps a small bore pistol mightn't have much of a recoil. So would the somewhat erratic shooting be the outcome of an unsettling emotional high that he couldn't simulate? A shaking hand, a thumping heart and a dryness of the mouth at the enormity of what he was about to do? Then what? And what had he expected to have happened? Did he run for it on the basis that the shots would certainly have been heard by somebody? That there would be an outcry? An immediate if cautious investigation into the cause of it? Would it not have been better for him to conceal himself in the inner darkness of the laurel bushes until his position apropos outside interference became clear?

And what of the woman he had just shot at through a window which was then open? Was that as fortuitous as might be her sitting in the chair she had hoped to occupy at that particular time? Had he as the intending killer to depend on that? Would he have expected her to fall from the chair at the shock of the striking bullets? To show at least something of herself in the convulsions of her wounding? And why should he come outside into a darkened garden to shoot a woman in the back? At what distance was he standing? Fifteen or twenty feet? Would there have been a lack of moral courage in choosing not to look the to-be-killed woman in the eyes?

Rogers laid a resigned and silent curse on the illogicality of it all, filling his ill-used pipe and flaring a small yellow flame in the darkness in lighting it. When he had got what he'd always considered to be his second-best friend drawing well, he held the flame to his wrist and checked his watch. It was one-fifteen and he guessed that Sloane would leave him for bed or succumb to an alcohol-related incomprehensibility were he not to get cracking on his interview.

The youth was back in his chair when, blinking his eyes' bedazzlement, Rogers re-entered the room, being slumped inelegantly with his feet up on the coffee table. His part-emptied glass of wine was balanced on the chair's arm at his side and he yawned without concealment at the detective's approach.

Rogers sat on the sofa vacated by Mrs Horsbrugh. Hiding his irritation at the youth's gaucheness, he said with a touch of forced amiability, 'It does seem after all that there was substance in what you told me me up at the Gibbet. And not a moment too soon either.' He looked wryly at Sloane. 'In fact, it was very short on the heels of your complaint, wasn't it?'

'I told you it was going to happen. If I'd known how soon I certainly wouldn't have been up at that frightful place being disbelieved by you.' He regarded Rogers with the arrogance he could let show on occasions. 'You'll agree that I was right and that you were wrong and that he *is* trying to kill her. And I did say I wanted her guarded. So what have you decided to do?'

'Not quite that. But certainly periodical checks here for as long as I think necessary,' Rogers answered him, urbane in the face of this sudden offensiveness. 'And, of course, to investigate the circumstances of what has already happened. Which is what I'm doing now.' He relit his gone-out pipe and blew smoke upwards at the ceiling. 'You said that your stepfather's gun is missing. That's rather important, so tell me how you know.'

'By looking,' he said. Rogers was able smell stale wine on his breath and he kept his pipe in his mouth as an antidote to it. 'When I'd been told that mother had been shot at, I knew it must have been him. I went to his study and found the metal box empty, that's all.'

'You touched it?'

'I had to, hadn't I? To look. Is that for fingerprints?' He smirked and drank from his glass.

Rogers thought that it must be the wine promoting his attitude. He hoped that justice would prevail in giving him a doom-laden headache and a bout of vomiting just before his breakfast. 'Where is your stepfather's study?' he asked.

'It's an office really, but the stupid old fart hides in there and calls it a study.' His mouth was loose as he spoke.

'Perhaps not so stupid if he wished to avoid your sort of unpleasantness,' Rogers said, frowning his displeasure at what Sloane had said. Here was a quite different version from the sometimes anxious youth he had spoken to at the Gibbet. 'He had visitors to his study?'

'Why not?' he replied sullenly. 'It could be that as the Director of Studies' – he gave a snort of derision – 'he had to speak to all the students at one time or another. Being all foreigners, I shouldn't think he'd understand what they were talking about.'

'Possibly not.' Rogers was stern, his amiability fled. 'But take my question seriously, will you?' Seeing Sloane raise his eyes to the ceiling in mock submission, he said sharply, 'Would they, or any of them, know that he kept a gun there?'

Sloane locked stares with him, Rogers recognizing in his a returned dislike. 'They'd all know. He was forever cleaning the damned thing, whoever might be there.'

'And you said that the box he kept it in was often insecure?'

39

'Did I? I don't think I did. But it was occasionally left without the padlock in place.'

'Are students attending here at the present moment? If they are . . .' Rogers broke off at a knocking on the door and the entry of WDC Witheridge, a tall angular woman with oatmeal-coloured hair who was a self-proclaimed feminist currently reading for the Bar. She was one of his staff, an efficient enough detective officer for whom he face-savingly dodged any discussion on criminal or civil law.

'I'm not interrupting, am I?' she said, as usual avoiding addressing him as 'sir'.

Rogers rose from the sofa, said 'Excuse me for a moment' to Sloane and crossed the room to meet her. 'You've a statement from Skinner?' he asked, lowering his voice. He would take up later the question of what the hell she had been doing for the past couple of hours.

'Yes,' she said, the second policewoman that night to appear anti-Rogers. But then she had, on some sort of feminist principle, always been so. 'Do you want it?'

'I'd like to see it, please.' He held out his hand, taking the pocket-book she gave him. Skimming through what was a highly detailed account of the evening's happening, he saw that shorn of its superfluity of words it agreed generally with what Mrs Horsbrugh had told him. Giving back the book, he said, 'A copy of it on my desk tonight, please, before you go off duty.' He gave her a cheerful smile as an encouragement for one from her – it failed – and returned to Sloane.

During his brief attention to Witheridge at the other end of the room, the youth had slumped back in his chair with his eyelids closed, his hands clasped behind his head. It appeared to Rogers to be another contrived posturing. Resuming his seat on the sofa, he said, intending to place him firmly in the age bracket that wasn't necessarily to be equated with knowing everything, 'I'm back, Willie, if you'd give me your attention.'

Sloane's eyes opened and he affected a mouth-open yawn, his hands remaining behind his head. 'I'm nightcapped,' he complained, 'and it's past the time for my sleepy-bag.'

'I was asking you where the students live,' Rogers pointed out, ignoring the complaint. 'Do you know?'

'No, of course I don't. Only that they're either in lodgings, guest houses, or with friends. It'll all be in the office records.'

'Where is the actual school situated?'

'In the tower. On the two lower floors, that is.' He yawned again.

'What's above them?'

'You're wanting to know a lot, aren't you?' Sloaned reached over the arm of his chair, retrieved the half-glass of wine from where he had put it on the floor and drank from it.

'Yes, I am.' Rogers was stern again. 'If you know, tell me.'

'The staff. There's usually three of them. Except for Skinner they'll be away for the weekend. Where, I wouldn't know.'

'Who are the other two?'

'Molly Traill and Constance Coppin.'

'Both teachers?'

'Yes,' he agreed impatiently. 'They wouldn't be students, would they?'

'You used the word foreigners just now. What nationalities are the students?'

'Christ! It isn't my bloody school!' Sloane said, irritation straining his words. 'Germans, Japanese, Thais, Italians; an occasional Hungarian or Pole, Arabs from around the Gulf; male and female and in between, if you understand what I mean. Is that enough for you?'

'Thank you,' Rogers said with irony, then giving him a sort of shark's smile. 'I'd always though that drinking wine tended to civilize, making a chap more amiable. You wouldn't agree with me, I suppose?'

Sloane, surprised, jerked his head towards Rogers and stared at him for long moments. Then, in a quite different voice, an overdone courteous voice that articulated carefully, he said, 'I . . . I do apologize most profoundly. I imagine that I might be more than a little pissed and that my bad manners are showing. I'm also dreadfully tired and worried about my mother.' He smiled his not-too-white teeth at the detective.

'Yes,' Rogers replied ambiguously, not taking his apology too seriously, for he suspected there could have been mockery behind it. 'Shall we go on?' He frowned irritably into the bowl of his gone-out pipe. 'What is the significance of Mr Skinner?

41

Why is he . . . well, you know.' He was recalling Mrs Horsbrugh's face and the strong message of her distaste or dislike it had shown him.

Sloane blinked, as if at the unexpected. 'Do you mean about me?' he blurted out. 'And Angela Annetts?'

'Naturally,' the so-far-foxed Rogers said, feeling that he had hit a nerve or two.

There were deep creases in Sloane's forehead. 'Was that what he told the policewoman?'

'You mustn't question from where we get our official information,' Rogers told him sternly. Since he had torn a minor strip off Sloane, he seemed to have sobered up. 'I couldn't tell you even if I wanted to. Not even if you were right, which you aren't. Tell me about him and you and Angela Annetts.'

'It was nothing really,' Sloane said lightly, with Rogers believing that it only came out after some moments of soul-searching. 'He got stupid one night and accused me of bedding down with Angela in the Lodge.'

'And were you?'

'No, I jolly well wasn't,' he said, suddenly heated. 'He banged on the door when I was in bed, listening to a play on the radio. I had to get up to convince him I wasn't entertaining his Angela or anybody else. I don't think I really did at the time but he went away and apparently sorted things out with her later on. He had to apologize in the morning, of course, so I didn't say anything to mother, who would probably have sacked him there and then.' A faint grin appeared on his face. 'He was in a hell of a bait that night and if I hadn't shut the door in his face I think he'd have tried to plant one on me. Naturally, I'm glad he didn't though I wasn't frightened of him.'

'How long ago was this?'

'Two to three months. I was home on a long weekend.'

'Don't be bashful about it,' Rogers said straight-faced, 'but did Skinner have the slightest justification for thinking that you and Angela would be in bed together?'

'Not in the slightest; not with anyone. I'd chatted her up on an occasion or two; sort of joked with her about that kind of thing.' There was an undertone of caution in his voice.

'Do I assume that she visits here?'

42

'She used to work here with the students.'

'Used?'

'She was sacked.'

Rogers thought about that. 'After the non-incident in your bedroom or wherever?'

Sloane looked as if about to object to that but, instead, said shortly, 'This month.'

'Why?'

Sloane made a snorting sound in the back of his throat. 'You'd better ask mother about that. She's the law around here.'

'Or should I ask Skinner?'

When there was no reply to that, Rogers said, 'Perhaps you'd show me Colonel Horsbrugh's study or office. I want to see where he kept his gun.'

Sloane pushed himself up from his chair. 'Won't it do tomorrow?' He sounded churlish and was clearly uninterested. 'I really am bushed.'

'No, just lead the way,' Rogers said. 'I want to get to bed too.'

Following Sloane from the room into the passage, he was led through a door on its opposite side into a square hall, being apparently now in the tower. It contained a short flight of stairs climbing upwards into darkness and an open office with a varnished wooden counter, manifestly used as a reception desk. Opposite the stairs, a panelled door had a name-plate on it that said *Director of Studies* in tarnished gold-leaf, with *Lt. Col. Henry F. Horsbrugh, BA* below it in more recently applied lettering.

Sloane opened the unlocked door and Rogers trod his heels in following him in. The blondwood desk in the room was imposingly large and topped with tooled red leather, its accompanying captain's chair leather-upholstered. A glass-fronted case showed the spines of books in such mint condition that Rogers judged that they must have been bought by the yard as decoration. Otherwise, the files, papers and equipment were standard office. The air in there carried the faint odour of a smoked cigar.

Pointed out by Sloane, a black steel box stood on the carpet behind the desk, its back flush with the wall. Rogers reached down and moved it. 'It should be a fixture,' he commented while opening the lid. 'Bolted down against possible removal, and locked. He could have his firearms certificate revoked.' Cynically, and to himself, he added, 'He must be sweating blood about that.'

The box was empty of a gun as Sloane had said it would be, though containing two cartons of Target .22 bullets. Stickers on them showed that they had been issued by the Abbotsburn Small-bore Rifle and Pistol Club.

'Is there an exit to the garden from here?' Rogers asked.

'To a separate garden, yes, though there's a gate in the fence that's never locked. You don't want to see it now, I hope? Not at this time of the night?'

'No, but I'd like to see the bathroom and bedroom your stepfather uses,' Rogers said.

Sloane stared blankly at him. 'I don't think mother would approve of that. Why do you want to?'

Rogers was trying to be patient with him. 'To see whether his intent to go missing is supported by his taking clothing with him; his shaving equipment – stuff like that?' He had a sudden gust of irritability at having to spell out his actions for this awkward adolescent. 'Do I have to wake your mother to get anything done here without your questioning it?' he growled, his eyes dark with his change of temper. He thrust his chin forward. 'Show me where they are without any more bloody argument or I'll look for myself and explain to her afterwards.'

Sloane's face had twitched his alarm at this unexpected hostility from the hitherto reasonably amiable detective. 'Yes, of course,' he agreed hastily. 'I suppose it'll be all right.'

Colonel Horsbrugh's bedroom and *en suite* bathroom led off from the same passage as did his wife's bedroom. It took Rogers – dogged by a sullen Sloane – only a few minutes to note a seemingly undisturbed wardrobe of clothing and the presence of a safety razor and accompanying brush and soap bowl, together with toothbrushes and aftershave lotion. Horsbrugh, it seemed, had fled in only what he had been wearing at the time of the shooting.

'I don't suppose you'd know if he'd have his cheque book and credit cards with him?'

'I wouldn't, but you could find out from mother.'

44

'No,' Rogers said brusquely. '*You* find out from her and let me know.'

He was returning down the stairs with Sloane behind him when the sound of a car being braked to a halt outside broke the heavy silence of the small hours. 'That', he said to Sloane without pausing in his stride, 'will be Detective Sergeant Magnus who is our scenes-of-crime-searcher. To satisfy your curiosity about what we do, Sergeant Magnus will be here with me for the next hour or so and we shall be engaged in an undoubtedly boring scrutiny of any evidence we consider relevant to the attempted shooting of your mother. Further, I shall, as soon as I can, use the telephone to arrange for the security visits for the rest of the night.'

'You can't do better than that?'

Rogers didn't like the way he said it. 'It's as much as I judge the situation to need. The likelihood of a repeated attack is minimal and we've a shortage of night patrols anyway. You're here and you're big enough and old enough and she's your mother.' He was stern with him. 'Now's your opportunity to do something yourself for her.'

Waiting in the lower passage for Magnus's arrival – he had only guessed it to be him from the distinctive sound of a Land Rover's engine – he said to Sloane in an effort to establish a less hostile atmosphere, 'If you are about to make yourself a coffee – which you may feel you need – two more cups would be most acceptable to us. When you've done that, it'd be useful if you could dig out the photograph of Colonel Horsbrugh I asked you for earlier last night.'

Rogers in his present mood thought him a detestable little sod. Well, probably not so little, but it was how he saw him. With the photograph excepted, he didn't want what he had asked for so much as Sloane's absence while he briefed Magnus on what he considered to be a rather peculiar set-up in the house. That and the necessity for a meticulous search of the garden for two cartridge cases which would have been ejected from the pistol used in the attempted shooting of Mrs Horsbrugh.

Rogers, reaching his flat in the now moonless pitch blackness of a half-past four warmish morning, sprawled fatigued and stale in an easy chair with a hastily made cup of coffee. With it, he smoked a last pipe of tobacco to give solace to his palate, epiglottis and nerve-ends before getting into his bed.

His eyelids closed, his overactive mind was unwillingly visualizing the mouths and wagging tongues of those he had spoken to and interviewed. But with remembered pleasure – of a sort – in thinking of the sensual mouth of Mrs Horsbrugh, his recalling of it being done in a none too virtuous manner. Something about her affected him strongly, leading his mind into thinking of her in erotic fantasies while his body struggled to express its response to it. In one sense it was an encouraging sign, possibly indicating that his believed menopausal period could be on the wane.

Considering what he thought might be an overly fatigued man's lust, he analysed it as much as his tiredness allowed him. It had, he recognized, little to do with a facial or bodily attractiveness though, fair enough, she couldn't be called unattractive. It had to be the inner something in a woman which neither he nor anybody else could identify, though its resulting in an increase in the numbers of *Homo sapiens* was known well enough. Whatever was leading him into this unwelcome attraction, it was something he didn't want. It was just his bloody bad luck that he had it.

His troubled off-duty mind shut down on him while he was still in his chair. Holding his coffee cup he drifted into sleep, unaware of the tepid dregs wetting his thighs. When he awoke, unrefreshed and stale-mouthed with sunshine trying to enter through his curtained windows, he recalled that his dreaming self had, in a confused nightmarish sort of way, biblically known Mrs Horsbrugh. While his fully awakened showering self had deplored it, been ashamed of it, his recollection of it was accepting that it hadn't been too bad an abstract activity at that. And, somehow, it assured him that he might not have reached the grand climacteric after all.

After a late breakfast of coffee and unaccompanied hard-boiled eggs – usually his *chef d'oeuvre* – which sat not too comfortably inside him, he was in his office in a mostly deserted Headquarters building at eleven o'clock. It was a depressingly and relatively new office in soulless hard plastic, enamelled steel, anodized aluminium and emulsion paint as yet untinged a golden brown by his tobacco smoke. The walls were visually dispiriting with taped-on sheets showing statistical columns of crimes committed in his bailiwick, and a board to which were attached specimens of dangerous drugs in capsule, tablet and pessary form.

Made slightly displaced by the eye-aching sunshine streaming in through the venetian blinds and the clangour of a Sunday's church bells coming to him over the roofs of the town, he was facing a preliminary review of his investigation and the future action to be taken. Now, he thought in his disgruntlement, while others of his acquaintance would be playing golf under the blue and cloudless sky.

Rogers's second-in-command, Detective Chief Inspector David Lingard, was making up for ten days' absence on an intensive course on the importation of illegal drugs by taking the day off. Rogers thought that his being a bachelor, and not subject to a married man's strictures and obligations to go places and do things, made him a man who would suffer no grief in being called out to help with the investigation, and he had sent for him.

Waiting for his arrival, he fired his pipe to what he hoped would be a nice steady burn and then pulled papers from his in-tray. The most interesting one was the combining in a report by DS Tomkin of a faxed reply from New Scotland Yard and the result of an enquiry made of the Special Investigation Branch of the Royal Military Police. Horsbrugh – Henry Fraser Horsbrugh and undoubtedly the same man – was not, and never had been, a lieutenant-colonel. Thirty-six years earlier, as a twenty-eight-year-old Captain Horsbrugh H F, he had been serving with the Prince Nicholas's Own Gurkha Rifles, attached to the Brigade

47

of Gurkhas Headquarters in Hong Kong. There, he had been court-martialled on three charges of larceny from Mess Funds, found guilty and cashiered. His unavailing defence had been that he had incurred heavy debts for medical treatment and a stay in hospital for his wife – who had since died – and that he had borrowed the money fully intending to repay it.

Twenty-two years later at the age of fifty and domiciled in England, he had been arrested as Henry Horsbrugh on criminal charges with no reference made by him or the police to his military service or rank. Employed in the management of an estate at Trumpton Beck, situated in a neighbouring county, by Lady Caroline de Vaugh, then a widow of sixty-eight years, he was the subject of her complaint to the police concerning alleged misapplied estate cheques. Arrested and charged, he was released on bail after strenuously denying the offences which had involved considerable amounts of money. His full anteced-ent history had not been obtained, due partly to Horsbrugh's determination to admit no more – he had said on account of his highly placed family – than that he had been educated in France and had been in estate management in different unnamed parts of the country for most of his working life.

Within days, Lady de Vaugh had withdrawn her complaint, her solicitor stating that there had been a misunderstanding about the authority she had given Horsbrugh to apply the cheques for estate purposes. Horsbrugh – who was later known to have been on more intimate terms with Lady de Vaugh than his employment might warrant – resumed his management of the estate until her death five years later. Several months afterwards, having been left £20,000 from Lady de Vaugh's estate, he left the area without disclosing to anyone a forward-ing address.

He had, Rogers mused speculatively, lived an interesting if not very revealing existence. And, almost certainly, he had made happy the last remaining years of an elderly Lady de Vaugh's life. Without wishing to extend his suspicions too far, he thought that he would later seek out the police officer engaged in the enquiry and have subjected to further examin-ation the circumstances of Lady de Vaugh's death. He made a note to that effect on his blotting pad before retrieving from between the pages of his pocket-book the photograph of Horsbrugh handed to him by Willie Sloane.

Postcard-sized and in monochrome, it was a head and shoulders portrait of an unsmiling and lean-featured grey-haired man wearing a conventional dark jacket with a white shirt and what appeared to be a regimental tie. Though he had not been one, he looked the archetypal lieutenant-colonel, his face taut and lined with an inner discipline and the slightest touch of intolerance. And, as an unsurprised Rogers saw, with nothing of his surface persona suggesting the dishonesties recorded against his name. Rogers felt, putting Horsbrugh's apparent light-fingeredness to one side, that he would like him on a closer acquaintance. Up to a point, that is, he qualified to himself; even believing that he could see from the photograph what had attracted the then widowed Mrs Sloane to him.

There was one other reference to Horsbrugh in the local records. Four years earlier he had been involved at night in a multi-vehicle road accident at Hutton-on-the-Moor when his passenger, a Mrs Primrose Booker, had been injured and admitted to hospital.

A computer printout with the details of Horsbrugh's firearms certificate gave his unchanged address as the Houston-Landorf Hotel at Thurnholme Bay, and authorized his possession of a .22 Browning target pistol and 1000 rounds of .22 ammunition. It seemed to be perfectly normal and there was nothing in it for Rogers to get excited about.

Nor was there anything to cheer him in Daniel Skinner's statement, committed now to a typed witness form. A name and date of birth check at NIB by the male-allergic WPC Witheridge showed nothing recorded against him. This would be filed mentally by the often overly-sceptical Rogers as NYFO, his acronym for Not Yet Found Out. It went with his permanent belief that almost nothing is as it seems on a first looking. Skinner would, he decided, be further interviewed about his spat with Willie Sloane over Skinner's girlfriend, Angela Annetts. Rogers had wondered at the time – not too deeply – why Sloane was telling him that he hadn't been entertaining Angela 'or anybody else'. He thought that he hadn't been heavy-handed enough in his questioning of him.

49

Using the descrption of Horsbrugh given to him by Sloane and drawing on the photograph itself, Rogers prepared with a doubt or two a *Wanted for Interrogation* notice for circulation throughout his own and neighbouring forces. He hadn't lost sight of Horsbrugh's having apparently gone on the run without, it could be presumed, taking a change of clothing with him or much else of substance as a support against the slings and arrows of what he might now be considering as dire misfortune. As an afterthought, he added *Believed to be in possession of a small-bore hand gun*.

He was drafting notes for his report on his interviews and his and Sergeant Magnus's unproductive search of the garden for evidential marks and the cartridge cases which would have been ejected by the automatic pistol, together with the sergeant's recovery of two distorted bullets from the television set and sitting-room wall, when his door was knocked on and Lingard, his second-in-command, walked in.

A tall slim man, he was dandyishly elegant in a well-tailored lightweight off-white suit, a check shirt high in the collar and long in the cuffs, a cream-coloured silk tie with a matching breast-pocket handkerchief, and highly burnished oxblood shoes. His parents' genes – undoubtedly elegant genes – had given him narrow features with a patrician nose, and yellow hair worn – in Rogers's opinion – a little too long for a policeman. He had daunting blue eyes and a jaunty temperament that had behind it some quite rough edges. He admired the very late George Brummell, the Regency dandy, to the extent of adopting the taking of snuff and some of his foppishness of dress, keeping both just short of provoking the ridicule of his peers.

'Bless my soul, George,' he said cheerfully, sitting in the visitors' chair on the opposite side of Rogers's desk. 'You've troubles, of course?'

'I want to unload, David. We appear to have a gun-happy husband running around and possibly waiting for a second chance at the target.' He was refilling and lighting his pipe as he spoke, then settling back in his so-called executive chair that squeaked mouselike at his every movement. Careful not to indicate his opinions of anything to Lingard, he gave him most of what he knew and had been told.

'Well, David?' he said when he had finished.

'I don't see much point in any of it,' Lingard replied bluntly.

'Neither do I,' Rogers agreed. 'Not unless we accept that Horsbrugh's really unbalanced. And yet, if you look at his photograph he doesn't look the sort of chap to do it even if he's that. Nor is he too much of a bogus colonel. He made it to captain with a pretty tough outfit until he was cashiered, since when he's re-enlisted himself and only moved up a couple of ranks. And what he's done in the past is a far cry from attempting to shoot his wife in the back.'

'He might have also promoted himself in the criminal activity stakes,' Lingard murmured, not too impressed with his senior's rationale. 'I'm interested in young Sloane though. Have you told me all?'

'I don't like him. I don't trust him either. He can be a cocky sod. And devious.' As soon as he had said it, Rogers reminded himself that Sloane was still only seventeen and could be forgiven some of his resentments and occasional arrogances. Even his gaucheries, he conceded.

'You say he doesn't like his stepdaddy?' Lingard took a tiny ivory box from his jacket pocket, pinched snuff into his nose and then flapped loose grains away with his handkerchief.

Rogers could smell the Attar of Roses perfumed air from where he was sitting. 'Is there any stepson that does? If he's right about Horsbrugh having attempted to kill his mother earlier on, it'd be understandable.'

'What isn't to me is why the self-styled military gent should want to kill her? There's a motive, George?'

'Jealousy? According to Horsbrugh's own statement to her he believes she's been sharing her favours on the side. Though I admit that her attitude in telling me this makes it difficult to believe.' Even as he said it, Rogers accepted that he had allowed partiality to colour his judgement.

'You're not forgetting the immortal Kipling and his "The Colonel's Lady and Judy O'Grady are sisters under their skins," are you?' Lingard quoted, almost under his breath.

51

'I'm glad you reminded me,' Rogers said drily. 'And thank God for it. I'd never thought differently.'

'I had the feeling from you that she wasn't too happy accepting that her husband was the party taking potshots at her?'

'In the beginning she rather held back from pointing the finger at him,' Rogers conceded. 'And admittedly I had to drag it out from behind a sort of old-fashioned wifely loyalty. Now she seems convinced it couldn't have been anyone else.'

'A bit more than you are?'

Rogers nodded. 'True, I'm not wholly convinced. I've an open mind and all that.' He frowned his indecisiveness, tapping at his teeth with the stem of his pipe. 'There's something else too. Young Sloane being with me up at the Gibbet when it happened doesn't mean that somehow or other he isn't a part of whatever was going on.'

Lingard raised his eyebrows. 'His own mother? Egad, George, you're pushing it a bit, aren't you?'

'Not his mother, of course not,' he said impatiently. 'I did say a part because he was with me when it happened. But what if somebody other than she was expected to be in the chair watching what was on television? Horsbrugh himself perhaps, though that's a pretty long shot even for me. Or, if I've misjudged him – and it is possible that I have – Sloane?'

'Shouldn't we be interested in finding Mrs Horsbrugh's lover if there is one?' Lingard suggested. 'Or what about that cove Skinner you mentioned?'

'Ah, I'm glad you reminded me, David. He's yet to be bunged through the mincer.' Rogers gave him the details of what he had been told by Sloane about Skinner's girlfriend Angela and her non-involvement at the Lodge. 'Flawed, I guess, because it stinks and makes no sense. My instinct tells me he lied and that he *was* entertaining a female, so friend Skinner's all yours. Preferably today because I'm struggling.' He brooded for a few moments, scowling at something outside the window at his side. 'Nothing of which explains why Horsbrugh's on the run, of course. Or just plain missing.'

'You said that he's also supposed to be having a bit on the

side,' Lingard reminded him. 'Might he not be holed up with whoever she may be?'

'It has possibilities and I'm already fretting about it. He crashed his car four years back – the details are in the records – and put a passenger, Mrs Booker, in hospital. She might be a likely, and if the accident didn't create any ill-feeling, whatever association it was may have continued. I think I'll see her in any event. She'll probably be able to give me an opinion of him which isn't his wife's or stepson's.'

He yawned behind a closed mouth. 'For you, David, though there isn't much at the moment for either of us, I want you to be in the picture. One thing I'd better have – and it can be done by one of our chaps who's *au fait* with who holds what official documents – is some background to Mrs Horsbrugh's two marriages and any changes of address or circumstances we can dig from her past. Also I'd appreciate your help in finding out some details about Sloane. We must have one at least of our graduate entries who attended St Wulfric's School, so sort out one of the more reasonably civilized for me, will you? I want him to chat up his old tutors or whoever and dig out some background on Sloane who'll be returning there in a week or so.'

'I think I know of one who might do,' Lingard said. 'He's probably familiar with a couple of two-syllabled words and I know his jaw doesn't hang too noticeably loose. I'll find out whether he can ask a question or two and push him up there.'

'Good, and I want it done today. I suppose you should also know that Horsbrugh's usual pothouse is the Rodmaris Arms. You might pick up some useful information there about any girlfriend he has.' Rogers looked doubtful. 'I imagine we might be capable of taking an active interest in that sort of thing in our sixties, mightn't we?'

'I'd be astounded if *you* couldn't.' Lingard had no illusions about Rogers's occasional interest in attractive women.

Rogers beamed. 'Life's not all black then, is it? While you're at it, will you detail one of the DCs on to finding the garage repairing his car? It's a grey Rover CKZ8817M. I think we should have a look inside it, apart from anything else. You can cope?'

Lingard stood from his chair. 'I couldn't have chosen a better way to spend my rest day,' he lied cheerfully. 'I take it that you're pushing the boat out for a meal at the Minster this evening so that I can call it quits?'

With his second-in-command gone, Rogers looked out from one of his windows at the largely deserted streets baking in the afternoon's sun. He was wondering what he could do further about Mrs Horsbrugh, who he had to see again as a source of information about her missing husband. He should, he knew, have passed the further interviewing of this hot potato of a woman to the unflappable Lingard. That he hadn't was beginning to worry him.

8

Sending for the road accident report filed under *Horsbrugh, Henry Fraser*, Rogers noted that his bogus rank was nowhere mentioned, that his sole passenger had been Primrose Booker, a married woman aged thirty-nine years, residing at Two Beeches, Spye Green Crescent, Abbotsburn, and that the accident involving two other vehicles had occurred late at night in September four years previously. 'Be sure our sins will find us out,' he muttered under his breath. Mrs Booker, concussed and bruised, had been admitted to hospital, being discharged two days later, seemingly as a walking wounded.

Finding the telephone number against the name *Booker, G. B.* – he assumed it to refer to her husband – he tapped it out. Should a male voice answer his call he was prepared to disconnect rather than walk into, or to reactivate, a marital problem. It was answered by a woman; a woman he judged, because she said a hesitant 'Yes?', to be cautious of telephone callers.

Asking if she was Mrs Booker, he gave his name and rank. 'I'm sorry to bother you,' he said, 'but is it possible for me to see you? In a way it's in connection with the road accident in which you and Colonel Horsbrugh were involved.' Rogers of

54

the Corps Diplomatique, he thought. And a tired and gently sweating one at that.

'Oh?' She obviously hadn't liked that. 'What on earth is that to do with you? Or with me, if it comes to that?' Her voice was light and seemed to affect a girlish ingenuousness.

'There are matters I have to enquire into, Mrs Booker, and Colonel Horsbrugh isn't available.'

'Are you doing this on behalf of my husband?' She was definitely hostile and not sounding like anyone called Primrose. 'If you are, you must please speak to my solicitor.'

Rogers, seeing the light, spoke more stiffly than he had intended. 'I'm a police officer, madam, not an enquiry agent. If my calling on you is an inconvenience perhaps you will say so.'

There was a short thinking silence, then, 'It isn't that. Is there anything . . . has anything happened to him?'

He softened. 'I'm sorry, but not on the phone. I'll explain when I call. In fifteen minutes if that suits you.'

It had seemed to, and driving his car into Spye Green Crescent – it was only a shortish road away from Horsbrugh's home in Kingfisher Avenue – he identified the Booker house as being the only one overshadowed by two immense beech trees. Built to stockbrokers' Tudor design it was showing signs of neglect, its doors and windows needing painting, its roof tiles acquiring a covering of moss. The uncared-for garden had been burned brown by the summer's sun, its grass and plants straggling.

Leaving his car in the road he entered the drive, seeing the front door being opened before he reached it by a woman whom he presumed to be Mrs Booker. She appeared to be what Rogers called a flouncy woman. She was diminutive in build though otherwise big-hipped and intimidatingly breasted. Her hair was tawny and worn in a contrived dishevelment around a small pointed face in whose features, possibly fancifully, he read a not too chaste interest in men. The dress she wore was of a wispy semitransparent material patterned in large flaring scarlet poppies.

Near her, his mouth readying itself for a smile, he saw that her eyes were a cool pale grey, her lightly painted lips thin with discontent written in their corners, neither yet ready for friendliness. Keeping his own smile on holdback, he said, 'I hope I haven't kept you waiting,' and followed her through the door into an enclosed hall. 'Now, Mr Rogers,' she said, sharp-tongued, 'perhaps you'll tell me what this is about.' She had kept the door open as wide as it would go.

Rogers could see no profit in his being pussy-footed in his approach and he plunged. 'Colonel Horsbrugh has been miss-ing from his home since yesterday morning under unusual circumstances,' he told her. 'I understand that it's possible that you may be able to help me locate him.' He thought he had seen surprise in the pale eyes before, rather theatrically, she put one of her hands to her mouth.

Seemingly worried and her voice sounding more schoolgirl-ish, she said, 'Are you telling me that something has happened to him?'

She was another woman who made him feel huge and clumsy and, in a way, overbearing. 'I don't know. I don't imagine I will until we find where he is. How well do you know him, Mrs Booker?'

She looked him over in a sudden transition to cool calculation. 'You wouldn't be here unless you knew, would you?'

'I don't suppose I would,' he agreed, smiling amiably and trying to look like a man who definitely knew something or other. 'I'd like to ask you a few questions about it. None of which should commit you to anything.'

She reacted to his smile with a grudging one of her own. 'I'm sure they won't for I wouldn't permit them to. You had better come inside and ask your questions sitting down.'

Following in her footsteps – Rogers had the illusion that the diaphanous dress floated her along – he entered a tall-win-dowed sitting-room appointed with rosewood reproduction furniture, green and gold fabrics and furnishings, and bowls and containers of flowers in scented profusion which could never have come from her own garden. Casually untidy, the room suggested that whoever did the housework wasn't too enthusiastic about it. He could see no signs of male occupancy, nor smell tobacco smoke.

Indicating him to an easy chair near one of the open windows – dust motes rose golden as he sank into it – she sat in one near enough for him to stretch and touch her were that his intent. Kicking off her shoes she tucked her bare legs beneath her. With the dress pulled taut, he could see the outline of the skimpy briefs she wore and he tried to think of something less unsettling. Such as what she was clearly about to say to him.

'I know that you'll be as kind and as nice as you are able,' she prompted him, widening her eyes. 'I really do wish to help you find poor Henry. I happen to be awfully fond of him.'

'I'm sure you do,' Rogers said, yet to be convinced. 'And are. Forgive my asking, but was there anything special about your relationship with the colonel at the time of the accident?'

There was an immediate touch of injured reproach in her face. 'Oh dear,' she sighed, looking up at the ceiling. Her fingers, thin and pink-tipped, were fidgeting with the gold snake-chain she wore around her throat. 'How men do tend to put the worst construction on a woman's friendship. I suppose you could say that we were very close friends, but that was all. I thought you knew that?'

'You say "were". Are you no longer very close?'

'Neither yes nor no. We are still good friends.'

'Do I understand from what you said on the phone that your husband no longer lives here?'

Her eyes flicked away from him to her thighs and back again, and she clenched her teeth in what seemed to be a painful grimace. 'We are legally separated,' she said as if it hurt her.

He had the feeling that she was acting out a part in presenting herself to him. He had met her type of female before and, apart from when it suited their self-seeking purposes, they were steel-plated beneath the softness of their flesh.

'Presumably as a result of the circumstances of the accident, I imagine?' he suggested, showing his teeth encouragingly.

She nodded. 'He was absolutely furious, screaming at me while I was lying in a hospital bed believing I was dying. He hadn't even thought to bring me a few miserable flowers.' Her face had reddened at her recalling it, her voice abrasive. 'When I was discharged – before I was ready to be, naturally – I was unable to get into my own home. The uncaring pig had taken his things and gone into lodgings, as I was later to find out.' She paused as if allowing the bile she had shown to recede.

Then, more calmly, she said, 'Though it was a complete misunderstanding and certainly did not call for him to go to those lengths, it would have been something else had it not been that. Gerald and I hadn't been temperamentally compatible for some time.'

The sad little smile she gave him demanded some sympathy and he responded with a straight-faced ambivalence. 'I'm sorry to have opened up old sores. That sort of thing does need some sensitive understanding from everyone concerned.' He thought sardonically that without any doubt it was a case of poor old cuckolded Gerald; bad luck and all that jazz. 'Your husband,' he said as if her extramarital peccadilloes were of intense interest to him, 'I imagine he was livid about the colonel? Wanting to sort him out and all that?'

She gave a trilling laugh that had derision in it. 'You mean Gerald being aggressive? For heaven's sake, no! He was mad at Henry for a time, but it was all words with him. I don't think he would hurt a fly.'

'That was then, of course. Possibly time – it must be all of four years – has given his losing you a bit of an edge?' It wasn't difficult for Rogers to imagine that Gerald, were he robust enough, could have spent long hours in his lodgings brooding a massive dislike for the seducer of his wife. Apart from which, the detective wished that this particular seduced wife wouldn't wear a diaphanous dress without putting on a bra. The ever-present protuberance of her nipples was distracting.

She seemed amused. 'If you're thinking that he might be responsible for Henry being missing, you're wasting your time.' She was suddenly anxious, Rogers thinking that it wasn't too soon. 'You're sure you don't think something's happened to him?'

'It's early days for that,' he said, dodging the issue. 'How did you come to meet him?' He moved in his chair, slowly sweating in the sun that was roasting him where he was sitting too near the window.

She had noticed his discomfort. 'Do take your jacket off if you are hot,' she suggested. Watching him take it off and reseat himself in shirt-sleeve order appeared to meet with her approval. He had, in truth, nothing to be overly modest about in the masculinity of his chest.

'You were about to tell me how you met the colonel,' he reminded her.

'Actually, I met him through Gerald before he'd married Rachel Sloane. We found we had similar interests and, well, our friendship developed from then. Later, Henry became involved with her in some advisory capacity – when she was supposed to be a widow – and Henry and I saw less of each other with no ill-feeling on either side. Then, about a year ago, he called me by telephone and said that the receptionist at the Language School was going to have a baby and would I be interested in standing in as a temporary receptionist.'

She was girlishly self-deprecating. 'Poor little me. It was silly and unnecessary, but I was so terribly bored with being on my own that I looked on it as something that could be rather exciting. During that time – it was only about three months – Henry and I became rather closer, particularly as I then realized that his marriage was not one in the true sense of the word.' She was occupied by silence for a short while, apparently in thought. Then she said, 'She wanted a man of substance to support her in her business, and he wanted a proper home and not the hotel room he was living in.'

'Did Mrs Horsbrugh know or suspect about your further association?'

'I'm sure not. I do hope not. Henry certainly didn't tell her about the accident.'

'How do you feel about her?'

'About Rachel?' She half smiled. 'I thought she was terribly sweet and considerate, although not everyone did so. And perhaps she could be thought a teeny wee bit inadequate in some things.'

Rogers was certain that her smile had had a touch of sourness in it; her words one woman's dissimulatingly barbed opinion of another. He said, 'And her son, Willie?'

'I hardly know him. I've only seen him once or twice. He's only a boy, isn't he?' Her voice had been dismissive of him.

'He's certainly young.' He smiled understandingly. 'Given

that the colonel's now missing, could you force yourself to give a straightforward opinion of him?'

The light blusher on her cheeks deepened, though Rogers couldn't tell whether it signalled annoyance or an unlikely embarrassment. She said, quietly earnest, 'He is a man whom I have always trusted. I have found him most genuine and modest about what he is and does. He happens to be very attractive to women and generous and considerate when he is with them. I have nothing but good to speak of him and you should accept from me – for I have known him for years – that he is a true and honourable gentleman.' There was an unspoken 'So there" behind her words and it seemed that she had discarded much of her ingenuousness.

It had sounded Jane Austen-ish to Rogers and he said disarmingly, 'Never doubted, Mrs Booker. When was the last time you saw him?' During the interview he had given ear to any odd noises that might be suggestive of an occupation of the upper part of the house. There had been none, but that could not lessen his in-built suspicion that Horsbrugh might have flown for shelter to his mistress.

There was another short period of silence before she said, 'I think about three weeks ago. Yes, at least that.' Her eyes, held wide and unblinking, had made that a probable lie.

In an apparently disinterested manner she had been stroking the tips of her fingers along the partially exposed thigh in Rogers's view and the sensuousness of it riveted his attention. Not enough to give him a nosebleed, yet certainly enough to distract his or anybody else's attention. He couldn't be certain whether it was with intent or not and, because she may have seen him looking, he coughed to cover whatever she thought she had read in his expression. 'Where did you see him?' he pressed her. 'Or would he visit you?'

She hesitated. 'Always here. Not very often, and you must believe that Henry would never have taken advantage of our being together.'

While he was questioning that in his mind, her eyes were telling him things – or so he imagined – that he didn't wish to know or to respond to. 'Did you ever meet him in the Rodmaris Arms?' he asked her.

She shot him a glance of surprise. 'Never,' she protested. 'There would be no point. I don't drink.'

'Are you back on speaking terms with your husband?' With her earlier mention of a solicitor he could guess she wasn't.

'Of course not,' she said, abruptly on the defensive. 'Not how you mean it, though he'd like us to be.'

'Is that why there hasn't been a divorce?' With his jacket off, the sun was burning his shoulders and he was sweating again, rivulets of it dampening his collar and the back of his shirt.

'There hasn't been because we can't come to an agreement about the house – neither of us wishes to lose a part of it.' She put on an air of self-satisfaction. 'I may have him back as a husband when it suits me, though certainly not for a few years.'

'You think he'll wait?' he asked incredulously. He thought her a mercenary little bitch, much like his own divorced wife. She had definitely put Rogers on the side of the unfortunate Gerald.

'Yes, I do. He's absurdly jealous, though he knows no different than that it's all over between us.'

Just the woman to turn the screw on the poor bugger, Rogers mused. He would have liked to tell her that even a mild man can be pushed into viewing the prospect of a dead wife as a quite pleasant one. 'For our records,' he said. 'Where does your husband live?'

She frowned, then pouted. 'You aren't going to talk to him, are you?'

'I can't think at the moment of any reason why I should, but I would like his address, please.'

'If you must. He's at present at a guest house in Hockton Hill.'

Hockton Hill was, Rogers knew, on the far side of town and that, for her husband, should be far enough away to allow her to copulate unmolested with her immensely attractive, generous and quite bogus lieutenant-colonel.

'And he's working?' he asked.

She gave another trill of laughter. 'You should know. He's a veterinary surgeon and your people call him out often enough.'

'A different department. And a different question, too. The last one,' he promised. 'In your association with the colonel

61

these past few months, have you noticed that he might be under a strain? That he's been acting rather peculiarly?'

Life seemed full of surprises for Mrs Booker, for she looked startled. 'No,' she said, frowning apparent incomprehension. 'What on earth do you mean?'

'Nothing other than that occasionally a man or woman will go missing because of some relatively minor thing like a depression or a loss of memory.'

'No,' she said firmly. 'You're wrong there. I know him so well and I would have known.'

He was standing and putting on his jacket to leave when she rose from her chair and moved to him, unnecessarily helping him to shrug it on. It could, he thought as she walked him to the door, have been his imagination in thinking that in helping him her hands had somehow contrived to be under the jacket and to slide lingeringly over his body. He was light years from complaining about it, but a married woman who had somehow parted from her husband could be one of the hazards of his profession; occasionally quite a dangerous one.

Getting into his car – which felt as hot to him as one of hell's furnaces – he thought himself neither too conceited nor too imaginative in believing he was probably fortunate in getting out of the house with his trousers still on and fully zipped.

Assessing the interview as he drove back to his office, he had to accept that she had told him nothing of significance. Probably, he conceded glumly, because he was as yet unable to ask her or anyone else searching questions based on knowing exactly what had been going on in the Horsbrugh/Sloane ménage.

9

Beneath his customary jauntiness, Detective Chief Inspector Lingard was suffering the trauma of a bereavement, not made less by the resulting huge increase in his personal finances. He had been forced to sell his cherished veteran Bentley, the *grande dame* of his affections and his surrogate mistress for half of his adult life. She had been – still was, he reflected sadly – elegant in her racing green livery, her long strapped-down bonnet with its polished brass radiator shell and her leather upholstery as soft and warming as a woman's skin. But she had begun to suffer the infirmities of age, even though not all her parts were of the year of her manufacture; her arteries being worn out and subject to clogging, her troubles under the bonnet having been diagnosed as incurable and having an alcoholic's thirst for petrol.

He had sold her with a deep feeling of shame to a collector of antique cars for a sum he would have been unable to match in several decades' salary in his rank, comforting himself only by an acceptance of the future inevitability of her being stolen, or being smashed to a metal ruin by another's carelessness in his daily driving of her. Because affection as such could not be replaced, he bought a red Alfa Romeo Spider convertible, not yet endowing it with a femininity he thought might eventually prove appropriate and hoping that they would grow to like each other. There was a considerable doubt in his hoping.

Now, driving it out of town with the hood folded back and the warm airstream whipping at his yellow hair, he was thinking out one of the reasons for his losing his rest day. He had telephoned Tower House and had spoken to Daniel Skinner. He, it appeared, had been half-way through the door and singlemindedly intent on continuing through it to pick up his hang-glider and his friend, Miss Annetts, and making a meet with other friends at High Platt where there were, favourably, thermals to be flown. He had said that he had no present objection to being interviewed so long as it didn't interfere with his and Miss Annett's flying programme.

'How will I know you?' Lingard had asked.

'I've a beard and moustache,' Skinner had told him, anxious to close down, 'and my glider's blue.'

High Platt, fourteen miles inland from Abbotsburn, was a ridge extension of the Great Morte Moor. Its contours were apparently so shaped as to promote the rising of the warm air needed by people wishing to fling themselves and their

63

undoubtedly dangerous contraptions soaring into whatever turbulence the sky then offered.

Finding the rugged climb to the moor's ridge towering over him seemingly too near the vertical for anything but a mountain goat in good condition, Lingard parked his Alfa Romeo with the seven other vehicles already there. The climb under a baking sun of a steep gradient fleshed green and purple with bracken and heather, and littered with sharp-edged rocks, was nothing Lingard would wish to do twice.

Hot, sweaty and irritable at the presence of thirsty flies, and also short of breath on reaching the plateau at the top, he saw small groups of men and women, most sitting on the ground, none of whom was wearing a beard. Obviously uninterested in his arrival, two couples of them were busy separately assembling spidery frames of metal tubing. Neither of the coloured wing fabrics, spread out for later fitting, was blue. Looking upwards, he could see five gliders soaring high in the sky in great curves, too dark against its brightness for him to discern colour.

Even as he was regaining most of the composure and well-being he had lost in his scramble up there, he saw a man climbing the slope of the ridge towards him. When an arm had been raised in greeting, Lingard moved towards him and, nearing him, took in his physical appearance. Skinner – for it had to be him – was lean and muscular and somewhere in his early twenties. He had no discernible hips and possessed the thin legs of contemporary young man. With longish blond hair tied at the back in a thumb-sized pigtail and a beard and a moustache, he looked to be of way-back Saxon origin, giving to sporting a gold ring in the lobe of his left ear. He wore lightweight green overalls and a silk neckscarf with something of the detective's own panache, only the ugly white and mauve trainers on his feet detracting from it. He carried a bulky white helmet by its chinstrap.

'Hi!' Skinner said. 'You're the fuzz, I take it?' His eyes were a startling blue in the shadow of their sockets and he had the look of a man very sure of himself.

'Lingard,' the detective said, shaking hands with him. 'Thank you for seeing me. I'm not interrupting?'

64

'Not yet.' Skinner led the way to a pile of nylon wrappings and a cool-box and sat sprawling on a clump of heather. 'I've just seen Angie off – that's Miss Annetts – and she'll be gone about twenty minutes. That's the time you've got, sport, for then I'm taking off on my own.'

Lingard sat, careful to interpose nylon between his immaculate trousers and the ground, a dusty and stony bed for the stunted heather and sparse needle-grass. 'Good,' he said, taking from a pocket his tiny ivory box and charging his nostrils with Attar of Roses against the smell of the parched heather and hot earth. 'As I mentioned to you on the phone, we are rather concerned about Colonel Horsbrugh being missing.'

'You want him, do you?' Skinner's expression was serious and thoughtful. 'I mean, is he wanted for trying to kill Mrs Horsbrugh?'

Lingard raised his eyebrows. 'You think it was him then?'

'Not me,' Skinner disclaimed hastily. 'In fact I don't, and I told the policewoman as much. I get on well with the old boy and I'm of the opinion that whoever shot at Rachel – Mrs Horsbrugh – it wasn't him.'

'We haven't said it was, though he is coincidentally missing.' He waited and when nothing came, said, 'You heard the shots, I understand? I haven't read your statement, so if it's not too much of a bore, perhaps you'd tell me what you told the policewoman.'

Skinner fumbled in his overalls and produced a slim card box from which he took a cigarillo as thin as a pencil and put it between his teeth. Then he snapped a gas lighter at it, the light breeze blowing the flame perilously near his beard. He said, 'You probably know I've a pad at the top of the tower which is a sort of half-perk for us teachers if we want it. It was ten o'clock or thereabouts and I was reading with my feet up when I heard two bangs sort of on top of each other. So far as I knew then or was particularly interested, they came from either the garden below or the road outside it. You know, it didn't hit me what they might be until a minute or so later, my interest still being in the book I was reading. When it did I couldn't be sure what it was I'd heard, other than it didn't ring a bell that I'd heard the same sort of thing before.' He put on a look of

65

puzzlement that he must have had at the time. 'There'd been a dead silence after the two bangs and that worried me, though I suppose I was worrying for the wrong reason. If there had been something wrong I'd have expected at least to hear yelling and shouting about it. Another factor was that at the time I'd be accepting that, in addition to Rachel, Henry could have been in the house. And Willie, if it comes to that. When I'd decided that I should look and see that all was OK, I went downstairs and into next door.'

He grimaced sheepishly. 'Mind, you could say I crept down all ashake, not wanting to have my head blown off if somebody was shooting real bullets. When I reached the passage I could hear Rachel in the sitting-room calling out "Help me somebody, please" and then repeating it. Not loud, but enough, as if she didn't want whoever it was to hear her. I went in then, still ready to duck and run, and saw her on her hands and knees cuddling her dog with the telephone on the carpet in front of her and nobody else there. She was pretty badly shocked, but did manage to tell me that somebody had shot a gun into the room and smashed the television set – which I could see for myself – and that she had already dialled Emergency for the police.'

He paused, inhaling lengthily at his cigarillo, then trickling out the smoke to be blown away. 'I asked her where were Henry and Willie and she said that both were out and that she was on her own. I did look out of the window into the garden – kind of cautiously, I admit – but so far as I could see in the dark there was nobody there. Still, there could have been someone in the bushes, of which there are more than enough. I sat her in a chair and kept an eye on her until the policewoman who interviewed me afterwards arrived and I let her in.'

'And that's it?' Lingard queried. He thought Skinner a chap he could be friendly with.

'Apart from being chivvied back to my room by the policewoman and told to wait there, yes.' He looked apologetic. 'I'm afraid it's not much, is it?'

'It's what you heard, saw and did and that's useful in anybody's book,' Lingard assured him. 'You say you popped your head out of the window in the line of fire so to speak. Yes?'

'I don't think, and I didn't think then, that anybody'd hang around waiting. I certainly never saw or heard anyone.'

'There was nobody else in the house?'

'Not in the house, nor in the tower.'

'And from what you said when we started, you don't believe the colonel had anything to do with the shooting. Why?'

'I just don't.' Skinner was positive. 'In fact, he's the kind of man I admire, whom I'd wish to be like. When I'm older, naturally.'

Holding fire a moment, Lingard had seen that one of the gliders on the ground – a yellow and black contraption – had been assembled and was being carried to the middle of the plateau. To the detective, it looked like an unwieldy headless pterodactyl and he knew with an inner certainty that he could never be persuaded to have it take him off from the safety of solid earth.

'I'm sorry,' he apologized. 'I was about to say that you must have noticed what his relationship was like with Mrs Horsbrugh. How did it strike you?'

'Good, as you'd expect. As I saw it – which was often – he was always courteous and affectionate.' He looked uncomfortable, tapping ash from his cigarillo with his forefinger. 'This isn't any of my business, you know. No offence, but I'd rather drop it.'

'As you wish,' Lingard agreed affably, 'though we aren't here for just a spot of gossip, are we? How about Mrs Horsbrugh? I understand that there'd been something of a contretemps between you and her?'

Skinner's expression was all surprise. 'Was there? If there was it was only because she and Angie had words about her precious Willie,' he said defensively.

Lingard, having noted that Skinner definitely didn't like Sloane, looked him straight in the eyes that were as blue as his own. 'Was that anything to do with your suspecting – wrongly, so I'm told – that Angela was in the Lodge with him?'

Skinner glowered and was suddenly unfriendly. 'Christ! I'm never going to live that down, am I? I made a mistake, that's all

67

there was to it, and I'm definitely not having Angie know about it. It'd finish everything.'

'You have my word,' Lingard assured him, 'though that's contingent on your telling me what the brouhaha was all about.' He smiled to take any sting away. 'I want it exactly as it happened and unexpurgated of anything you fear I may want to know.'

What he had said seemed to have relieved Skinner of his unfriendliness. He said, 'That's blackmail in anybody's language, sport.'

'So it might be,' Lingard conceded amiably, 'but not anything a lawyer would call unlawful. You can say that it's demanding information by menaces, if anything. So tell me about it.'

'I'm glad I haven't anything serious to be worried about,' Skinner said, now equally amiable. 'That business about Willie isn't recent history, you know. I'd say it's three months old, though exactly when can be pinpointed easily enough because he was home from his school at the time. Angie was working at the Language School then and being a local girl was living with her parents. We weren't engaged or anything, but she was my girl and accepted as such by everybody there. I hadn't been with her on the evening we're talking about and I'd had a few drinks with some friends in town. A few too many, I'd say. I was walking back and passing the Lodge where Willie beds down when he's home when I heard sounds that made me stop. It's dead quiet in that area and people joke that at night you can hear the fieldmice coughing, so hearing what I heard wasn't so unusual.'

He grimaced, manifestly not enjoying the taste of the cigarillo dying on him. 'He must have had a window open somewhere' – his face was suddenly flushed at its recall – 'and I could hear those groaning and heavy breathing noises some women make when they're enjoying being rogered. It was definitely a woman and I could swear to it. And, God forgive me, it came into my head that he had Angie in there.' His face showed the working of the inner turmoil which had moved him at the time. 'The more I thought about it, the more I was convinced and it led me into making a bloody fool of myself. I don't know what came over me unless it was the drink, for I'd no reason to suppose that Angie would do that sort of thing to me, though that bastard Willie would. Actually, Angie and I don't anyway because of her religion, and I respect her for it. It must have been in my mind at the time that, because I hadn't with her, it wasn't really what she wanted and she'd decided to find somebody who would. You know what I mean?'

'With some difficulty,' Lingard said, glancing at him sharply and wondering if he were serious. What he was saying sounded too naïve to be true, but then, one never knew. 'You found that you were wrong, of course?'

'Yes, but I wasn't mistaken about hearing a woman in his bedroom.' He groaned and banged his forehead with the clenched fist that held his now dead and cold cigarillo. 'God! If she ever gets to hear of it I wouldn't know what to do.'

'She won't hear from me, old son. Not unless somebody starts pulling my toenails off. Nothing of which, it seems, leaves you liking the much misjudged Willie, eh?' He held up a finger. 'Hang on a moment, will you? I see some suicide-motivated fella about to fling himself into outer space.'

He narrowed his eyes against the sun's dazzle, watching one of the helmeted characters – he only thought it might be male – fitting himself into the framework beneath the newly assembled triangular wing. Then, with the help of his fellow eccentric and overshadowed by the tilted-up wing, he stood upright and started a laboured run towards the slope falling away in front of him. As his running speeded up to what resembled a canter so there was lift-off and he was suddenly hidden beneath the wing that was carrying him over the valley dropping steeply below.

Lingard turned back to Skinner. 'You're all raving mad,' he said genially. 'You were about to tell me what happened next.'

'Yes, though there isn't much to my credit. If I could have got around to where his bedroom window was I would have, because I think it must have been open for me to have heard. But I couldn't, so I tried to open the door. That was locked and as I wasn't able to hear anything through it I had no option but to bang on it. I had to do it again because though I wasn't getting an answer I knew he was in there. When he did open the door he acted scared to death. That was understandable, for

69

I can imagine how I looked, being in the mood to have smashed his face in. I nearly hit him then, but thank God I didn't, because when I asked him if Angela was with him – I'm sure I was shouting – I could see from his face that he was completely surprised. He then changed completely and laughed at me and said that I was a silly bugger and why should she be.' His fingers scratched at his scalp as if he was still bewildered at his own attitude.

'Before you go any further,' Lingard said, 'how was he dressed? I mean, if he was doing what you thought he was, he'd have to put something on to answer the door. And there'd be a delay in answering it, anyway.'

'I don't know,' Skinner said helplessly. 'I was so choked up that I didn't really notice. He was dressed in something, of course; not pyjamas, but what in I just don't know.'

'Understandable,' Lingard agreed. 'What then?'

'Well . . . I was preparing to back off by then, but I had to say something, so I said it was because I had heard that I thought it might be Angie in there with him. He did lie though, because he said I was a fool – which I accept I had been – and that what I'd heard must have been a play he was listening to on his radio. I said that I couldn't hear it and he said of course I bloody well couldn't because he'd switched it off before answering the door. He was being nasty by then and said that not only was Angela not with him, but it was unlikely that she ever would be, seeing that she wasn't the type in which he'd be interested. He was being sneery then and I could have hit him for that. But when all's said and done he is only a schoolkid and I'd always be in the wrong if I had.'

Skinner shook his head and was silent as he relit his cigarillo. The hand holding the lighter had a distinct tremor and Lingard noticed it. 'I was still being stupid and arguing with him why I'd thought he'd had Angie in there when he suddenly told me to push off and leave him alone, slamming the door and leaving me standing there.' He pulled a doleful face. 'I then did what I should have done in the first place if I'd had any sense. I went into the school and rang Angie's home number and it so happened that she answered it. You won't want to know of the excuses I had to make for calling her up at eleven at night, but

70

she certainly hadn't then or since any suspicion of anything being wrong. The next morning . . .'

Lingard interposed. 'While I think of it,' he said, 'who else in the school might the woman in his bed have been?'

'Nobody I could remotely think of.' He was positive. 'There's only Molly Traill and Constance Coppin – they are also teachers – and for all I remember they were both there, though they do go away weekends.'

'Sorry. You were saying something about the next morning.'

Skinner hawked disgust in his throat. 'I had to eat dirt. I apologized to him through clenched teeth and then let him walk all over me so that he wouldn't crow about it to Angie. Something I'm sure he'd be capable of doing.' He managed a weak grin. 'There you have it; the unabridged confessions of a bloody idiot.' He was watching a blue glider descending in a wide curve, an affectionate anxiety in his expression. 'Angie's getting herself in the landing circuit, so you'd better finish now and push off.'

'A couple of quickies, old son,' Lingard said firmly. 'Why was Angela sacked from her teaching job a short while back?'

Skinner looked surprised, then irritated. 'She wasn't sacked, sport. She left for another job in town which I already knew about. I should have told you though that Willie had been chatting her up – you know he's as sex mad as a bloody rabbit, don't you? – and that was why I suppose I made my horrible boob about her being in bed with him. Because of his age – Angie's four years older than him – I didn't originally take him too seriously, though it did seem to annoy her.'

He spoke more quickly, having glanced up at the glider still high in the sky. 'After she left the school she told me that in telling Rachel why she was leaving she pushed in a bit – unnecessarily, I thought – about her son acting above his age and having some quite nasty ways. I imagine you'd know the sort of things that a boss's son can try on with women employees? Angie was surprised by Rachel's reaction and it seems that they had quite a female up-and-downer. To be honest, I thought afterwards that I might have to go, but nothing was said and it seems to have blown over.'

'The other quickie,' Lingard said. 'Why are you at the school?

71

Forgive me, but you don't look the archetypal teacher-wallah to me.'

Skinner smiled, then spoke briefly. 'I'm not by profession. My parents are in Bavaria for the next two years or so; and me, I'm reasonably independent with no particular qualifications, needing temporary accommodation and something to do. Right, sport?'

He had been watching the blue glider flying smoothly in a wide downward sweep towards the landing area. The slim helmeted figure of his Angie, prostrate in her harness beneath the tilted wing, was dark against the shining blue of the sky. 'I'm going,' he said, flipping away the stub of his cigarillo and clipping on his helmet, then pushing himself up on to his feet. 'I don't want you to see Angie about what I've told you in confidence. If you absolutely have to, then I shall want to know so that I can do something about it.'

Lingard, staying seated on the ground, flapped his hand languidly with whatever meaning the other chose to read into it. He waited, watching Skinner – a man he still liked, though not so much that he believed his every syllable of every word – take what seemed to be his pre-ordained place on the landing area. To Lingard, it contained in it all the reckless disregard of standing in the path of a charging bull.

The blue glider, almost head-on and looking more like a headless pterodactyl than ever, appeared to be coming in faster than Lingard thought necessary or safe, its frame audibly creaking and its fabric swishing in the airstream of its passage. Angela Annetts, now upright in her harness, her legs cycling away at the yielding air in anticipation of meeting the more solid ground, was pulling back on the control bar. When her feet – she wore lumpish trainers too – hit the ground she ran, seeming to support the heavy wing on her slender shoulders. With the nose lifting in a stall and checking the glider's speed, the fluttering wing appeared to drop on her, forcing her into the safe reach of the earthbound Skinner who had been running with her.

Lingard, using the occasion to descend to the skirting of the ridge and his Alfa Romeo, had been impressed by the seeming disregard the hang-gliding coterie had for the well-being of tender flesh and fragile bone. 'Absolutely raving bonkers,' he commented sententiously to the Alfa Romeo, giving off heat waves from its glittering enamel and metalware, as he put it into gear and joined the trunk road traffic back to Abbotsburn. Checked to a crawl in a slowly moving tailback, he had time to think over his interview, deciding that while he wouldn't go behind Skinner's back if ever it was necessary to interview Angela Annetts, he would certainly do it without her somewhat unlikely slow-off-the-mark boyfriend being there.

10

Rogers, broiling damply at his desk, had telephoned his opposite number, Detective Superintendent Park-Davis stationed at the neighbouring County Police Headquarters, telling him briefly of the circumstances of Horsbrugh's disappearance, of his known antecedent history, and asking for any information recorded about Lady de Vaugh's death some nine years earlier. Not unkindly, he thought that he might, metaphorically, have put a firework under Park-Davis's tail-end.

Then there was the must-be-done paperwork of his office were he not to sink into an administrative sea of tardily dealt with crime files, in few of which he had any direct interest and none of which was likely to set his pulses pounding.

That part of his mind not occupied with the compulsory reading of reports was, in parallel, reflecting on the happenings at Tower House. Particularly, he was trying to make sense of why a man of Horsbrugh's background – such as it was – and presumed intelligence could leave his house for the garden, there ineptly to fire two shots through an open window at a chair which only possibly could be presumed to be occupied by his wife. Then, having blundered his way through what appeared to be an attempt to murder, to seemingly vanish into another dimension for all that had been seen or heard of him. It sat uneasily in Rogers's thinking. That Horsbrugh was now a missing person, presumably with no clothing but what he was wearing, without taking his shaving gear and toilet necessaries, was only an unsatisfactory surmise. The whole episode appeared to be pointlessly stupid, only perhaps explicable should Horsbrugh be as unbalanced as his wife thought him to be. That he should have showed that side of himself to her and not to Primrose Booker or his stepson was, perhaps, something else altogether.

It all seemed to be against logic, though that did not necessarily make it illogical, only that Rogers himself might – at the moment – be too dimwitted to understand what it all meant. He kept his mind resolutely from thinking of Mrs Horsbrugh as anybody but an injured person and a potential witness. It wasn't easy, but his intuition was telling him that she could constitute a definite hazard to him as a police officer working under the constraints of the Police Discipline Regulations.

Pleased to get out of an office he regarded as being claustrophobic, he drove his car to Kingfisher Avenue with his jacket off – for him, a rare excursion into casualness – and every window opened. Seen in sunshine and set back from the road, Tower House was an impressive three-storeyed building of warm red brick and large white-painted windows. Taller than the house, the tower had clearly been built on to it at a later date. Architecturally, it didn't harmonize, its shape being four-sided with room only for a single window overlooking the front garden at each of the three levels. Its roof was steeply pitched and, for anyone prone to thinking that way, the whole thing could be held to suggest a giant quadrilateral phallus. The Lodge, occupied by Willie Sloane and situated immediately inside the double gate, was revealed as penny-pinchingly tiny and almost completely hedged in by the garden's shrubbery. The Volkswagen he had seen there the previous evening was no longer there.

Putting his jacket back on and leaving his car in the shadow of a tree growing from the footpath, Rogers walked the drive to the house, passing the raised shutter of the garage and seeing in there Mrs Horsbrugh's white coupé. Receiving no reply to his repeated knocking on the front door, he walked to the side of the house.

Without the distorting effect of moonlight, impenetrable

shadows and veiling rain, the sunlit garden presented to Rogers a very different picture. Without entering, he stood taking it in. It was spacious and enclosed by a high weathered pink brick wall in which, near to him, was the wrought-iron gate he had tested the night before. At the far end, there was a second gate in a length of panel fencing which gave access to a separate enclosure at the unseen foot of the tower.

The garden's centre piece – the Cedar of Lebanon – stood tall and massive and densely foliaged, with, at each side, a shrubbery of glossy-leaved laurel bushes. Wide borders under the ground-floor windows of the house were thickly planted with roses. The asphalt path ran alongside a raised expanse of sun-baked lawn on which had been placed an iron white-enamelled table and two chairs. Also on the lawn, but nearer to the house, was a plumply padded lounger in a floral-patterned linen with a huge fringed sun umbrella at its head. In its shadow, propped up on the lounger's inclined rear, lay Mrs Horsbrugh, staring straight ahead of her and apparently unaware of the detective's presence.

Rogers, holding his still-burning pipe in his hand and without a door to knock, coughed loudly and walked towards her, the asphalt soft under his tread. When she turned her head to him he could see a haunting sadness in her face. He said, 'I hope I'm not disturbing you, Mrs Horsbrugh. Can you spare me a few minutes?'

'Of course,' she replied with no change in her expression. 'You can see I'm doing nothing at the moment.'

Rogers had the feeling that his presence there was not too deeply welcomed, that as masculine man he had not made a particularly lasting impression on her.

Wearing a vaguely pinkish dress that went well with the brownness of her skin, her make-up not quite so colourful as it had been the day before, she remained unmoving in her propped-up posture beneath the umbrella. She looked to be in a profound depression, though to the unshown admiration of the detective she was still as he had imagined the Egyptian Queen Nefertiti might have been. On the grass beside her were an open book, a packet of Gauloise cigarettes, a lizardskin-covered lighter and a pair of white court shoes she had been wearing.

Standing at her side and looking down at the top of her glossy black hair and the length of her excessively slender body because he hadn't been asked to sit – which would have had to be disadvantageously on the grass anyway – he said, 'I needed primarily to see the garden in daylight, but I would appreciate your help with some questions I have to ask.'

While she had not lifted her gaze to him and there was no change in the sadness of her expression, he had seen that she had quite noticeably jerked her head at his words. 'It is no matter. I expected that you would want to see me again.'

'You haven't heard anything of, or from, your husband, I suppose?' It was a stupid question, but he wanted to see her reaction to it.

Her eyes, now meeting his, showed what he thought to be a spark of apprehension. 'Had I, Mr Rogers, I would have told you. Or, anyway, told one of your men who are visiting here.'

'Of course, forgive me.' He metaphorically put on velvet gloves. 'It would be understandable had you not, but did you ever mention to Willie that his stepfather might be mentally ill?' He felt the sun's heat on his shoulders and a dampness down his spine. Unlike him, Mrs Horsbrugh was doing nothing so commonplace as sweating.

She said, after a brief hesitation, 'I'm afraid not. I wanted them so much to get on with each other, but . . .' She shook her head and reached down, picking up her cigarettes and lighter and holding out the opened packet to Rogers.

'Thank you,' he said, 'but I use a pipe. May I smoke that?' With the tobacco in it only half burned, he put a match to it after receiving her unsmiling approval and her rejection of a light for her cigarette. Returning to his questioning, he asked, 'Do you know of anyone who might hold a grudge, or an imagined grudge, against your husband? Anybody who might feel wronged by something he'd done?'

Her eyes reflected her surprise at his question, her fingers twisting around the lighter she had retained in her hand, which Rogers saw as a sign of an inner agitation. 'I don't understand. I don't see the purpose of your asking me that.'

'Truth to tell, I don't myself,' he said amiably. 'Other than that I have to investigate the possibly unlikely as much as I do the likely. You see, there are aspects of the attack on you which might actually have been aimed at another person. Who, I wouldn't know, but it's a possibility I have to consider. As for your husband's subsequent disappearance, he doesn't quite fit the picture of a man on the run from having attempted to murder his wife, if that is what it was.'

When she spoke her voice was suffering, and Rogers was uncomfortably aware that he hadn't exactly made her day. 'There is no one I know who could possibly wish to harm him. Nor, I should say, to harm myself.' Her fingers looked as though they were intent on rubbing the lizardskin from the lighter. 'I don't know what to think,' she continued. 'I did tell you how difficult I find it to believe that he would go so far as to try to kill me. I would give much to be convinced that he hadn't.' She paused, her over-mascara'd eyelids half closed as though she were brooding on what he had said.

Rogers, chewing on the stem of his pipe, let the oppression of a disquieted silence extend until she should decide on words to fill the emptiness.

'I would want to be fair to Henry,' she finally said haltingly. 'Whatever I told you doesn't detract from his being normally a considerate and understanding man. He is quite a religious man, though not in the Christian sense, and he wasn't free of faults. Few of us are, Mr Rogers, as in your profession you must know. I may have said things – exaggerated them a little – in the unusual circumstances in which I found myself.' She eased herself more upright, screwing her unfinished cigarette to extinction in the turf at her side, and looked around her. 'He loved this garden, you know. When he could he would sit out here and smoke his cigars. He loved flowers too, and he planted those roses you see in the borders.' She bit at her bottom lip. 'I have to tell you this also, for it may help you in finding him. When I said he was religious, I hadn't intended telling you this, but I think part of it was in holding the cedar in great venera-tion. He said that that was how it was with the Nepalese for whom he'd always had an admiration. I wasn't supposed to know, but he used to come out here after dark – he always said

77

that he was taking a stroll – and stand in front of the tree with his head bent as if praying. A tree?' she said with a faint edge of puzzlement in her voice. 'Would you know about that?'

Rogers had been watching the sad sensuality of her mouth as she expressed what he thought must be the last fragments of a wifely loyalty. He was aware of the possibility that she was shunting him off from whatever she had thought he was about to ask her. Nevertheless, whatever her motive, his interpretation was that she had relieved herself of some of the guilt she obviously felt about her earlier accusations of his misdoings.

'I have heard of something similar,' he answered her untruthfully, 'and of course I accept that Colonel Horsbrugh has all the attributes you've spoken of. There is one other matter I . . .'

'Please no,' she interrupted him, showing a sudden resolution. 'I really must ask you to excuse me.' Picking up her book and cigarettes, she stepped lithely from the lounger on the side away from him, then stood and faced him. Blinking her eyes, she looked near to tears – he thought he must seem to be a tactless and clumsy lout – and he winced his discomfiture. 'I have one of my migraines,' she said, 'and I must go to bed.'

'I'm sorry,' he sympathized with her, though, in truth, his former wife had made him almost paranoically suspicious of headaches as an excuse. 'May I see you again when you are feeling better?' He wanted that, for there was much more he needed to know about her and her husband. So far, his investigation had profited little from his interviews with her.

'People lie, Mr Rogers,' she said as if she hadn't heard his question. 'We all do to a certain extent. I want you to know that.'

'I think that off and on I've known them to,' he told her gravely. 'Are you accusing anyone in particular?'

'I think . . . no, I'm sure that one of my employees might; Daniel Skinner.'

'In what way?'

She managed a sad brief smile, one almost of apology. 'You wished to see the garden and I've kept you from it. I believe I can manage my own way back to the house, so please feel free to do what you wish to do here.'

She turned to go, then abruptly faced him again. 'I hadn't

meant to speak of it, Mr Rogers,' she said, 'but I believe it to be necessary. If it happens that you get to the truth of this matter, which I think you may, you should know that there is a mental condition which may not be immediately apparent, but which you must be sure to have taken into your reckoning.'

'I do understand, Mrs Horsbrugh,' he assured her, wondering why the devil she should keep on about it.

'Perhaps you do not,' she contradicted him with a sudden intensity, her eyes reflecting an inner passion. 'I want you to remember that. You will understand when it happens. *Please,*' she added as she turned away.

Puzzled, he watched her walk from him in her bare feet – that, somehow, emphasized her apparent vulnerability – and enter the house through the porch, suddenly tinged green from its glass. Seeing her disappear gave him, he had to admit, a pang or two – was it of Hamlet's dispriz'd love? – though nothing that couldn't be made bearable by a cold shower or being hit on the head with a heavy hammer.

He snorted a sort of contempt with himself, thinking that he was a bloody fool, putting his momentarily straying mind back to the main purpose of his visit. With Sergeant Magnus and his team of searchers having earlier flea-combed the garden in their search for the two cartridge cases and any other evidence relevant to the investigation and finding nothing, Rogers accepted that he could suppress his own impulse to make a physical search of his own.

Viewing the backs of both the house and the tower, he took note that in the latter building there were no windows overlooking the garden. Moving to the six-feet high panel fence separating the gardens, he unlatched its communicating gate and walked through to a kitchen garden with a greenhouse and toolshed. Largely neglected, the few plants growing there were wilting in the sweltering heat. There was no other entrance to the garden but for a door at the base of the tower.

Returning to the house garden, feeling that his underclothing and socks had resolved themselves into hot wire wool, he pushed his way into the tall and now wilting laurel bushes. Thus placed, he was not only concealed, but also directly opposite the window into which the shots had been fired. There was a carry, he judged, of about twenty yards and to hell with using un-English metres. Looking from behind the stiff-leaved foliage at the window as if aiming a pistol, he could see framed in it only the lower half of one of the high-backed chairs. He was, clearly, nowhere near the position from which the pistol had been used.

Moving towards the window until he was on the lower level of the garden path, he was able to confirm his earlier opinion that Mrs Horsbrugh's assailant had stood there to do whatever had been intended. And, that close – Rogers could see that the distance from himself to the window was no more than fifteen feet – anyone standing there would be within the ambit of a brightly lit window and could, if seen, be recognized.

'Um,' he muttered to himself, and that said it all as he walked thoughtfully from the garden to his waiting car.

11

Having gone back to his apartment for a shower and a thin slice of refrigerator-chilled game pie which he made do for a late lunch, Rogers returned to his office no more knowledgeable for the thinking he had been doing about Horsbrugh in the intervals between.

Being told by the duty chief inspector that PC Rutter was in the Parade Room waiting on his return, he said, 'Send him up', and suspended operations pending his climbing the two flights of stairs to his office. He recalled that Rutter was one of the force's university graduates on an accelerated promotion entry and would certainly be Lingard's choice for the digging out of information from some academic at St Wulfric's School. He might, in fact, be the one who had previously attended there.

Rutter, knocking authoritatively on Rogers's door and entering, gave immediately the impression that he was an achiever, a constabulary high-flyer. His immaculate uniform sat on him like an army officer's regimentals, his forceful personality showing out from behind his officially issued impassivity. Rogers guessed that unless Rutter was extremely careful he was far too youthfully good-looking to last the distance in any walk of life bringing him into contact with predatory women. Bearing in mind that caveat and given a fair wind, he was almost certainly destined to be some force's Chief Constable. Rogers thought, not too seriously, that as with large bosomy women, Rutter tended to make him feel a little inadequate.

'Good afternoon, Rutter,' he said pleasantly. 'I take it you've some information about young Sloane?'

'Yes, sir.' His voice already had the listen-to-what-I'm-saying intonation of a senior officer. 'I believe you'll find it useful.'

'That's the general idea we have about information,' Rogers said more drily than he had intended. 'Sit down and give it to me.'

Rutter sat, empty-handed and without taking his pocket-book from his tunic pocket. 'Two things first, sir,' he started. 'My informant has family connections near here and for that reason and the obvious one insists on anonymity. He also made it a condition that at no time would I write down anything of what he said. I consented to this and, if I may, shall call him Mr Jones.'

'That's usually par for the course and nothing to be concerned about,' Rogers said. 'Just so long as you can remember precisely what your informant told you and he didn't say anything of evidential value.'

'I can do that, naturally,' Rutter assured him, though not quite so confidently, 'and I'm sure he said nothing that would be admissible in a court of law. Mr Jones was my form master at Wulfric's in my final year before I went up to university. He is still one of the sixth form masters and Willie Sloane is well known to him. His opinion of him as a boy – he'll be a boy until he leaves school – is not too good, though academically he is intelligent and diligent and should definitely be good for his university A levels. Mr Jones said that Sloane was self-contained – possibly beyond his years – and not inclined to mix sociably with his fellow students. There is an oddness, an apartness about him, he says, that he cannot understand. I asked what college activities Sloane took part in and he told me that he was a reasonably active member of both the Draghound Hunt and the Rockclimbing Society, and that he regularly took part in track events as a middle distance runner.'

Rutter paused pointedly as if waiting for Rogers to detach his interest from methodically refilling his pipe and then scratching matches at it. 'Go on then,' Rogers said brusquely, for Rutter wasn't a Chief Constable yet. 'Get on with it, I'm still listening.'

Rutter looked injured. 'I'm sorry, sir. I was about to say that I asked Mr Jones why he said his opinion of Sloane was not a good one. He didn't appear too keen about answering that, but when he did he told me much more than I had expected. He said that in his considered opinion there was an element of depravity in him and that he was a rather unstable boy with a potential for violence. Apparently a few months previously, Sloane's room was ragged by a couple of his fellow formers. Knowing or guessing who had done it, he assaulted both rather more badly than was warranted. It wasn't on, naturally, that they should complain about it, but it did get put around by the usual sneak and it did reach Mr Jones's ears. He decided to do nothing officially, but to have a quiet cautionary word with Sloane. In the event, Sloane proved to be quite unrepentant, saying that the two other boys – whom he refused to name – had, among other things, ruined a photographic portrait of his mother by adding an inked moustache and beard to her face.'

'Distasteful as that is,' Rogers commented with irony, 'it hardly amounts to depravity.' He had the impression that he was listening to the anonymous Jones's actual phrases and words as recalled by Rutter. No bad thing, of course.

'No, sir,' Rutter said, not too successfully hiding a sudden irritation with Rogers. 'I wasn't suggesting that it did. Possibly what I persuaded Mr Jones to tell me wasn't the whole of it, and probably not meaning much at all.' He sounded dismissive of it.

'Still, we'll have it,' Rogers told him firmly. 'Anything about Sloane has to be potentially useful.' He scratched another match to fire his gone-out pipe, thinking that Rutter had lost some of his earlier forcefulness in his telling. Perhaps he might prove to be an ordinary mortal after all.

'I'm sure it must be,' Rutter agreed hastily. 'Mr Jones had heard a strong rumour that Sloane had been seen wearing women's underclothing. I think he meant panties, though he didn't say. He didn't wholly believe the rumour because he couldn't see Sloane as that type of boy. But, because he had heard about this more than once, he feared an unpleasant scandal in the college and spoke to Headmaster. Having received his approval, Mr Jones put the nature of the rumour to Sloane. In his favour, Sloane was quite unabashed at the accusation. In fact, it appears that he treated it lightly, saying that it had happened once and once only and then solely because of a shared joke with another unnamed boy. He actually offered in a rather aggressive manner to drop his trousers to show that he was wearing a normal male's Y-fronts, but Mr Jones – he had obviously been most agitated at the time – sensibly refused to allow him to. He then cautioned him about the possibility of a misunderstanding of his motives in wearing such an article, even of his standing in the college as a normal boy, in any repetition of his so-called joke. Mr Jones told me in passing, declining to elaborate on it, that he considered the boy to have had an emotionally disoriented childhood.' Rutter looked expectantly at Rogers. 'That's it, sir. I imagine that it's what you wanted?'

'It adds substance to a youngster I consider to be an unpleasant little sod, if that's what you mean,' Rogers said. 'Why do *you* suppose he was wearing a woman's knickers?'

Rutter was surprised. 'If he was lying about its being a joke, I suppose it could be an aspect of a suspected homosexuality.'

Rogers shook his head. 'Not so. I'd say anything but. Look up fetishism if you're interested enough. Did your Mr Jones think to question him about who donated the knickers? Or whether he had bought or stolen them?'

'I did ask him, but he said that it wasn't the sort of question he would put to a boy.'

'That was a pity, don't you think? A disappointment? It might have been the interesting answer to some questions I already have in my mind.' He showed Rutter some affability in dismissing him. 'You did a good job and I'm grateful,' he said. 'If you do happen to pick up anything more about Sloane, let me know, will you?'

With the PC having left the office, Rogers indulged himself in projecting his thoughts forward to when Rutter might have achieved the rank of Chief Constable. 'Ah, yes,' he would drawl, apropos of something relevant, 'I remember Rogers very well. A bit of a prat actually, and devilishly thick between the ears.'

He was still smiling at the thought when his telephone bell rang. 'Park-Davis here, old boy,' his caller said. It was his opposite number from the county covering the village Trumpton Beck, who then remarked how pleased he was to have found Rogers in his office on a Sunday afternoon. Which, he would know, was not the most tactful thing to say. Park-Davis was a man who had manifestly burned tyre rubber in searching out what he thought promised to have been an overlooked cock-up by his predecessor. He sounded just the slightest apprehensive at what he had found, though prepared to fight his corner against any outside assertion of unnoticed or undetected villainy in his bailiwick.

Rogers scribbled notes as he listened. From a reading of the file papers of Park-Davis's predecessor's investigation and his visit to the scene, it appeared that Lady Caroline de Vaugh had been found lying face downwards in an ornamental fishpond in the garden of her house by one of the estate workers. She had been seen alive and well by a house servant less than an hour before the finding of her body. It was evident that Horsbrugh – there was nothing in the file to suggest that he had then claimed any military or other service rank – had been elsewhere on the estate for two hours or so before the dead woman had been found. A post-mortem examination had been made of the body, the pathologist having no hesitation in deciding that the death had been an asphyxial one due to drowning. There were no marks on the body to suggest the use of physical violence and it could only be presumed that, being elderly, her fall into the water had been caused by fainting. A coroner's jury had brought in what the former detective superintendent had considered to be a proper finding of Death by Misadventure.

'I shouldn't think there's anything in it for you, old boy,' Park-Davis had ended, more confidently than he had started, and that was something that Rogers couldn't argue about. Not, anyway, without having more information than was apparently in the file that Park-Davis was set on hanging on to until his Chief Constable gave him the authority to part with it.

It was following his disconnection from Park-Davis that he realized he had overlooked in Rutter a useful source of research.

He used his internal telephone to call the Parade Room, catching Rutter before he left it for whatever beat duties he had been assigned for the good of his soul. 'I take it that you're reasonably well up on tree worship?' Rogers said, always a good opening for nonplussing somebody.

'Sir?' Rutter replied after a couple of seconds' puzzled silence and clearly taken off balance. 'Indeed I'm not.'

'Nothing about it at university?' Rogers made himself sound astonished at discovering an obvious shortcoming in Rutter's education.

'No, sir,' he said in a manifestly controlled voice. 'I graduated in Philosophy, Sociology and Economics. None of which touched on tree worship.'

'That's good. You can research what I'm asking for with an open mind. I'll clear it with your chief inspector that you do it for me today.'

'On tree worship?' Rutter clearly doubted Rogers's seriousness.

Rogers laughed. 'Bear with me, Rutter,' he mollified him. 'It actually is relevant to our investigation, though nothing to do with Sloane. I want to know if any of the Nepalese, in particular the Gurkhas, go in for tree worshipping; specifically the Cedar of Lebanon or whatever it might be called in Asia. You understand?'

'Naturally, sir.' Rutter was plainly relieved. 'It sounds interesting.'

'It is. Colonel Horsbrugh was supposed to be one such. I know it's Sunday and most sources will be closed to you, but no doubt your ingenuity'll get you over that. I need it urgently, which means today, even if you've to do it in your own time. And on paper on my desk, please.'

He closed down, being more doubtful than he had sounded. Finding out that Horsbrugh was genuinely a tree worshipper, or that it was a manifestation of his supposed barminess, seemed unlikely to further his investigation more than a whisker or two. But, he knew, it would at least suggest to uninvolved higher authority that he was, as the cliché should have it, exploring every bloody avenue.

12

The Lord Nelson Dining-room in the Minster Hotel served undoubtedly expensive meals above the restaurant proper, keeping its club-like exclusiveness by requiring reservations from its patrons. The room had a perceptibly, almost dangerously, tilted floor of ancient highly polished boards, ceiling beams against which the tall and incautious could sustain brain-ringing impacts, and its complement of seven tables and their chairs. In addition there were six dimly lit and shadowed cubicles formed by grouped together linenfold-decorated church pews for diners of a secretive or reclusive temperament. Each cubicle was furnished with a blackwood table with iron legs and fitted with wine-coloured curtains on brass rings which could be drawn closed at a diner's discretion. The gravy-brown walls were heavily concealed by black-framed mezzotints and steel engravings of Admiral Lord Nelson, HMS *Victory* and different flag-flying, smoke-filled naval actions engaged in during the Battle of Trafalgar. Where the walls had shelving between the small diamond-latticed windows, these held old pewter tankards and flagons. The two elderly waiters – reputed exaggeratedly by regular diners to have served under Lord Nelson in the *Victory* – were spryly efficient, obliging with an old-fashioned courtesy and necessarily discreet when serving any male diner who appeared to have reserved a cubicle at different times for markedly different wives or girlfriends.

Rogers, having earlier reserved a cubicle, sat in it with Lingard opposite him, the curtains left open. The small table lamp between them gave a greenish cast to their features, reminding Rogers of his last view of Mrs Horsbrugh entering the porch of her house after her apparent dismissal of him.

Not as hungry as he had thought he would be and bearing in

mind that he was picking up the non-tax-deductible bill, he had ordered Eggs Benedict with smoked mackerel pâté and a Waldorf Salad. Lingard – an uncaring gormandizing sod, Rogers had called him – chose, despite this, the hideously expensive Lobster Thermidor and Salade Niçoise.

At their coffee, with Rogers's nerve-endings anaesthetized by tobacco smoke and Lingard's nostrils fully charged with Attar of Roses, Rogers spoke in a voice not to be overheard and apropos of each of them having briefed the other on what had gone before. 'You wouldn't think that a former captain of the Gurkha Rifles and a present member of a small-bore pistol club could miss putting a couple of bullets into the back of a chair at five yards, would you?' he said.

Lingard, comfortably bloated, said, 'Impossible, George. If he hit the television set, he was aiming at it.'

'That's what I think, only I don't know why he would.' Rogers was fishing not too subtly for his second-in-command's opinions. 'And apparently taking the used cartridge cases away with him.'

'To prevent identification of the cases to a particular pistol?'

'I'd assume so, but we've a contradiction there in that he seems to have taken the pistol away with him. If', Rogers said carefully, 'by "he" we mean Horsbrugh.'

'As we've already agreed, there's at best only a piddling motive for what he's done. And a piddling execution too of an attempt to shoot holes in Mrs H.'s back.' Lingard shook his head. 'Stap me, George, a schoolgirl could've done better.'

'Or somebody like young Sloane if he hadn't been at the Gibbet with me and if we had some suggestion that he didn't like his mother.' Rogers was looking into the bowl of his pipe as if for inspiration. 'There could be Booker, of course, who may, if he's that sort of a character, nurse something of a dislike for Horsbrugh. His wife says he's a wet, but at the same time is extremely jealous. None of which explains why he'd want to shoot at a chair presumed to be occupied by Mrs Horsbrugh who would have nothing to do with her husband's having it off with his wife.' He creased his forehead as if in pain. 'Even were that explicable, it makes no sense that Horsbrugh and his pistol should, coincidentally, both go missing.'

'A dead end there, I think. Nothing fits.' Lingard was clearly unimpressed.

'No, it doesn't. However, I've put a watch on Mrs Booker's home – her name's Primrose by the way and it doesn't suit her – in case Horsbrugh's still around and is hiding up with her.'

'He could be, George. We do tend to flee to the friendly bosom in times of trouble. Of which, more later. Have you considered Skinner?'

'I have. Mrs Horsbrugh suggests that he's a liar. A liar full stop, and no less.'

'I don't think he was lying about young Sloane having a woman in his bed. Apart from which, I'm wondering if there's not a link there between him and Mrs H.? I've heard that detestation's often a close follower of infatuation.'

Rogers frowned, not wishing to believe it. 'That he and she were lovers? That she'd possibly made him redundant? Anguished despair and all that? Driven to trying to shoot her?' He beckoned without any suggestion of customer bossiness at the whiter-haired of the two waiters, asking, when he arrived, for more coffee, please. 'Though why not in the name of human frailty?' he conceded. 'I imagine a failed love affair might well provoke a mutual dislike.'

'Well, he's a good-looking cove, a blue-eyed macho type and blond with it,' the blue-eyed, blond-haired macho Lingard said without a change of expression. 'Even taking into account his doubtful claim not to ever do anything unbecoming with the fair Angie, it wouldn't surprise me.'

'I suppose that we should remember too that he was in the house at the time of the shooting.' Rogers shook his head in irritated frustration. 'Admittedly, he'd know about the pistol and could no doubt obtain access to the ammunition, but what would he have done about Horsbrugh? Hidden the bugger under his bed?' He paused as the waiter arrived with a tray of fresh coffees, resuming when he had left them. 'Still, it mightn't be a bad idea though to have the tower searched. The roof-space, too. Anywhere capable of hiding a body; even the kitchen garden and outhouses. He wouldn't be the first unlucky husband to be finished off and buried under the cabbages. All presupposing, of course, that he does happen to be a corpse.

Get it done, David, will you? Without advertising it, naturally. We mustn't aim the finger of imagined suspicion at anybody in the house. Perhaps you could suggest that we're still looking for the missing cartridge cases.' He put his pipe down and drank coffee while his thinking was ticking over. 'I'd be a lot happier if I knew from whom Sloane got those knickers. I've a feeling we'd learn something useful from them.'

Lingard raised an eyebrow. 'Would we? Don't you think he might have had them as a sort of gage? Much as the love-smitten knights bachelor used to wear a lady's scarf around their throttles, or carry her glove into battle? Or he might just see them as his baccalaureate in adolescent seduction.'

'True, but it still might be a rather queer case of fetishism,' Rogers said, his earlier conviction that it was a little lessened. 'I knew a chap – he was a retired naval commander – who had a somewhat similar thing about women's high-heeled shoes. Except that he didn't wear them of course. I sorted out his house once after a breaking and entering there and saw that he had a fine old collection of new shoes and photographs of women's legs wearing them stored in his wardrobe. They obviously didn't belong to his wife who slept in a separate bedroom. She – a lovely little poppet with big dark eyes – told me later on about her husband's fixation on shoes.' Rogers's voice had an echo of wistful regret in it when speaking of the woman. 'Apparently he wasn't sexually demanding as we know it where his wife was concerned, but contented himself with putting the shoes on her feet when she was fully dressed and doing whatever it was she was quite determined I shouldn't be told. There was a sort of justice in it when she later packed her bags and took off with a well-built, primitive-type fella who'd been doing some landscape gardening at the house next door.'

Lingard, in the act of pushing more Attar of Roses into his nose, laughed. 'You're making it up as you go along.'

'No, it's true. And I'll tell you this. I was a detective sergeant at the time and quite a few years younger than she was, but she took a pretty determined shot at getting me into her bed. I was bloody idiot enough to back off, though I was regretting it even as I was closing the front door behind me. That's when she must have looked over next door's fence at the gardener fella who probably had more sense than I had then.'

He shrugged off the memory of gloriously rewarding opportunity lost. 'Back to Horsbrugh, if we've ever actually left him. I've had words with DC Lewis at Thurnholme about him. He's made enquiries and he confirms that Horsbrugh had a room at the Houston-Landorf Hotel for about three years. He'd registered there as a lieutenant-colonel retired, paid his monthly tab on the dot, was very popular with the management and staff and also, it's known, popular with a succession of well-dressed women who dined frequently with him at the hotel. He owns a reasonably good Voyager four-berth sailing boat that's moored at the Bay Sailing Club. The retired Rear Admiral who runs the club let Lewis get aboard and do a search. Horsbrugh, dead or alive, certainly wasn't in the cabin, in the bilges or anywhere else, and he hadn't been seen near the clubhouse or the boat for the past fortnight or so.' Rogers tapped the stem of his pipe against his teeth, a sign of his hesitancy. 'I'm getting a very different picture of our missing lieutenant-colonel than the one I've been given from Tower House,' he said.

'He might be schizophrenic,' Lingard suggested. 'All baring of teeth and bad temper at home, and being the *gentilhomme parfait* away from it.'

A little tentatively, Rogers said, 'It might be useful to consider that he may have left home with a temporary loss of memory; the result perhaps of the unendurabilities of an unhappily married man's life. A mental fleeing from the unpleasant and traumatic he couldn't face up to. A fugue, I think the head-shrinkers call it.'

'I've not met with it myself,' Lingard answered him, 'and I'm sure it would strain the limits of my credibility if I did.'

'I suppose it would mine too,' Rogers agreed. ''T'was but an idle thought. Whichever, I don't believe there's anything at Thurnholme for us.' He looked at his wrist-watch, concealing a hard-earned yawn behind his teeth. 'I've an enquiry to make, David. Have you anything before we go?'

'Yes. Our missing friend's Rover is tucked away safely in the workshop of the Bearsbridge Garage. It has had clutch problems, but they've been dealt with and it's been ready for collection since last Friday, the day he was notified about it by telephone. Odd that, don't you think?'

'It's odd that he didn't pick it up then, or on Saturday. At the time of the shooting and afterwards I don't suppose he'd have been able to. But there's certainly something a bit puzzling about it.' Rogers wasn't happy about that at all, and he needed to brood on it. 'Is there anything else?'

'There is. Our former military gent never ever in historical time – that is, for about the past two years – missed visiting the Rodmaris Arms on a Saturday evening; walking there and back and drinking his three whiskies and sodas. No more, and no less. Except, naturally, last night. He was well liked there and, as the landlord, his wife and the barman help all told me all at once, never ever had he brought a popsy in with him, he being their beau ideal of a happily married man.'

Rogers frowned. 'It seems that I've been misled about that too, unless it's never been more than one of my unfounded suspicions. There's more?' he asked, reading that there was in Lingard's face, though hoping he had finished.

'Only this. What do you feel about my friendly bosom theory? And a thwarted, frustrated, bloody-minded, jealous or exasperated husband banging off a couple of warning shots at a chair he knows to be unoccupied, and then heading for the consolation of the more loving bosoms than those his wife gives him. Even if only for a few days?'

Lingard's theory, flippantly delivered though it had been, deserved some serious thought. Rogers gave it some while he refilled his pipe, scratched matches at it and blew out smoke to deepen further the gravy-brown staining on the ceiling. 'It's a possibility, David,' he finally said. 'I feel no more than that. That is, unless he's gone over the top and is knee-deep into the irrational. In fact, I don't go overboard for any of our theories. It damn well irks me to say it, but none gives me any conviction that it's right. And if you believe in intuitive guesswork, I've the feeling that we've a dark and nasty something in the whole stupid business that I don't even begin to understand.'

' A fiver on my warning shots theory?' Lingard suggested, not yet unconvinced of it.

'After I've settled for your meal and mine I won't be left with anything like a fiver to bet with.' Looking at the window at the far end of the dining-room and seeing the setting of a reddening sun, he pushed back his shirt cuff and checked his watch again. 'I've to see a man about a gun, so I'd better be going,' he said.

Not only had he to see a man about a gun, but he had also to attend an unarranged meeting where he was to force a somewhat spineless resolution into facing up to an existing impasse. His six feet and two inches of reasonably sturdy bone and tissue and a normally confident and thrusting temperament were going to mean little to his advantage in the coming hour or so.

13

In the darkness of the as yet moonless night, the heat of the just dead day not yet dissipated, Rogers drove his Astra into the hard-standing parking area at the back of the offices – from which lights still burned – of the *Daily Echo*. There, parked in a row of five cars and illuminated in his headlights, was the violet-coloured Volkswagen Beetle whose presence he sought. Positioning his front bumper within inches of its exhaust pipe, he cut his engine, switched off his lights and lit his pipe to ease the tedium of his waiting. Easing it also would be his consideration and evaluation of the information arising from his meeting with Percy Ruddle, the captain of the Small-Bore Rifle and Pistol Club.

After he had told Ruddle only that Horsbrugh was missing from his home, Ruddle had said that he, of course, knew him well, considering him to be a pleasantly friendly man; rather phlegmatic and carrying his authority as a retired colonel with a proper modesty.

Ruddle had shown Rogers the long and narrow room used as a shooting range, heavily sandbagged and metal-plated at its end. Shots were routinely fired at seven-inch circular targets placed against the buffer from twenty yards. Producing what he said was almost the twin of the .22 pistol owned by the man he called the Colonel, he had handed it to Rogers for his examination. It was a glossy black, evil-looking long-barrelled weapon, more angular than the detective had recalled seeing before, with an oddly shaped anatomical grip and a solid weighty feel to it. Its grip held a slim magazine of ten rounds which, when fired by Ruddle wearing what he called his ear defenders, made a much louder noise than Rogers had anticipated.

Asked to give an opinion on Horsbrugh's target-shooting ability, Ruddle had said that he was rated as very good for his age, able on average to group a cluster of shots in a three-inch diameter circle on a target sixty feet distant.

Questioned about the social side of the club, Ruddle said that the Colonel had been originally introduced to the club by a then member, Mr Gerald Booker, who had, about a year ago, ceased attending. Earlier, he had amplified, Mr and Mrs Booker and the Colonel had attended the club's social functions together, but this had ceased of course when Mr Booker no longer shot his pistol on the range. Asked for an opinion on Booker, he had said that he was quite a pleasant bloke and normal in his attitudes towards other members.

That had left Rogers with much on which to brood. Knowing now that the cuckolded Booker also possessed a small-bore pistol made him a slightly more interesting character to think about. But only to think about for the time being. Yawning away the growing fog in his brain, he stiffened at the sight of the dark silhouette of a woman appearing in the yellow rectangle of an opened door, shutting it off as she emerged.

Approaching the Volkswagen and seeing his car, she halted, indecisiveness in her attitude. Rogers, quite certain that anyone within fifty yards of him must hear the banging of his heart, switched on the parking lights of his car and climbed out to meet her.

She was thin, not much bigger than a splindly schoolgirl, but emanating for Rogers all the femininity and sexual attraction of a woman of what were her thirty years. Her hair was a glossy black, her dark eyes, dark brows and unsmiling mouth giving an appearance of cynicism to her unmade-up elfin features. Her white dress, emphasizing her seemingly fragile litheness, made her wraith-like in the darkness. Apart from the cynicism, her appearance could be deceptive. She was very much her own self-assured woman, one who could quickly disabuse a man's conceit of his own stature and importance. She was Elizabeth Gallagher, investigative journalist and Rogers's quondam lover. It had been his memory of the captivating thinness of her body and the manner in which she could use it that had led him into being attracted to Rachel Horsbrugh, in so many respects her physical double.

'Hello, Liz,' he greeted her, as unsmiling as she was. 'Sorry to jump on you, but I think I may need your help.' She was near enough for him to smell that she had recently put on scent. It was unsettling stuff.

'I'm not so sure that I believe that,' she said. She held her car keys in her hand. 'I'd like to get my car out, please.'

He felt awkward, stifled of what he had intended to say, but stubborn with it too. 'I'm sorry. What I said wasn't quite the truth.'

'So spell it out for me so that there won't be any misunderstanding.' There was an undercurrent of distrust in her voice.

'I wanted to see you.'

'So it appears,' she said drily. 'It does rather depend on why, doesn't it?'

'I suppose I've been a bit of an idiot.' Rogers was in the mood to admit with a qualification or two any minor frailty he thought he might possess.

'Yes, you have. And you know that if I'd any sense I'd tell you to go to hell.'

He winced, thinking it rough on him to have to listen to those words from so kissable a mouth, held exaggeratedly in his memory as a tasting of summer flowers. Their earlier parting was never because he had been discovered hot from the arms of another woman. 'You haven't died on me have you, Liz?' he asked.

'It's been very near it.'

'It's also been a long time.'

'Yes. Quite three weeks,' she answered him, not willing to give an inch.

'I've missed you.' In truth, he had, but he had never thought he would be led into admitting it. 'Can you leave your car here?'

'Oh? Why?'

There had been an almost perceptible softening of her voice, and he was encouraged. 'I thought we might go somewhere.'

'To do what?' Her shadowed eyes were watching him unwaveringly.

'It's too late to do much, but I thought to talk.'

'At your place, I take it?' she said, her face wooden. Her voice hadn't sounded encouraging.

'I thought you'd prefer it there.'

'Did you? Hadn't you ever considered that I may have gone back to Michael since I saw you last?'

He felt the suffocation of angry jealousy in his chest, and its effect showed in his face. 'Have you?' he asked in a voice he tried hard to control.

There was silence between them during which she had studied his reaction. Apparently satisfied with what she saw, she said, 'No, of course I haven't.' There was a waiting silence again before she added, 'I'll follow in my car if you like. It does depend, and I might choose not to stay.'

Leading the way through the centre of the town, checking frequently that he wasn't losing her in the late evening traffic, he worried about what he had done in chancing his arm so recklessly. It wasn't eighteen holes of golf he was hoping to be playing with her, but something where his suspect ability at a different activity altogether might possibly be put to embarrassing proof.

As had been her earlier habit in visiting Rogers's apartment, she fitted her Volkswagen into the first vacant Residents Only parking place she found. Joining him at the entrance to the apartment block, she climbed the stairs with him; unspeaking and, as was apparent to Rogers even in the dim light allowed the building's tenants, preoccupied with some sort of decision-making that went on behind her shut-off face.

It had, unexpectedly to Rogers who knew little about women anyway, resulted in something most pleasantly positive, for, on entering his sitting-room, she had looked up at him, her perfume heady in his nostrils, and said softly, 'You don't have

95

to put on the lights, George.' After that, his physical and mental fatigue, the occasional depression caused by his fretting about the imagined menopausal clap of doom, the attraction of the now put-behind-him Mrs Horsbrugh and the nagging improbability of his ever breaking his ninety at golf, were as of nothing when, in bed, he was held tightfast in the affectionate embrace of her arms.

Struggling up from the dark tunnel of his exhausted sleep to the sound of his hated telephone bell, Rogers groggily checked the time on his wrist-watch, the only thing he was wearing. It was one twenty-something – his eyes were incapable of focusing properly – and Liz had been gone for less than an hour. When the ringing of the bell showed no signs of going away, he climbed from his bed, padded unsteadily into his sitting-room and lifted the receiver.

'Rogers here,' he said into it in as civilized and composed a voice as he could muster when risen from interrupted sleep.

His caller was Lingard, unbearably cheerful for that time of the night, telling him that he was about to gallop post-haste to Tower House, having just received emergency telephoned information that an as yet unknown somebody had broken into the Lodge slept in by young Willie Sloane and fired shots at him. He had not been hit apparently, but it had been a close-run thing and he was badly shaken.

Disconnecting, Rogers returned to his bedroom to dress, wanting to rail against the people who seemed always to insist on killing, or on trying to kill, other people in the middle of the bloody night; particularly so when a grossly fatigued and irritated Rogers was still trying to catch up on the sleep he had lost the previous night.

14

When Rogers braked his car to a halt in Kingfisher Avenue, the pallid newly risen moon hung large over the hump of the shadowed moor behind the town, its background of inky-blue starlit sky clear of clouds. Apart from Tower House and its Lodge – from which lights were showing – the houses in the avenue were in unlit sleep.

Leaving his car and approaching the drive gates, he saw that the door of the Lodge was open. Passing through it, he noticed that the door lock socket had been torn from the door stile, the tongue of the lock casing on the door itself being extended and the key secure on the inside. On the door's exterior, at the side of the handle lever, were the dusty confused imprints of the sole of a shoe.

The Lilliputian sitting-room in which he found himself was furnished with not much more than an elderly easy chair, an eating table which would be crowded in use by more than one person, a wooden cottage chair, what looked like a food cupboard for somebody with a small appetite, and an electric fire standing on the border of a patterned carpet. On an otherwise empty wall was a short wooden shelf of paperback novels and a telephone. Apart from the door through which he had entered, there were two others side by side; one ajar and revealing a glimpse of an old-fashioned white-enamelled bath; the other wide open and framing Lingard intent on his examination of a bed's green velvet, padded headboard.

Rogers joined him in the narrow half-sized bedroom where Lingard showed his teeth in greeting. He looked well scrubbed, his suit and shirt immaculate. 'I've just arrived myself,' he said. 'Well, ten minutes or so ago. You want the picture? As much as I've had it from PC Orton?'

'PC Orton?'

'Yes. He was doing his security check at the house when it happened.'

Rogers nodded, taking in his second-in-command's turn-out, feeling himself not nearly so scrubbed and immaculate. He had looked briefly at the room as he had entered, noting the single bed, with its disordered sheets and one blanket, set alongside one wall which had an open curtained window in it. A narrow wardrobe stood against the wall opposite and, next to it, a plant pot table having on it a mirror and toilet articles. This room, Rogers considered, had to be where Skinner had alleged that Sloane had been making love to a woman who had been so audibly enjoying it, but who had manifestly not been his Angie.

Now his interest was focused on the bedhead and the apricot-coloured pillow resting on it. There was a small hole in the padding of the headboard two or three inches above the pillow and apparently continuing through into the wall. The pillow, impressed from a head having been lying on it, had two dimpled holes in its cover. Three empty small-bore cartridge cases in polished brass lay on the blanket at the foot of the bed.

Having remained silent while Rogers was seeing for himself, Lingard spoke only when his senior's interest in bullet holes and cartridge cases had obviously exhausted itself. 'When I arrived,' he said, 'Orton was in the next room, having switched on all the lights to make sure that nobody was concealed here, and seeing what there was to see.' He looked around him. 'Egad, George, anybody not a three-foot gnome would have a job, wouldn't he? It seems that Orton had been doing his wandering around the back of the house at about one o'clock, both ears cocked on his surveillance thingy, when he heard three spaced-out shots coming from somewhere – he wasn't sure from where – and he broke into a constabulary gallop for the front of the house. In his hurry he tripped over his feet or some such and knocked himself silly for a moment or two. When he did get around here – he was bleeding a fair bit – he met young Willie running in his pyjamas and bare feet as if the plague dogs were after him. Definitely in a fair old tizzy and yelling that he wanted Orton to save him from somebody who'd been shooting at him in his bed.'

Lingard, as if exhausted with talking, took out his tiny ivory box and pinched snuff into his nose, flapping away loose grains with a crimson silk handkerchief. 'First things first, I suppose,' he said, still sniffing, 'and I'd have probably done the same, but Orton took Willie into the house, obtained a rather shattered account of what he was flapping about, and then used the phone to dial for some assistance. Orton left a badly shaken-up Willie with his mum, who had come down from bed by then, and then trotted down here to see what it was about. That was when I came into the picture.'

Rogers indicated the three cartridge cases. 'I doubt that these were found where they are now.'

'No, I was coming to that. Orton found them just outside the bedroom door. He said he realized they might be walked on and disturbed so he marked where they were and picked them up. Taking care, of course, not to wipe any fingerprints from them.'

'Stout fella,' Rogers said approvingly. He said it despite having forgotten to bring his pipe and tobacco with him and recognizing the need to control any future gusts of irritation his body's craving for nicotine might provoke. 'Sloane obviously had something to tell Orton?'

'Yes, he had, though it seems it wasn't much. He was asleep in bed when the noise of his front door being kicked in woke him. He says that it scared him and that sort of half-asleep he scrambled out of bed in the dark and found himself behind the side of the wardrobe here. Understandable, I feel, for a youngster. He then heard whoever it was moving in the other room and this was immediately followed by the three shots Orton heard. He tells Orton that they were fired very close to his bed. When he heard departing footsteps or whatever coming from the other room, he poked his head out from around the wardrobe and saw what he thought might be a man high-tailing it out of the open front door. He's not at all sure about that apparently. He waited a bit, then decided that he'd best make a run for the house.' He added, 'I've checked what can be seen from behind the wardrobe and, as you can probably see, the front door does come into the picture.'

Rogers frowned. 'He's not saying that it was his stepfather?'

'I don't think Orton had the time or inclination to dig too deeply, but Willie did apparently say that, while he hadn't actually recognized who it was, he was sure it must have been

99

his stepfather.' Lingard seemed not to have too many uncertainties about it. 'No doubt he'd be justified in assuming that it was. The gallant colonel would know where he slept of course, and the exact whereabouts of the head of the bed. It's a presumption that he'd believe Willie to be still in it, waiting for his head to be blown off.'

'Compared with the shots fired at Mrs Horsbrugh's chair, these were much better aimed,' Rogers commented. 'Particularly so being aimed in the dark, which the others were not.'

'You're going to lose your fiver, George,' Lingard predicted. 'The colonel might well see a difference in aiming at a chair, perhaps to frighten or warn his wife, and aiming at a stepson he may have cause to dislike or even fear.'

'You've a point,' Rogers admitted. 'Switch off the lights and we'll see, or not see, what may be what.'

When Lingard returned, having put the rooms into darkness, they waited. When their eyes had adjusted to it, it could be seen that the night's darkness contained within the rooms was only tenuously lightened by the phosphorescent blue of reflected moonlight entering through the windows. A man would not be seen as much more than a shadow for all his clothed flesh, and with Lingard having gone into the sitting-room to test it, Rogers thought that even he might not recognize him for who he was if suddenly wakened from sleep.

Rogers said, 'I'm not exactly hysterical about any of this, David. In fact, I haven't been happy at all about any of the motives it's been suggested that Horsbrugh might have had for popping off at his wife, or for disappearing .' He made a sound indicative of his exasperation. 'And why should he turn up from being somewhere else for nearly forty-eight hours and then try and blow his stepson away? There again, what the hell's the motive?'

He hadn't been asking questions, but letting off steam, and Lingard knew that, contenting himself with recharging his nostrils with snuff and making small noises that could be taken for cheerful agreement. 'You'll be taking over now, will you?' he said. Rogers had started the investigation and it wouldn't be considered heavyweight enough by higher authority to warrant the efforts of both a superintendent and a chief inspector.

100

'I'd better, I suppose,' Rogers told him, asking him to return to the office and to call out Sergeant Magnus for a fingerprint search and photographic survey of the scene. While he was at it, he could also call out a sufficiency of other CID bodies who, a sardonic Rogers felt, should not be left to hoggishly snore in bed while their departmental superintendent was getting no sleep himself. Too, he said that he might need the attendance of a policewoman, being neither Doust nor Witheridge who would both be likely to shrivel whatever self-esteem he thought he might still possess. Before leaving by the shattered door he handed his house keys to Lingard. 'A favour, David. My pipe, tobacco and matches are in my sitting-room. You'll save my sanity if you can have them ferried up to me just a little faster than the speed of light.'

<h1 style="text-align:center">15</h1>

For Rogers, it was very much as if circumstances were repeating themselves when he entered the house and made his way to the lamp-lit sitting-room. Mrs Horsbrugh, predictably no longer giving off a discernible sensuality to the *après*-Liz depleted Rogers, occupied the sofa with her son; she in her cream satin robe and looking as washed-out as a faded sepia photograph; and Sloane, in a white towelling bath robe over red pyjamas, hunched as if smoulderingly defensive against a not-yet-gone-away threat. He held a half-empty glass of red wine cupped in his hands. PC Orton, in his uniform and with one side of his face showing a gravel rash, was in the background, as darkly inconspicuous as he must have been in patrolling outside the house.

Despite the air of cheerless gloom there, Rogers managed a reasonably encouraging 'Good morning' to Mrs Horsbrugh in particular – she said something in reply he couldn't quite catch – and included by a nod of his head the other two.

Sloane, apparently waiting on his arrival, was flushed and obviously chewing on a grievance. 'You told me you were going to look after us,' he said to Rogers with a barely concealed hostility that must have been overriding the shock that Orton had reported he was suffering. 'To protect us. I was nearly killed in my bed and nobody did anything to stop it.'

Rogers, now well into nicotine deprivation and never at his sunniest at two in the morning, wanted to diminish his hostility with stern words but, mindful of his mother being present, said reasonably mildly, 'Not you, Willie, not you. You'll remember that you never were the target. We were here to protect your mother on your own complaint of possible future violence to her.'

'It's the same thing.' Behind his dishevelment and what remained of his shock, Sloane was manifestly unappeased.

Mrs Horsbrugh, intervening rather spiritlessly, whispered, 'Please be quiet, Willie. Mr Rogers is perfectly right.' Turning her gaze to the detective, she said, 'He is so upset. He wouldn't be like it normally.'

'I'm sure not,' Rogers answered her, lying as one did with troubled mothers. 'Who else is in the house?'

She looked to her son to reply, her mouth reflecting a deep sadness, and he complied, speaking to Rogers without further hostility. 'Only Mr Skinner and he's obviously still in bed. Mrs Traill and Miss Coppin aren't due back until the morning.'

'He's in the tower?'

'At the top. If you want him, his bedroom's got his name on the door.' Sloane had finished his wine and was fussily balancing the glass on the fat arm of the sofa.

Rogers spoke to Orton. 'Find your way into the tower, will you, and knock up Mr Skinner. He seems not to have heard the gunfire. Tell him what's happened and that I'd like him to come down here.'

As Orton left, apparently knowing already how to get there, Mrs Horsbrugh said, 'I'm dreadfully tired, Mr Rogers, and I would like to return to my room.' She appeared only half-awake, the flesh on her face slack, her brown eyes lustreless and heavy-lidded.

Even in her spiritless, washed-out mood, without the enhancement of her make-up, he thought her an attractive woman and one not to be considered too lightly. 'Of course,' he said sympathetically, 'though I'd be obliged if you'd tell me first what you know about the attempt to shoot Willie.'

She winced at that and, in an expressionless voice, said, 'So very little. I was only half-asleep when I heard the noise of a gun going off; several times it seemed, though I didn't then appreciate that a gun had been fired. After that, I thought I heard somebody running, but I can't now be certain. It could have been something else.' She turned her head to look at her son. 'Then I heard Willie calling out for help, though I couldn't be sure of the words he was using. So I came downstairs when I must admit to being very frightened, and he told me what had happened.' Her thin body shivered. 'I don't understand what is going on. It's got beyond . . .' She stood from the sofa, a haunting fear in her eyes, looking what Rogers would call bereft.

'Take your mother up,' he said to Sloane. 'I'll speak to you when you come back.'

'No.' She managed a firmness in her voice. 'I am quite able to see myself to my room.' She turned, swaying a little and leaving her son standing where he had risen to go with her.

Rogers, waiting until she had left the room, dragged a chair near to the sofa and motioned Sloane to sit; seating himself with, he thought gloomily, all the stiffness of an octogenarian in splints, 'I've been told more or less what happened this evening,' he said, trying to emanate a kind of matiness in his search for a non-hostile gabbiness. 'After you'd been fired at, you looked out from where you'd been hidden and saw who-ever it was going out through the door. Is that right?' Sloane had folded his arms after sitting and Rogers was wondering what the hell that was supposed to be telling him in body language.

'Yes. I saw a man in the dark. I couldn't actually see who it was, but you can't have any doubts yourself, can you?' For a moment, the expression on his face had been ugly.

'That it was Colonel Horsbrugh?' Rogers pursed his lips as if entertaining a doubt or two though, in truth, he had to admit to himself that he hadn't a damned clue. 'Have you?'

'He did the same rotten thing to mother, so it's not so strange that he should do it to me, is it?'

'Assuming that he did, why? He'd need a reason, wouldn't he?'

'*I've* given him no reason I can think of. I'll admit I've never liked him though, any more than he's liked me. I think he's touched in the head and, if he is, he wouldn't need a reason.' He reached for his wine glass and stood. 'I must have another,' he said, then, though not too invitingly, added, 'Will you have one?'

This interview was one of the occasions when, for Rogers, Sloane held himself and spoke – give or take a gauche discourtesy or two – as if older than his seventeen years. Rogers shook his head, refusing a drink with 'Thank you, but no.' He waited while Sloane filled his glass at the sideboard and then returned; his need for a smoke was beginning to do unpleasant things to his nervous system.

'Speaking of your not liking your stepfather, would that be solely because of what you told me about his threats to your mother?'

Sloane looked as though he thought there was a catch to that question. 'Yes,' he said carefully. 'Wouldn't that be enough?'

'It's reasonable, I suppose, though in addition you wouldn't like him over-much for having married your mother, would you?'

Sloane's face flushed red. 'No, I wouldn't,' he ground out. 'I told you that when I first saw you. And now I've even more reason to hate the bastard.'

There was silence between them while Rogers waited for him to regain his composure. 'What time did you go to bed?' he asked, leaving Colonel Horsbrugh in the wings for the moment.

Sloane had drunk in one swallow half the wine in his glass and he hiccuped without apology. 'Elevenish,' he said. 'About that. I don't make any effort to remember something that means nothing to me.'

'We don't, usually, do we? Had you been in the Lodge long before that?'

'Half an hour or so.' He shrugged. 'I'd been out earlier on and when I returned I called in on mother for about twenty minutes to see that she was all right.'

'And she was?' Rogers had been watching Sloane as he

spoke, seeing that he had dingy teeth behind unpleasant pinkly-moist lips, neither likely to attract a fastidious female interest.

Sloane looked surprised. 'Naturally. She was in bed.'

'I thought she didn't look at all well and . . .' Rogers stopped when Orton re-entered the room and came towards him.

'Sir,' he said. 'I don't think Mr Skinner's there unless he locks his door when he's in.'

'You presumably knocked loud enough?'

Orton looked injured. 'He'd have had to be deaf not to have heard it.'

'Does he lock himself in?' Rogers asked Sloane.

'I wouldn't know, would I?' The youth showed irritation. 'Though there's no reason why he shouldn't, whether he's in or out.' Clearly his mind was on his own troubles and not to be bothered with Skinner's living habits.

'It's gone two o'clock,' Rogers pointed out. He didn't like this at all, not when it was coincident with the shooting at Sloane, and when he wasn't yet prepared to exclude Skinner as a suspect of sorts. 'Is this normal with him?'

'Again, I wouldn't know, would I? It's my mother who employs him. If his car's not here then he must be out. If it's here, he could be in bed and entertaining a friend he doesn't want embarrassed by an interfering somebody poking his nose in.'

'Is that what he does?'

'For God's sake,' Sloane muttered under his breath, shaking his head at Rogers's apparent naïvety. Aloud, he said, 'This isn't a prison, you know, and if my mother doesn't wish to know what must go on now and again, then why should anybody else worry?'

'Where does he normally keep his car?' an unruffled Rogers asked.

'In the road at the side of us.' He jerked his head, indicating its direction. 'Behind the Lodge. There's a small hard-standing there he uses.'

'And the car? It's what?'

'An old green Ford Estate with an aluminium roof-rack,' Sloane said impatiently. 'I don't know it's number, but it's got hang-gliding stickers inside the rear window.'

105

Rogers caught Orton's eye and jerked his head at him. It signified that he should get on out and look for it. 'Right,' he said to Sloane. 'I was saying that your mother wasn't looking at all well.'

'She isn't,' Sloane said as if that were Rogers's doing. 'None of this has done her any good and she's back on her antidepressants.'

'I'm sorry.' That, he thought, must explain her lacklustre attitude to the night's violence. 'When you were woken by whoever it was kicking down your door, what did you think was happening?'

Sloane shot him a sharp look, the look of somebody who thought that there must be a catch in the question. Then he said, 'First of all, I didn't know what was happening. I didn't know it was the door that had been smashed in until later. For all I knew then, it could have been the roof caving in.' His face was working as if he was reliving his waking experience. 'All I know is that I was scared rotten. It was like one of the worst of my nightmares. I found myself on the floor without knowing how I had got there, knowing that something pretty frightful was going on. I don't remember why – I think I must have heard him knocking into something – but I knew I mustn't stay on the floor. So I wriggled on my hands and knees to behind the wardrobe and stood up where I couldn't be seen, trying not to breathe too loud.' He was doing it now, his eyes holding a hunted look. 'That was exactly when the gun was fired. It was so loud that I knew it had to be close to me. I was expecting to be killed, but the bullets missed me and I didn't know where they went. I remembered mother then . . . how she must have felt and been frightened.' He frowned. 'Where did the bullets go?'

'Into the bed,' Rogers said, not too informatively. 'Was that when you looked to see who was shooting at you?'

Sloane grimaced and, holding the glass in both hands to steady it, finished off the wine. 'No,' he said, shaking his head. 'I didn't. I wasn't thinking properly, but I was terrified that he would come into the bedroom after me, so I looked from behind the wardrobe to see where he was. That's when I saw this shadowy figure going out through the door. I waited for a few minutes – it seemed a long time – then decided to run for it in case he came back.' He grimaced again and shuddered. 'Going out through that door was the most terrifying thing I've ever done in my life.'

'This man who shot at you. I understand that while you couldn't actually identify him, you thought he had to be your stepfather?'

'I can't imagine it could have been anyone else, could it?'

'Rogers stared at the youth who appeared to be so visibly shaken in his telling of the attempt on his life. He would have expected, he decided, a little more braggadocio at his age. 'Did you hear a car being started up, or anything like it?' he asked.

'Nothing. There was nothing.'

'We'll leave that now,' Rogers said, feeling that Sloane might be milked of information more effectively after he had had some sleep and recovered completely from his shock. 'If there's anything more you remember you can let me know later. I asked you yesterday to find out if your stepfather had taken with him his cheque book and any cash or credit cards. Had he?'

'Yes.' He bobbed his head, his unruly hair flopping over his forehead. 'He's taken them. At least, I couldn't find them, so it seems he did.'

Rogers, feeling that he was now about to start twitching his deprivation, wanted to ask him of the possible significance of his wearing a woman's knickers at school; something about which he had to be very careful. It could definitely be held to be out of order to question hostilely a person who was a complainant or injured person in the investigation, and not a suspect. Every man – and every youth too – was entitled not to have his vices exposed to a policeman without reason. Nevertheless, he was about to approach it indirectly and with persuasive subtlety when Orton returned.

'There's no Ford Estate on the hard-standing, sir,' he said, 'or anywhere near it.'

'Is there a spare key in his room?' Rogers asked Sloane. 'I think I should have a look at it.'

'If you're thinking that it was him who shot at me, I don't think so and I'm sure you're wrong,' Sloane said with unconcealed derision. 'I said who it was, and because Skinner happens to be out when you want to see him doesn't alter that. And anyway, why would he want to shoot me?'

Rogers gave him something like a down-putting stare. 'As you wish. You were the chap shot at after all. If there is a spare key, go with PC Orton and get it, please.'

'I don't need any help; it's in the school office.'

Rogers shook his head at Orton as Sloane, his white bath robe flapping, left them. On his almost immediate return with the key, he seemed sullen and withdrawn.

Rogers said, 'If you're unhappy about this, Willie, you may, of course, come with us.'

Sloane, retrieving his empty wine glass from the arm of the sofa, said, 'No, thanks. I'll wait here, but I am tired and I want to go to bed. Will you be long?'

'I shall be around the house and in the Lodge for some time yet.' Rogers felt – in a minor sort of way – sorry for him. It wasn't every night that he would be shot at and have policemen tramping over his and his mother's homes asking awkward questions. 'If you like, find somewhere away from this room where you can have a catnap and I'll be in touch if I want you.'

Sloane had moved over to the sideboard and was pouring wine into his glass. 'I'll be putting my feet up in Colonel Horsbrugh's room,' he said. 'If I don't see you again tonight, it won't necessarily upset me.'

Rogers, despite his now-nagging need for tobacco smoke, smiled at the unaware Sloane's back. 'Thank you for your co-operation,' he said, amiably enough for his condition. 'We'll keep in touch.'

That wasn't exactly a reflection of what he thought inside his tiring brain of the awkward and occasionally churlish toad. Moving off to enter the tower next door, he hoped sardonically that he wouldn't be reduced to asking Orton to support him as he would a feeble old lady in climbing all the stairs to the top of the tower. Having made love to Liz a couple or so hours ago wasn't exactly the right training for stair climbing. All he felt he wanted now was bed and undreaming unconsciousness.

He managed the three flights of mostly steep and unlit stairs with Orton following, suffering nothing worse than aching calf-muscles and a mild sweat. With the low wattage light bulb switched on as they reached the landing at the top floor of the tower, Rogers could see in its ochre dimness four doors. Each was labelled with a small white card; one with *Bathroom*, and the remaining three with the names *Mrs M. Traill*, *Miss C. Coppin*, and *Mr D. A. Skinner*.

Rogers banged his knuckles thumpingly on Skinner's door and waited, his ear close to it. From inside there was only silence and he used the key he held to open the door, fumbling inside for the light switch and looking into the room. 'Empty,' he said to Orton. 'Go back and look after the front door, there's a good chap. We should be getting our reinforcements by now.'

With Orton gone, his footfalls dying to silence on the carpeted stairs, Rogers looked carefully around the room. There was a bed, its bedding undisturbed, a small two-drawered table with a companion wooden chair pushed under it, a wash-basin set flush in the top of a cabinet, and a shabby easy chair. The window above the bed was open to the moonlight, its curtains riffled by a light breeze, and, despite this, he could detect the scent of tobacco smoked not too long ago.

The table contained on its varnished top a shaded lamp, a portable typewriter, a gilt-framed photograph of a smiling Skinner with a solemnly attractive girl who could be his virtuous Angela, and a pile of aviation magazines. In one of the drawers were papers detailing painfully dull exercises in the English language and notes on the psychology of teaching, a pair of battered Zeiss binoculars and items of largely unused stationery. Rogers decided to do a trawl of the papers later, or not at all if he could pass them with a clear conscience on to somebody else. In the other drawer, keeping company with neatly folded handkerchiefs and socks, were enough packeted condoms for a largish number of interesting weekends. These, Rogers felt satisfied, must give the lie to Skinner's assertion to Lingard that he would have no use for that sort of thing with his Angela. But, perhaps with someone else? Someone like Mrs Horsbrugh, so conveniently adjacent for a man's otherwise thwarted lust. Or, indeed, either of the two other teachers even more conveniently adjacent.

A long plastic container – just about the size of a body bag, he thought – hung on the back of the door and served as a zipped-up wardrobe with not a lot inside it. In a negative sense, the cabinet with the wash-basin was significantly revealing in that it contained nothing on it or in it a man would need to maintain himself in a shaven, well-scrubbed and masculinely scented condition.

Pulling back the bedclothing from the pillow, he put his nose close to it and sniffed, smelling the ghost of a distinctly feminine fragrance that would certainly not be a man's.

Behind the imperfection of his flagging brain – probably permanently crippled by the loss of sleep, he thought with a perverse satisfaction – he was hugely sceptical about any innocent reasons for Skinner's absence. He was experiencing what could be a premonition of something of significance that was beyond his capacity to identify. But of the significance of his absence he was in no doubt.

Leaving the room and relocking the door behind him, he crossed the gloomily shadowed landing to the other bedrooms. The doors were unlocked and he went into each, switching on the lights. He touched nothing else, but looked. There were single beds in each bedroom with no sign or smell of recent occupation, nor anything in the rooms but undisturbed emptiness to interest him.

Returning to the landing and recalling his earlier suggestion to Lingard, he checked unsuccessfully for a roof-space trap-door in the ceiling. From its only window he could look down on the moonlit forecourt on which, to his rising irritation, other vehicles had yet to arrive, one surely to be carrying his pipe and tobacco. Also within his view was that part of the roof and one of the windows of the Lodge not obscured by tree branches and the surrounding shrubbery. This might be the view seen by Skinner should he have felt the need to use his binoculars to confirm any suspicions he apparently had about Sloane's sexual activities with his Angela.

He thought about Mrs Horsbrugh, presumably now in her drugged sleep; whether he should have her roused from it now and not later, to be asked on mostly speculation just what her relations might have been with Skinner whom she could now dislike enough to have it show in her face at the mention of his

110

name. Rogers, though still sexually neutralized by his earlier activities with Liz Gallagher, could still feel a tiny pang of envy at the creeping thought that she might have had the undoubtedly good-looking Skinner as a resident lover.

It would be tricky, Rogers considered, pinching thoughtfully at his bottom lip, though faint heart had certainly never clobbered a fair lady. He shook his head and that didn't do it any good. There was a clamouring in his mind, almost a confusion, of what he thought he already knew and what he must now find out about the entirely fresh developments. It was called the investigative process, which didn't make matters any more simple or easier to comprehend. Even his earlier thinking about Mrs Horsbrugh and her son had to be flawed, for none of it could have taken into consideration the still missing colonel and Sloane's being shot at on the same night on which Skinner was now presumed to have fled from the premises. He felt again in his tired and aching bones a shadowy awareness of a darker will, an emotion of which he was ignorant, controlling or at least influencing the events unfolding in the house and Lodge.

16

Rogers had slept for a full four hours, uninterrupted by dreams of improbably demanding women or telephone calls requiring his presence at some scene of bloody violence. Waking not quite aware to a hot and glittering day – Monday seemed par for the course in not being overly welcomed – and finding himself lying half undressed on his bed, he made amends to his *savoir-faire* with a cold shower and a mowing of his emerged whisker stubble.

Doing so, he went over in his mind what he thought he could only imperfectly remember of the later non-events of the night. With his pipe and tobacco delivered by one of his DCs, he had smoked himself into a mood where he no longer felt that he was acting out what he called the Genghis Khan side of his persona. Sergeant Magnus, for all his meticulousness in finding or unearthing the most fragmentary or minute speck of evidential material, had come up with virtually nothing. The three cartridge cases and the brass handle of the Lodge's door were bare of any suggestion of fingerprint ridges. There were only poorly defined characteristics on the marks left by a slamming shoe against the front door, and a search of the darkened grounds of the house had drawn a blank. He thought that while it was all very dispiriting and tedious for those doing the searching in the small hours, it would no doubt be rewarding for their souls. As rewarding, no doubt, as the positively useless Wanted Notice he was derisively composing in his mind: *Arrest sought for Attempted Murder. A medium-sized shadowy figure, armed with a .22 firearm and wearing approximately size 9 shoes, believed leather-soled with no identifiable characteristics. May or may not be dangerous.*

He had not seen either Mrs Horsbrugh or her son again, but had left one of his more expendable DCs inside the house until one of them had decided that life simply had to go on and had got out of bed. Why that should necessarily do any good he couldn't fathom, but it might be justified in keeping Sloane's carping to a minimum.

He was far from satisfied with what he had discovered, or had had thrust upon him and, horses for courses, he had some difficulty in seeing either Horsbrugh or Skinner – the latter with the greater reservations – as figures of murderous intent. Horsbrugh was still apparently in the limbo into which he had vanished since Day One, and Rogers was thinking it increasingly unlikely that a man of his background could act in the way the facts in the case appeared to suggest. Skinner had not returned to the house and there now appeared no likelihood that he would. Slotting him pro tem as the man taking potshots at Sloane hadn't yet produced a motive acceptable to the detective. Angela Annett's home address had been obtained and a discreet – and unsuccessful – search for Skinner's car had been made of the area in and around it.

With an oyster-coloured dawn lightening the sky, he had driven back to his apartment, using his barely working willpower to keep his eyelids open, spending long minutes in finding the door keyhole he was convinced some miserable bugger had improperly moved. Reaching his bedroom – he couldn't afterwards remember that – he had managed to pull off his jacket and tie before giving up the struggle and falling wholly uncaring into a welcomed unconsciousness.

Far from being fully recovered, he had, for the sake of his morale, put on a new white shirt with the charcoal-grey suit he usually reserved for court appearances; his first chore on reaching his office being to enter notes in his official pocket-book of what he had seen and had been told at Tower House. That there could be gaps in his recollection of events due to a fatigued brain at the time worried him, the possibility existing that he had forgotten something which might later prove to be of significance.

Finishing that, he prepared a *Missing from Home* notice for circulation throughout the force, giving Skinner's description and that of his green Escort Estate. He had already farmed out to Lingard an early interview with Angela Annetts and – just in case – he was also to initiate an investigation into the private activities, the publicly-known character and the previous evening's movements of Gerald Booker. After the attack on Sloane, however, Rogers was less inclined to fret about Booker's alleged jealousy regarding his wife's involvement with Horsbrugh. Though he could recognize a *non sequitur* when he came across one, his caution about being tripped over by the unlikely, by a reversal of all that was logic, still required him to go through the motions required in an investigation.

There were files and papers in his in-tray to be scanned and decisions to be made on them. One file, a four-page report from PC Rutter – he must have sat up half the night preparing it, Rogers thought – could be accepted by anybody who knew about such esotericisms as a near-doctorial thesis on what he referred to as the tree-worshipping aspect of animism. Getting to the pith of some obviously diligent researching, it appeared to a bemused Rogers that one-time tribal Arabs, the Burmese, the early Buddhists and the ancient Prussians – only a few of those mentioned – were known to have practised tree worshipping, holding some to be sacred, inhabited by deities or other spirits of a sufficient potency. And to these, in less civilized instances, human sacrifices had been bloodily made. Much of this was mind-boggling to Rogers who was inclined to the simplistic view that trees were woody organisms on which such things as fruit and flowers were grown. To the point, however, it had appeared that Rutter could nowhere find any reference to the Nepalese in general paying spiritual homage to what was in essence an overgrown vegetable; nor, in particular, to any nationality at all bowing down in prayer or cutting a sacrificial throat to *Cedrus libani* – Rogers liked that – known to the common herd, Rutter explained in a coded phrase, as the Cedar of Lebanon.

'Peculiar,' Rogers said aloud to an otherwise empty office and shaking his head. 'Bloody peculiar.'

A short report from WDC Sadler – she was apparently knowledgeable enough to know where and how to locate births, marriages and deaths documents and little more – said that Rachel Isobel Barr, a spinster aged twenty-three years of an address in Keighley, had married Gregory Sloane, a teacher of languages, at the Church of St Malachi the Martyr. Later leaving Keighley where she and her husband were partners in the Schenck English Language School, they transferred the business to Abbotsburn. Gregory Sloane died in a boating accident at Thurnholme Bay when his wife was thirty-seven years of age, leaving her a widow with their son, William, aged fifteen years. A year after being widowed – her husband's body had never been recovered from the sea – she had married Lieutenant-Colonel Henry Fraser Horsbrugh, an independent retired officer and bachelor aged sixty-two years, at the Thurnholme Bay Registrar's Office. Nothing was recorded on the national computer against either of her two married names or her maiden name.

The report was sparse in detail, uninformative, and Rogers felt that he could have done better himself with a couple of telephone directories. Finishing off his paperwork, most of the non-urgent stuff being temporarily laid to rest in his pending tray, he thought that he could justifiably consider his own needs for a minute or two. With the blood running hot in his arteries again, he dialled the telephone number of the *Daily Echo* and was put through to Liz Gallagher. Arranging to meet for a meal at the Restaurant Provençal, they agreed that she should afterwards return with him to his apartment for a brandy or two or three and, he said tongue-in-cheek, for an uplifting discussion on the high incidence of the illegal milking of goats in rural areas.

Replacing the receiver, he refilled his still-hot pipe and gave more minutes to thinking of his encounter with her the previous evening. It really had been a civilized come together and he could now recall that she had smilingly joked in the darkness of his bedroom – hugely exaggerated by affection, he thought – that he was a yummy armful, smelling so nicely of kitten fur and newly baked bread.

He was laughing inside himself at the absurd incongruity of it when his telephone bell rang. Answering it dispelled immediately his inner cheerfulness, for his caller, DC Lewis, stationed at Thurnholme Bay, was reporting the finding by a couple of snorkellers of a submerged green car in the sea below Spye Head cliff. So much of it that they could see had revealed that the driving seat was occupied by the body of a man with blond hair.

It wasn't bloody well true, he growled at his closed-down telephone. It damned well couldn't be. Malign fate had it in for him. It was his karma catching up with him and he was being hounded into an early grave, forever doomed to drift sleepless through eternity. Not feeling too martyrish and against having to suffer alone, he left a message with the duty chief inspector for an absent Lingard to follow close on his heels. Lingard was not an entirely suitable substitute for Liz Gallagher, but at least he might be able properly to unload some of the enquiries on to him. He was sure that that was what seconds-in-command were born for and not to spend their duty hours salivating to occupy a senior officer's chair of command.

17

Lingard, wearing with panache a tan twill suit, a coffee-coloured silk shirt and a yellow silk tie with a matching breast-pocket handkerchief and doing nothing so inelegant as sweating, paid a begrudged pound coin to park his Alfa Romeo for an hour on a melting asphalted rectangle of local authority-owned real estate a minute's saunter from Goatacre Park. He felt none of a car-lover's anxiety yet in leaving it unattended and exposed to somebody laying impious hands on a coachwork which shone a begorged tomato-red in the fierce sunlight as he would have done with the Bentley he knew now he had so regrettably sold down the river.

Passing into the park through the huge black and gold wrought-iron gates, closed at nightfall in an inadequate attempt to discourage acts of fornication on the manicured grass or in the concealment afforded by the decorative shrubbery, and threading his way through some of the town's citizenry, he looked for Angela Annetts who he had been told would be eating her lunch by the lake. He saw her – he had learned from her employer that she would be wearing a blue polka-dotted dress and white flat-heeled shoes – seated on a wooden bench backed against some of the park's orange-flowered bushes surrounding the lake. She appeared to be sharing her lunch with a pushing mob of ducks, pigeons and sparrows.

Approaching her, picking his way carefully through the unconcerned birds, he said, 'Miss Annetts?' showing her his warrant card with a friendly reassuring smile and introducing himself, taking in her description as he did so.

He considered her a rather attractive and pleasant-faced girl with short tawny hair that had been flicked across a smooth forehead, pale green eyes reminiscent of a placid cat's, thickish eyebrows darker than her hair and a too-pointed chin that might bode ill in later years for the husband she would undoubtedly have. Unfairly, Lingard thought in view of what Skinner had told him about her religious scruples, she had a most kissable unmade-up mouth and a pleasing amplitude of bosom. An open vacuum flask smelling of coffee and a blue plastic box of sandwiches and fruit rested on the bench at her side.

'I regret intruding on your meal,' he said, 'but I would appreciate a few words with you. They concern Mr Skinner.'

She looked startled, then apprehensive. 'Is there something wrong?' she asked. 'Is he all right?'

'I don't know,' he admitted, stepping further through the birds, one of his highly polished shoes acquiring a large splash of white on its toe as he took his seat at the end of the not wholly clean bench. 'Please don't jump the gun and assume that there's anything terribly amiss, or that he's done something wrong, but he has been missing from Tower House since last night. He certainly hadn't returned from wherever, nor slept in his bed.' He held her gaze, seeing in it bewilderment and the beginning of panic, her hand reaching up to her mouth. 'You wouldn't know why, I suppose?'

'Dear God!' she exclaimed. 'You must tell me if anything has happened to him.'

'Nothing, so far as we know,' he assured her, emphasizing his words. 'There's no reason at all why he shouldn't be spending the night with friends' – she was already shaking her head in negation – 'or he happens to be delayed in returning from somewhere. When did you last see him?' he asked before she might rightly tell him that he was talking a load of tit.

'Yesterday. We were flying our glider at High Platt.' Her eyes were moistening and Lingard cursed himself for his professional clumsiness.

'What time did he leave you?' he asked.

She bit her lip, reaching absently for a sandwich and breaking it up, tossing pieces of it to the birds and not apparently realizing she was doing it. 'He left me at nine. He had to get back to prepare his papers for today's classes. Something's happened to him, hasn't it?'

'When somebody's missing, Miss Annetts, nobody can be certain about what has happened and we, so far, are in that position.' He was concerned by the signs of despair he saw in her face. 'What may certainly help in finding him will be your

117

answering my questions, odd though some of them may appear.' He paused for a moment while she dabbed a wisp of a handkerchief to her eyes. 'Would you have any idea where he might possibly be if not at the school? Anywhere likely? Even unlikely?'

She shook her head dumbly.

Lingard had to tread carefully now. He took out his tiny ivory box and opened it. 'Do you mind?' he asked, his finger and thumb poised over it. She shook her head again, a little impatiently he thought, and he pinched the snuff he was badly needing into his nose. 'Please don't read anything into the questions I'm about to ask you, for it would certainly mislead you. Just believe me that they are being asked to perhaps help us to understand why Daniel is missing and to further his return. How did he and Willie Sloane get on with each other?'

She frowned. 'I don't think Daniel particularly liked him. In fact, I'm sure he didn't like him at all. There were reasons why.'

'Such as?' Lingard gave her a grave and encouraging smile. Although he kept his gaze on her, ready to detect any insincerity or evasion, he was conscious of the semi-circle of birds waiting at her feet in the manner of interested spectators.

Her chin came up. 'I shall be candid, Mr Lingard. Willie was on occasions disgustingly indecent in his speech and manners. Not only to me, but to the other teachers as well. You possibly know I worked at the school until a few months ago and I left because of him.'

'I understand you said as much to his mother.' Lingard needed to get to the crux, the possibility of a sexual relationship having existed between Skinner and Mrs Horsbrugh. 'I haven't met her so far, but as you've been employed by her, possibly you would care to tell me what sort of a woman she is. And how Daniel got along with her. Whatever you tell me would be subject to your continuing anonymity, naturally.' He gave her a confiding smile.

Her face was a picture of indecisiveness while Lingard waited in silence, not looking at her directly or doing anything to help her. After a long minute of this, she said, 'I'm sure Daniel knows something about her that he doesn't like, though before then I believe that he had been very friendly with her.'

118

'Do you mean very friendly in the way in which I as a policeman would understand?' He tried to look a man who knew something or other. And, beneath an unclouded sun, a man who was beginning to feel grilled.

'It was before Daniel and I started our flying together,' she said, manifestly dodging the issue. 'I thought he was about to tell me several times, but he didn't.' Her eyes moistened again. 'I didn't wish to question him about such a thing because I hoped he would do so in his own time.'

'You do mean his admitting to having been Mrs Horsbrugh's lover?' Lingard put to her, bluntly for him. He thought that she was mature enough to know that it sometimes happened between a woman and a man.

'I don't know,' she said helplessly. 'It was something I didn't understand and I hate myself for even thinking it. She is so much older than he is . . . it wasn't right and it wouldn't have been his fault.' She hesitated, seemingly in making up her mind. 'And then there was something about her that he didn't like. As if she had been hateful to him . . . or something.' She took a small sandwich from the blue box, bit at it and then put it back with a look of distaste. 'He did say recently that when he was sure about whatever it was, he would do something about it. Which he said would cause a terrible scandal.'

Lingard stared hard at her, seeking some kind of an answer from the expression in her face. 'But absolutely no hint of what it was?'

She shook her head, her eyelids closed as if she were in pain, opening them to say, 'No. It was really none of my business. And sometimes I wasn't even sure who he was talking about.'

He wasn't getting much from her about Skinner and he decided to turn back to the subject of Sloane. 'I was told that you were surprised at Mrs Horsbrugh's reaction to your telling her that young Willie was a sex maniac or some such?'

'I didn't say that,' she protested, apparently uninterested in asking from where he had got his information. 'I never would, but I did tell her that he had suggested some improper things to me. She was annoyed as I'd expected her to be, but I think she must have already known what he was like.'

'Mothers usually do, don't they? What was her relationship

119

with him like as far as you saw it? How close were they?' He could tell that she was beginning to be restless, probably not wishing to dwell on anybody but her missing Daniel.

'Well, Willie obviously adores his mother. I suppose in part because his father is dead and because he isn't often with her, seeing her only in between school terms.'

When a plump and sweating woman with two noisily loutish children stopped close to them with the obvious intention of sharing the bench, Lingard directed an unspeaking patrician loftiness at her, indicating by it that they would not be pleased to be imposed upon by her presence. Apparently getting the message, she scowled at his uncharacteristic churlishness and moved on.

When she was out of earshot, Lingard said to the girl at his side, 'And what about Mrs Horsbrugh's attitude towards young Willie?' Angela was patently holding back on what must be her inner turmoil at his questioning and he admired her for it.

'She is rather difficult to understand. She does try to make him keep his distance and not act in a way I would call sloppy with her. She snaps at him quite a lot. Unnecessarily so at times, I feel.'

'He'd react to it?' He fished for his snuff box and inhaled Attar of Roses. For a moment he had the expression of a man receiving a sacrament.

'He would laugh and be even more ridiculous, as if trying to irritate her. And, in a way, trying to boss her about.'

Lingard hoped that some of the stuff he was digging out from her apparent innocence was going to be useful to Rogers, deciding to get away from the two people he did not know and whom he had difficulty in visualizing. He put on an expression of bafflement and said, 'May I just ask one more question about Daniel, Miss Annetts? Are you able to hazard a guess or two as to where he might have gone?'

She looked at him, her green eyes bleak. 'His parents are living in Germany and he visits them occasionally. He wouldn't go there, I'm sure, without telling me. I know he wouldn't.' Her eyes brimmed with tears and she turned her head away to conceal them from passers-by. 'I think that somebody has made

120

him go away, or taken him away. I'm praying that he's all right. *Please*. Do you know that he might have been taken away?'

'I'm sorry,' he said. He was sensing the depths of her held-back distress and it was having its effect on him. God knows, he thought, how she'd react if Skinner were indeed the unknown and so far ineffectual man behind the shooting at Mrs Horsbrugh and her son. 'I honestly know no more than what I've already said.'

'Has this anything to do with the colonel being accused of doing such a terrible thing?' When Lingard remained silent, giving her only a noncommittal shrug to conceal his unknowingness, she burst out, 'I don't believe one bit of what is being said about him. I've always found him to be extremely kind and thoughtful. And so did Daniel.'

Lingard thought that he hadn't got too far with that and he looked at his wrist-watch and stood. 'I'm sorry to have kept you,' he said. 'And do forgive me for spoiling your lunch. Try not to worry too much about Daniel.' He gave her a reassuring smile. 'I shall be in touch and keep you posted.'

She was moist-eyed again and he thought that he had been right in not adding to her suffering by asking her if Skinner had had any experience with hand guns. And now, likely to add to her distress, would soon follow the almost certain disclosure that her flaxen-haired, possibly screwed-up non-lover may well have been fornicating freelance once out and away from the rather forbidding proximity of her sexual rectitude. For the moment, he confined himself to worrying about his shoe having been shat on by a careless lout of a pintail duck.

18

The Thurnholme Bay Police Marine Section of the force's underwater search team was staffed by a sergeant, two PCs, and an inflatable dinghy. Rogers had ordered DC Lewis to arrange to have the dinghy and crew standing by for him at the town quay, and he with it.

Thurnholme was a small town a good twenty minutes' low-gear drive over high terrain from Abbotsburn and situated on and between the steep slopes of a basin formed by enclosing rocky headlands. Geared as much to the short-stay, fast-food, liquor-derived entertainment of summer visitors as to the yachting and cruising fraternity using in large numbers its harbour and clubhouse, it proliferated in restaurants, pubs, cafés, ice-cream parlours and a couple of unusually respectable night clubs not yet taken over by the local equivalent of the Mafia.

The town made occasional claims to be a sort of English St Tropez, ignoring the sewage outfall not far enough out to sea, the usual smell of hot cooking fat and, with the tide out, of fetid wet mud, an amalgam of odours passed off by the local Chamber of Commerce as health-giving sea air. It owned to no street that wasn't cluttered with nose-to-tail cars or deserted of everything but No Waiting signs. It was, Rogers bore very much in mind, the missing Horsbrugh's former stamping ground.

Quite certain that his authority to investigate serious crime must override a local by-law or two, he parked his Astra on the double yellow lines in an absolutely and positively No Waiting street as near the town quay as he could get. He placed an acquired PC's helmet on the rear passenger seat as a visible prod in a traffic warden's ribs, though it would by no means be certain to result in absolution.

Lewis, tall and gangling with a blond crew cut and a twisted nose, was waiting on the quay with a heavily moustached and badly sweating Sergeant Lauder clad uncomfortably in his rubberized wet-suit. Their very presence had attracted a growing group of the morbidly curious.

'I'm late, sergeant,' Rogers said to Lauder, 'so let's get going,' then moved with him to the corroded iron ladder fixed to the stone blocks of the harbour wall. Moored to the ladder, the lower rungs of which vanished into the green depths of the gently heaving water, was the fifteen-feet long constabulary-blue inflatable dinghy with POLICE stencilled in white on its bloated flotation pontoons and an outboard motor fixed to its sternboards. A wet-suited PC Potter of slightly prognathous jaws that made him look vaguely Neanderthal, a one-time CID aide and an exacerbator of Rogers's nervous system because of his habit of hissing tuneless dirges while cracking his finger joints, stood at the foot of the ladder ready to assist aboard the senior officer he would think of as elderly.

Watched by the row of interested holidaymakers, Rogers grasped the rough iron sides of the ladder and prepared to descend. He said to Lewis, 'Sit with me and do your filling in while we're on the move.' Lowering himself on the rungs and stepping cautiously into the inflatable – he frightened off Potter's offered help with a frowning shake of his head – he sat himself on the rubberized fabric of a pontoon and waited for Lewis clambering down to join him.

With Lauder handling the wheel and the engine started, Potter pushed the dinghy for its stern to clear the harbour wall while an unstably seated Rogers grasped at the pontoon's lifeline. He could swim – it was a necessary qualification for joining any police force – but that wasn't the point with him. An accidental plunge into sea water would do nothing to improve the looks of his best suit and the new shirt he wore.

Under way and with Lauder turning the inflatable north to parallel the shoreline, Rogers, now fully exposed to the brazen sun and beginning to sweat in his suit, his eyes aching from the dazzle, told Lewis to fill him in. There wasn't, it appeared, much more than what he had been given over the telephone. Two brothers Oxford, locally known of suspect honesty, had been snorkelling from their unusually black-coloured sailing boat anchored in a rocky cove at the foot of Spye Head; a beauty spot of sad repute from the occasional suicidal leaps from its height. There they had seen the submerged car, almost concealed by kelp, between their boat and the base of the cliff; and, one had estimated, about four fathoms down. They had done an unbreathing dive to within nearly twelve feet of the car, obtaining a glimpse of a yellow-haired man sitting in the driver's seat. Surfacing, they had returned the seven miles back to Thurnholme and reported to the police what they had seen. Asked to return and mark the spot by staying there, they had shown a momentary unwillingness to do so, but had then agreed. Presumably, Lewis assured Rogers, they were now surely floating above the car and its dead occupant and awaiting their arrival.

Negotiating a high rocky point and turning into a small cove, they saw the sombre boat occupied by the Oxford brothers being held motionless by one of them with the aid of two very small oars, its slender mast with its tethered brown sail dipping and swinging gently against the warm pushing of a soft breeze. Lauder, throttling back on the inflatable's engine, drew alongside the boat while Potter grabbed and whipped a rope line on to its stern rail.

Where the two boats rotated slowly around each other on the translucent skin of the reasonably friendly sea, the huge mass of limestone cliff, studded with heavy outcrops of known-to-be-detachable rock, towered above them, threatening, it seemed, to topple and fall into the cove in which they floated. For Rogers, it held in itself a natural instability and probably a malevolent propensity for dropping large boulders on innocent detective superintendents.

The Oxford brothers with their weatherbeaten skins and hard looks could be taken for latter-day buccaneers and, because of their repute and villainous appearances, Rogers made a mental note – even as he showed his teeth in greeting to them – to later check on exactly what they were doing in this deserted cove.

Being questioned, they added nothing significant to their original report and, after Lauder had peered through a glass-bottomed viewing box into the depths below them and nodded an affirmation, Rogers thanked the brothers and said that he was sure that they had other more important things to do than to wait around in the cove.

On their leaving, and with Lauder and Potter each putting on his weighted belt, air cylinder, rubber fins and face mask, Rogers took the viewing box, leaning over the side of the inflatable and holding its glass base just below the surface of the water. With the sun hot on his spine and on the back of his head, feeling that he might fall asleep draped on the soft air-filled pontoon, he fitted his face against the foam-rubber seal of the viewer and looked down from a pellucid greenish height into a canyon forest of sinuously waving glossy-brown kelp anchored between a scree of fallen limestone boulders. He saw small schools of slate-grey fish moving through the kelp and a hazy mist of sand grains lifted by currents from the sea bed.

The green Ford car, which Rogers recognized as an Estate and fitted with an aluminium roof rack, lay on its side, wedged between boulders cast off from the cliff. One of its front wheels had broken off and its superstructure twisted out of alignment. The open window on the driver's side framed the shoulders and greenly pallid flesh of the head of a man whose long yellow hair waved synchronously with the kelp around the car. The safety harness was clearly in position over the white-shirted chest.

Primed by Lingard with a description of Skinner and having seen his photograph, Rogers had no doubts that this was the hang-glider-flying, backward-seeming lover of the girl Annetts. A sad end, he thought, for a man who might have had some extremely interesting answers to some necessarily penetrating and probably hostile questioning.

The backwards-plunging rubber-suited body of Sergeant Lauder, his mouth full of tubed breathing regulator, making his descent in a trail of bubbles, set the inflatable rocking and splashed Rogers with the spray of his entry into the water. With Potter following him – his splashing of Rogers was accounted to be less forgivable – Lauder finned himself down towards the car.

Holding the car's door handle to steady himself, Lauder looked long and thoroughly at the dead man's body, finally releasing the safety harness from around the chest and lifting the door open. With Potter's assistance the body was manoeuvred out from the car, its mouth an open dark hole seemingly expressing a screaming pain. Then, with each bunching a fist into the dead man's armpit and lifting him, they rose slowly towards the watching Rogers.

Putting aside the viewing box, Rogers waited until the two men and their burden broke the surface. Concealing his repugnance, he helped handle the body over the pontoon and roll its soddenness into the well of the boat, clear water gushing from the mouth on to the detective's shoes and socks. With the body now exposed to the brilliance of sunlight – there was no smell of death's rottenness though that might come later in the afternoon's heat – it could be seen in fine detail. Moustached and bearded and dressed in a tropical tunic shirt with pockets

125

and epaulettes, he wore with it blue skin-tight jeans and well-worn bicoloured trainer shoes. He looked as though he had died badly.

Searching the body with distaste, Rogers recovered a soggy leather wallet from a rear pocket of the jeans. It held three £10 notes, a bank cash card that confirmed its holder to be Daniel Skinner and a single packeted condom – a normal male's emergency equipment which, Rogers considered, every man should be born with. A side pocket contained an unhelpful handkerchief, a small penknife and a few coins.

Sergeant Lauder, a red-faced humanized walrus in his glistening wet-suit, his breathing regulator out of his mouth, his mask pushed up over his forehead, held on to the lifeline and said to Rogers, 'I see that chummy's been badly knocked on the back of his head, and there're some nasty cuts on the scalp.' He was patently careful in not committing himself to how they might have been caused.

Rogers frowned and turned the head sideways, pushing concealing wet hair away from the back of the skull. There were two splits showing white bone in the scalp. The major one was cruciform in shape, the other, a transverse laceration, was two inches or so to one side of it. Whatever blood had fouled the flesh and hair had been washed off by seawater. Grimacing his unease at touching dead flesh, Rogers placed his finger over the cruciform wound and pressed firmly against the underlying bone of the skull, feeling in its grating what he thought to be a severely comminuted fracture. It would be for Wilfred Twite the pathologist to pronounce on it, but Rogers was already of the opinion that the unfortunate Skinner had been killed by the forceful wielding of a tool such as a hammer or a steel bar.

Dropping the head back to its sightless staring at the blue sky, Rogers pushed at the lower jaw to close the mouth and give the features a less disturbing expression. He could see no signs of violence on the good-looking face in which he chose to read an apparently civilized decency and honesty. He said to Lauder, 'A fractured skull, sergeant. But never in the fall in the car?' That was a question.

Lauder shook his head. 'No. He was strapped in and there was a head restraint on his seat. A padded one. There's damage to the car body, but nothing that could have touched him in the driver's seat. Somebody's clouted him?'

'I'm almost sure so. After leaving Potter here to stop anyone stealing the wheels from the car or whatever, I want you to take me back to the harbour where you'll arrange for an ambulance to remove our friend here to the mortuary at Abbotsburn. When you return, I want you to search the car and to specifically check whether it's in any particular gear and if the ignition key's in the off or on position. I'll arrange for it to be photographed before it's lifted.'

With the tarpaulin-covered dead Skinner behind him, a nasty audibility of water moving inside his body, Rogers sat in the passenger seat at Lauder's side. He felt cooked to hell and overly full of ozone or whatever it was that made seawater smell of dead fish. With nothing to do but watch water move frothily past the blunt prow of the inflatable, he realized how physically bushed he was, how bloody tired; and how dispiriting it was to know that his blood was undoubtedly turbid and stale in his veins. He couldn't even appreciate how pleasant it was to be alive and almost *compos mentis* instead of slopping around unbreathing in the well of a police inflatable on his way to being cut up and disembowelled on a mortuary table.

Being dropped off at the harbour wall, a disembarking Rogers shared little of the gawping interest shown by the few holiday-makers in the tarpaulin-covered body in the inflatable. He had told the sergeant where he was going and that should Detective Chief Inspector Lingard arrive at the police mooring stage looking for him, he was to be asked to join Rogers at the top of Spye Head.

There was no traffic warden's ticket under either of his car's windscreen wipers and he had to impatiently wait for minutes with the four doors open in order to dispel the torrid head contained in it.

Spye Head, a much trampled-on beauty spot with a quite potent attraction for people needing to jump from its loftiness – one elderly woman cursed with loneliness had obtained a posthumous distinction by doing it on a bicycle – was approached by a winding road just wide enough for the tour coaches which most often used it. Driving up it, Rogers had several times to pull into lay-bys, manoeuvres that did nothing to calm a scowling irritation already made manifest by his underclothing sticking sweatily to his tired flesh.

Two coaches, giving off ripples of heat waves, were parked on an asphalted lay-by near a large white-painted board containing in red letters the warning *Danger. No vehicles driven past this point. By Order of the Thurnholme Bay Parish Council.* What bloody fool would, Rogers muttered to himself, seeing the slope of browning grass and stunted windblown shrubs leading to the cliff's edge. On a two-feet raised earth ridge, intended to be a barrier against cars entering the forbidden area, he thought he could discern in crushed grass the ghost of the twin tracks of a car's wheels. These petered out to invisibility after a few yards, though showing an unswerving objective for the drop into space.

There were people sitting and walking on the baked grass, among whom two youthful couples were finding the need and occasion for a distasteful gnawing at each other's mouths; none, he noted, stupid enough to get too near the patently dangerous brink. Walking through them, he followed a line drawn mentally from the ghost wheel tracks he thought he could see crossing the ridge, feeling himself to be the object of their morbid interest – was he an intended jumper or not? – though none showed any apparent concern to do more than stare. Standing as near the vertiginous edge as his aversion for dangerous heights would allow him, he sought for signs of the green car's descent down the irregular face of the cliff. Not easy to find, but they were there, well below the toes of his shoes in the form of a small crushed and broken shrub unwise enough to grow from a crevice a hundred feet or so on the car's way down. There was a further sign in a fresh scar on a boulder protruding from the cliff face, possibly the one from which Skinner's car had bounced to miss the rocky beach at its foot, invisible to Rogers from where he stood, and to find deep water. Over four hundred giddying feet below, a tiny PC Potter held station in a miniaturized one-man inflatable dinghy on the translucent green of the softly heaving sea.

Rogers was wishing that he knew more about the dead Skinner when he heard the expensively muted sound of a climbing car's engine and Lingard's Alfa Romeo drew up behind Rogers's more modest Vauxhall. Leaving the open cockpit of his car with all the panache of a well-dressed, well-heeled bachelor, Lingard approached his senior at the brink at which he grimaced his unease.

'I saw Sergeant Lauder at the mooring, George,' he said, 'telling me all and showing me poor Skinner. He said you'd thought he'd been banged on the old noddle and sent over the top. We've a multiplicity of problems I imagine?'

'There's a comminuted fracture there,' Rogers told him, not looking away from the cliff below them. 'He was belted in and there seems to have been padded head restraints fitted, so I don't believe he got it from the fall. Though Wilfred and his scalpels could prove me wrong,' he added with a proper caution. He was absently stuffing tobacco on to the hot ashes in his gone-out-again pipe as he briefed his second-in-command on the finding of Skinner's body.

He finished by gesturing at the evidence of the car's descent into the sea. With Lingard there his irritation with the world in general was dissipating. 'That's the way he went, David. I'm sure you aren't going to have me believe he drove himself up here and did a deliberate nose-dive over the edge?'

Lingard shook his head unequivocally. 'No way, George. He wasn't the type. Not only from what I know of him, but from his girlfriend too.' He pulled a face. 'It's a mite depressing, you know, when I'd seen him, spoken to him, in the flush of his virility or whatever it is.' He shook his head. 'I must take care. Us good types seem fated to get the chop early in our lives.' Charging his nostrils with Attar of Roses, flapping his yellow silk handkerchief at the grains escaping inhalation, he recounted to Rogers the details of his interview with Angela Annetts. 'My respects to the lady, but I'd say she was too bovine to be anything but honest. Skinner was apparently party to a mysterious something, obviously to do with the Horsbrughs, which, if he should tell all, would cause what she considered would be a five-star stink. She said it would be a terrible scandal, for what that's worth, though it'd have to be pretty embarrassing or shaming for it to be a motive for bashing him on the head and heaving him over the top.'

The waiting coaches had been reloaded with their passengers and were moving off. Rogers had been staring at them in their inoffensive curiosity in what he and Lingard were doing, willing them away from the scene he now held to be sacrosanct to his investigation into a violent death. 'Do you really believe that he's been having it off with Mrs Horsbrugh?' he asked Lingard. Why the hell should he worry, he thought. His sexual interest in her had been so short-lived, and misbegotten anyway. He moved away from too close a proximity to a brink of another sort and Lingard moved with him.

'It'd fit the circumstances, wouldn't it?' Lingard answered, having no doubts about it.

'You're bringing in the colonel, aren't you?' Rogers put a fourth lighted and unsuccessful match to his pipe, moving with Lingard towards their cars.

'It's an option. He could have caught them *in flagrante delicto*. Bonking, I believe, is the in-word for it now.'

'If it was the colonel – which I'm beginning to doubt – he'd have some rather awkward transport problems after Skinner and his car had been disposed of, wouldn't he? With his own car being under repair he'd need an accomplice with another car to get him back.' He screwed his face into doubt as he thought it out. 'Mrs Booker?' He shook his head, though not decisively. 'Without that, there's no telephone up here to call a taxi, no nearby bus stops and it's a damned long walk back to wherever he or she came from.' Rogers's reasoning, admittedly flawed at times, couldn't quite put an evidential finger on whoever it might be.

'What about Sloane?' Lingard suggested, mainly to show he was actively interested in an investigation which circumstances had led him into having been fed little information. 'He sounds a nasty little sod and, from what you and Miss Annetts tell me, he and my man Skinner weren't all that crazy about each other.'

'I don't eliminate him, David, but on the face of it he seems to be the injured party in the quarrel – if you can call it that – he had with Skinner. But one could argue, I suppose, that nothing need be too trivial these days to trigger off bloody violence.'

'For what it's worth, yes.'

'There is one thing that shouldn't go unnoticed.' Rogers was

130

kicking himself; not for overlooking it, but for not earlier appreciating the significance Skinner's death could give it. 'Consider Skinner a little more seriously. So far as we know he had as ready an access to the colonel's pistol as anyone else in the house. He was, apart from Mrs Horsbrugh, alone when the attempt was made to kill her and there's only his account of where he said he was when he heard – if he did hear – the shots fired.' He was tapping his teeth with the stem of his cooling pipe as he thought it out. 'Unlikely as we might think it is, he could, with the pistol he had already taken from the colonel's study, have gone downstairs and fired the probably deliberately misaimed shots at Mrs Horsbrugh's chair for God only knows what reason. That done, he could then time it to seem to have himself come downstairs, a man trying to find out what had happened.' He frowned, creasing his forehead. 'But *why*? I know we've said "why" to it before, but Skinner is significantly more in the picture now.'

'Bloody-mindedness?' Lingard offered flippantly. 'Jealousy? Having been told "Not tonight, Daniel" once too often? Feeling unloved? Egad, George, shouldn't we be thinking about the stupid and perverse for a change? Get our minds out of constabulary harness for an hour or two?'

'First,' Rogers said drily, 'we'll do our constabulary-harnessed probing at Tower House in depth. There are people such as Sloane, Mrs Horsbrugh and the two lady teachers yet to be seen.'

They had reached their parked cars and Rogers was kicking half-heartedly his still-wet Oxford shoe at a rear tyre that looked as if it had lost some of its pressure. 'You inconsiderate bastard,' he swore at it under his breath. To Lingard, he said less irritably, 'My mind's been doing that while we've been talking. Have you ever known anybody to be so thoroughly missing, yet able at the same time to be so cold-bloodedly active in shooting at what's left of his family?'

'You mean he's cold-blooded in the pathological sense?'

'Why not?' Rogers said. 'I might as well use my imagination as not. When we get back to the office we'll try and think out where one might dispose secretly of a dead bogus lieutenant-colonel of no large dimensions.' Somehow he knew he would feel happier having to deal with two bodies than none at all.

At his asking, Lingard trailed behind him in case the rear tyre became flatter still and stranded Rogers miles away from the tall gin-and-tonic with ice that he so badly needed to both pacify and stimulate his physical and mental needs.

19

Rogers, developing a fear of being thought too casual in his approach to a suspected murder, changed his mind about first returning to his office and, followed by Lingard, changed course for Tower House.

Entering the drive, he noted that Sloane appeared to be in, for his orange Volkswagen waited simmering in the late afternoon's sun. Speaking to Lingard who had drawn up behind him, he said, 'Take the two teachers if they're now back, David. They're Traill and Coppin and one of them's a Miss, though either may be the one who kept up poor Skinner's morale. And maybe Sloane's too. It's a fair bet that either could have been the apparently grateful woman heard in his bedroom by Skinner.'

'Bless my soul,' Lingard murmured to himself. 'What if one's a genteel and virtuous maiden lady, the other heavily into whatever sanctified side there is to marriage?' The elegant detective had never liked questioning a lady's virtue, no matter how free she appeared to have been with it.

Sloane made a delayed answer to the pulling of the brass bell knob on the door, appearing to Rogers something of a lout in scruffy denims and a stained twill bush shirt. His hair was disordered and there were creases of sleep in his face. 'It's you,' he said, not appearing to be over-pleased at seeing the two men.

Rogers said, 'We need to come in, Willie. We've some quite important information for your mother and you, and there are more enquiries to be made.'

For a moment Sloane appeared surprised, looking past

Rogers. 'You've got him then? I hope you haven't brought him here,' he gabbled, his surprise turning to anxiety. 'We don't . . . neither of us want him back in this house.'

'You mean the colonel?' Sloane obviously had, Rogers knew.

'Of course. We don't wish to see him ever again.'

'I imagine not,' the detective said with irony. 'Nor would we bring him here had we arrested him. It's something else altogether and we'll talk about it inside.'

The sitting-room, in a welcome semi-darkness with partly drawn curtains, had plainly suffered from a male's neglect of it; empty cups, glasses and newspapers littered its furniture. There was a dead smell of smoked cannabis hanging in the air, though not sufficiently strong for Rogers's nose to make an issue of it.

With the three of them remaining standing, Rogers said to Sloane, 'Are the two teachers back from their weekend?'

Sloane shrugged that aside with an irritated 'Yes, they are,' then said, 'What were you going to tell us that is so important? Was it about Skinner?'

'Yes it was, and I'll tell your mother what in a moment. Mr Lingard wishes to interview the teachers so, if the two ladies are in their rooms, he can go on up.'

'Not both of them. Mother had sent the students packing and there's nothing much for anybody to do. Mrs Traill's gone into town for something or other.'

'Had they been told about Mr Skinner being missing? And your stepfather?'

'My mother's husband,' Sloane corrected him, apparently objecting to any closer relationship. 'Yes, she told them both. And about the shooting.'

Rogers turned to Lingard and nodded at the door. 'Fire ahead, David, will you? Their rooms are on the top floor of the tower.'

With Lingard gone, he said to Sloane, who had shown his back to them in walking to and looking through one of the windows on to the rear lawn, 'Mr Skinner has been found dead and I'd prefer that I gave your mother the details first.'

Sloane had stiffened at Rogers's first words and had turned back to him, his mouth open and his expression clearly disorganized. 'You mean that he's been killed? That he, I mean my mother's husband, shot him too?' There was near hysteria in his words. 'You can't mean it?'

'He's dead, Willie, but your words about the colonel doing it are yours, not mine.'

The youth's face was gorged with his sudden anger, his eyes directing it at Rogers. He raised his voice to a shout. 'Why don't you tell me what's happened! I'm not a bloody child and somebody's trying to kill me too! I've a right to know!'

'Up to a point,' Rogers conceded, impassive against the tirade. 'But I'd prefer to give your mother the details first. She's his employer, not you. I assume she's in the house, so will you please tell her that I wish to see her.' He made his voice authoritative. 'Where is she, Willie? I want no nonsense about your telling her first.'

'She's in her room.' He was sullen. 'She's in bed with heat exhaustion and worry, and I'll see what she says.'

He moved towards the door and Rogers, joining him, said sharply, 'No. You'll say that I'm with you and that I'd like to see her on her own for a few minutes. And you'll say it with the door open while I wait outside.'

Apart from glaring venomously at Rogers and compressing his mouth to thinness, Sloane made no acknowledgement of his instruction.

Climbing stairs, which gave the following Rogers's already weary calf-muscles a beating, and reaching the door of Mrs Horsbrugh's bedroom, Sloane tapped and opened it. Standing just inside the heavily-shaded interior, within Rogers's view – the detective could smell what he thought to be eau-de-Cologne and the warm odour of a woman in bed – Sloane said softly, 'I'm sorry, mother, but Superintendent Rogers is with me and would like to speak to you about Daniel.' He paused long enough to swallow. 'Are you feeling better?'

'No. Please not.' Her voice was strained and exhausted. 'Tell him I'm sorry, but not now.' There was a pause before she forced out, 'What is it about Daniel? Is he back? Where has he been?'

'I can't say, mother, other than he's not back.' As before, he acted a different species of youth with his mother. 'Superintendent Rogers says that . . .'

134

Rogers interrupted him. 'I'm sorry to barge in on you like this, Mrs Horsbrugh,' he said from the outside the wooden door between them, keeping his voice gentle, 'but I do have to tell you myself that Daniel Skinner *has* been found, though tragically he was dead. He was found in his car in the sea at Spye Head cove.' Sloane's head had jerked around sharply at hearing Rogers's words. 'Because he lives here and is in your employ, there are one or two questions I feel it's necessary to ask you.'

There was a silence, a heavy almost telepathic silence in which he believed he could read agitation and distress above the sound of the pulsing of blood in his ears. Then, even as he saw Sloane's expression change from that of a son's sympathy for a suffering mother to an angry frown, he heard a soft whimpering that should never have come from the mouth of a woman such as she. He could, he supposed glumly, feeling as pitiless as all hell, be considered blood-brother to a bird-killer shooting at a sitting pheasant.

As Sloane went to his mother, closing the door after him and cutting off the unhappiness within, Rogers heard her almost indistinct plea, 'Please, Willie, no. Not now . . . later . . .', and then, walking away to return to the sitting-room, caught the sound of her son making gentle soothing noises.

Irritable now at the way matters had developed, with an obviously simmering Sloane rejoining him ten or so minutes later, Rogers said formally, 'I'm sorry about that. I had no idea she would take his death so badly.' That she had, he thought, would suggest the suspected closer relationship with Skinner than one of employer and employee.

He had necessarily spoken to Sloane's back, for he had gone immediately to the sideboard and was pouring red wine into a large tumbler with a shaking hand. While he did so, Rogers pulled out his pipe, tamped tobacco in it and lit it, his unwavering gaze fixed on to the youth.

When Sloane turned, his loose-lipped mouth glistening with the wine he had drunk and regarding Rogers with bitterness, he said, 'You're a bastard, aren't you? You should have let me tell mother. I told you. I told you before we went up that she couldn't see you.' His face worked with emotion. 'Does this

135

mean that he's the one who tried to kill me? And mother? That it wasn't my . . . not my mother's husband at all?'

Rogers simulated astonishment, ignoring most of what he had said and holding his smoking pipe poised. 'What reason would he have had for wanting to do that? Is there something you haven't told me? Some action of yours that would give him a motive?' His smile, meant as an encouragement to a flow of informative words, held little amiability in it.

Sloane thought it out for a long time, screwing creases in his forehead and manifestly worrying at it. 'It could have been that business about Angela,' he said. 'I'm sorry, I didn't tell you everything. She did have a bit of a rave on about me, though Daniel was mistaken in thinking I had her with me that night.' He returned again to the sideboard and refilled his glass, then sat in a chair away from the bar of sunlight entering the adjacent window.

Waiting while he did this, Rogers was certain that Sloane was using the small activity to compose whatever story he now had in mind. Stifling what would have been a huge jaw-locking yawn of tiredness, he said, 'So he could have had some justification at the time for thinking that you had?'

'I imagine so.' He was now appearing to be seeking some sort of an understanding from the detective. 'I expect that you've already guessed that there was somebody with me. Not Angela, of course, and it was none of his business. Nor yours either, if it comes to that. All I was worried about was that he didn't go blabbing to mother. Or to her husband either.'

'Had you told Mr Skinner who it actually was in your bed, would he have still wanted to thump you?' When Sloane was patently not intending to answer his question, he said impatiently, 'A name, Willie. I want a name.'

Sloane's expression took on insolence. 'I don't know anything about your own dealings with women, Mr Rogers, but from where I stand one would be a complete oik to name names in this sort of affair. Ungentlemanly, wouldn't you say?'

'Except in so far as Miss Annetts is concerned, of course,' Rogers said pointedly. 'Please answer the question I asked you. Would knowing the identity of the woman in your bed cause

Mr Skinner to want to thump you? In fact, later to wish to shoot holes in you?'

'Not knowing whether he'd ever had her in bed himself, I wouldn't know, would I?' He shot a hard look at Rogers. 'I take it that you'll respect the information I've given you? Not go sneaking to my mother when all I've done is to answer your questions in order to help you.'

'What you have told me, which hasn't anyway been much, remains with me,' Rogers said brusquely. 'Were the two lady teachers sleeping at the school that night?'

Sloane, immature though he was in some ways, was no fool. 'Were they? I'm sure you'll find out if they were.'

'Yes, I suppose I shall.' Rogers wasn't about to give him the opportunity of denying that one of the teachers – perhaps the same one who had been relieving the thwarted Skinner's lusts – had been in his bed. He said speculatively, 'If – and it is a bit of an if – Mr Skinner had taken a dislike to you because he believed, wrongly or not, that you were trespassing in what he thought to be his private access to a woman and tried to shoot you last night, why beforehand would he have shot at your mother? That'd have been a rather peculiar thing to do, wouldn't it? Unless there'd been some reason I don't know about?'

Sloane stiffened and laid the empty wine glass he had been nursing carefully on the fat arm of the chair in which he had been slouching. 'Possibly not so peculiar,' he said tightly. 'Mother took a dislike to him over something or other and I do know that she was looking for a good reason for giving him the boot. Don't ask me what it was over because I don't know and wouldn't tell you if I did.'

'I'll leave now,' Rogers said. There wasn't much more he needed from the awkward young bugger anyway. 'It's important that I see your mother today, so I want you to call me at my office when she's sufficiently recovered.' He made his voice authoritative. 'You understand? While your mother's well-being must be a matter of concern, she does have to be seen concerning Mr Skinner's death without too much further delay.'

He thought he could just accept the scowl he received as a sign of reluctant agreement and left it at that.

After he had secured the door to Skinner's bedroom and issued a dire warning against any interference with it, he left the house for an examination of the hard-standing on which Skinner had normally parked his car. He found what he had looked for – a patch of staining on the concrete which appeared to be mahogany-coloured varnish – and, in the looking, the thinking part of his not quite comatosed brain worried about the shooting at Mrs Horsbrugh. It could have been a kind of frightener with no real intent to kill by a subsequently luckless Skinner cast in the role of a dismissed lover. Undoubtedly she was the sort of older woman who would arouse and attract the fast-burning lusts of young men. And also the not-so-young men, he had to admit to himself. And the possibility of Skinner's involvement – had that been put forward by Lingard? – suggested to the detective on the wild side of logic that Skinner might have looked on Colonel Horsbrugh as an obstacle to be rid of. Or perhaps – he could visualize easily the situation – he had been surprised by Horsbrugh with his trousers down – that again had been Lingard's suggestion – in a suspicious proximity to the colonel's wife, reacting to discovery more violently than had the older man.

It was a neat enough theory other than that it had reckoned without a motive for Skinner to later shoot at Sloane, certainly in that instance with a murderous intent. No. He put the brake on that thinking. Say, hypothetically, that Sloane had learned of his mother's adultery with Skinner. Would that be enough for Skinner to try and silence him? Or, from another angle, would it be acceptable logic for him to consider Sloane to be the agent of Skinner's death; revenge for what he might consider the despoiling of his mother's virtue?

But what then of the youth's behaviour shown subsequent to his mother's giving herself to Skinner? His observed attitude, noted by Rogers, had been far from what he could imagine a son's would be, knowing or suspecting her to be promiscuous, a son being almost always highly sensitive towards the integrity of his mother's virtue.

It was all very well to theorize, Rogers told himself, and to then believe that he hadn't pushed at Sloane hard enough; but how could a man get around to questioning a woman's son about her possible adulterous affairs? He decided that he couldn't, not without some evidence to support it, though Mrs Horsbrugh could not by any means be protected by the same restraint. And that was something he wasn't looking forward to with any pleasure.

20

Two matters were niggling at Lingard's inner contentment as he climbed in the dead air of the winding stairs to the top of the tower. They weren't worries enough to give him high blood pressure, but were irritatingly persistent.

One – the more important – was his growing disquiet as belief hardened into conviction that the Alfa Romeo was not for him, that he had ill-advisedly bought a welded and bolted together assembly of expensive hardware which was to remain for ever in his mind as a sexless 'it' car and not a 'her'. This was little to his taste and there was a growing determination in him to somehow dispose of it before it began to register in his mind as a male.

The other worry – more of a fretting – concerned Rogers, his senior colleague and friend. Massively bushed during the past twenty-four hours or so after a sleepless night, he was now believing himself capable of going on for a further twenty-four. While admitting that self-praise was no recommendation, the elegant detective had long thought that Rogers, deplored by him for his subfusc taste in wearing dark mourning-style suits and white shirts, had a better tailored, more efficient and much under-used second-in-command. He believed himself, not immodestly, to be equal in professional stature to Rogers, if not rather the better, and admitted to a friendly peevishness at not being passed the information and opportunities to which he was entitled. In the interests of Rogers's well-being – and he was sincere in that – Lingard considered that he should retire sensibly to either his own bed or that of the skinny black-haired and sardonic female journalist he shared, seemingly unaware, with a singularly hairy house-doctor from the local hospital.

Knocking on the door labelled *Miss C. Coppin*, he waited nearly a minute during which he heard hurried movement and soft bumping noises within the room as if she were tidying it. When she answered his knocking, looking a mite flustered Lingard thought, he went into the showing of his warrant card routine, asking if he might come in. While he sat in the only chair in the underfurnished room – a bloated easy chair almost big enough for two and covered in a hideous sulphur-coloured patterned chintzy fabric – she told him her name was Constance Coppin and offered to make him a cup of tea. That being declined politely, she sat herself on the edge of her single bed and smiled brightly at him.

While explaining to her the purpose of his visit he took the externals of her and his assessment of her persona into his consideration. Overall, she looked a nice young woman dressed in a pale-blue linen skirt and a white blouse with a ruffed collar. Other than for slightly oversized hips, fat thighs and a plump behindness she was of a slim build. With her chestnut hair worn hanging in a thick braid down her back, pale tea-leaf freckles, a pleasant unpainted and partly opened mouth that showed her large square teeth, and saucer-sized spectacles cradled over a snub nose that magnified her green eyes, she was Lingard's idea of a twenty-five-year-old schoolgirl. Despite her smelling of an erotic perfume – freshly put on? Lingard wondered – which seemed at distinct odds with her appearance, he liked her, though preparing to be deceived.

She had said a tiny 'Oh' with her hand quickly up to her mouth, shock whitening her face and sudden tears brimming her eyes, on being told that Skinner had been found dead and was warranting a few questions of his associates. Lingard waited patiently, taking snuff while her face was averted and pretending to be engrossed in the view from the solitary window of the leafy tops of a neighbour's silver birch trees.

She had asked him halting questions such as how had Skinner – she called him Daniel – died? Had he been shot? Where was he and how had it happened? These Lingard parried away from any suggestion that he had been murdered, implying that he had died as the result of an accident in his car; which, he supposed, was somewhere near the truth of the matter. And no, he assured her, it needn't have anything at all to do with Colonel Horsbrugh's disappearance. Nothing of which sounded convincing enough to him to satisfy even a credulous half-wit.

When she appeared to have largely recovered, and Lingard was satisfied that she wasn't grieving deeply enough for him to put off firing his questions, he said carefully, 'I had met Daniel of course, and I understood from him that you and he were close friends.' He cocked his head, his companionable smile inviting her to understand what he meant, despite the fact that it was a blind shot in the dark.

She searched the vivid blue eyes intent on hers, then dropped them in a female appraisal of his immaculate suntan-coloured twill suit and Italian hand-stitched shoes. 'Are you asking were we lovers?' she said, looking back at him and raising her eyebrows.

She had disconcerted him with her directness. And her insight, he supposed. 'Sort of,' he conceded, relieved. 'Though not unpleasantly, I trust? I assume that you were?'

'You consider that unusual?' There was a touch of crispness in her words. She was a woman obviously not to be judged only by her appearance.

'Oh Lord, no,' he said hastily, near to have been losing some of his aplomb. 'It's as we want it, isn't it?' He smiled reassuringly. 'With poor Daniel no longer with us, could you be obliging enough to say whether he was the jealous type?'

She had blinked still-moistened eyes behind her lenses at his 'poor Daniel'. 'Not of me. He had no reason to be. Our friendship was one of convenience though affection was obviously there. It began and ended here at this school.'

'It had ended then?'

'Yes, a few weeks back,' she said curtly. 'That's not up for further discussion.'

'You would know of another association of his?'

'You mean Angela? Poor girl, she must have taken this badly.' She seemed to wince. 'Naturally I knew. There was no conflict of loyalties there.' Her fingers were kneading at the fabric of her skirt.

'She knew then?'

'I doubt it,' she said, almost witheringly. 'Daniel's loyalty was to marry her sometime in the future. Mine was elsewhere, and Daniel wasn't changing it. We never felt the need to be bound by the mores of our profession.'

Lingard, thinking her too well-scrubbed and ingenuous to be overly promiscuous, said, 'I'm afraid that *my* profession occasionally forces me to ask questions which may sometimes be taken amiss and . . .'

She cut him short, grimacing wryly. 'Which means, I'm sure, that you are about to be dreadfully offensive about something.'

'Unwillingly, Miss Coppin, I assure you.' She was a woman already putting him on his best behaviour. 'I rather need to know how you feel about Willie Sloane.'

'Good Lord,' she said, looking up at the ceiling, not too far above her head anyway, 'not him as well?' Her expression showed distaste. 'I'm not to be quoted on this, but I don't like him. Not a wretched boy who can only talk to a woman in barely concealed indecencies . . .' She broke off, her features reflecting anxiety. 'You understand, I *am* employed by his mother.'

'Your words will only grace the pages of my notebook,' Lingard murmured. Her obvious honesty effectively dismissed from his mind any suggestion that she may have been sexually interested in Sloane. 'I'm sure Daniel wouldn't mind my saying this, but he told me that about three months ago he heard Willie apparently making love to a woman in the Lodge. Quite noisy love, in fact.' Searching for signs in her eyes of an existing awareness of what he had said, he smiled disarmingly. 'He may have told you of this? Or, perhaps, you heard of it from a different source?'

She had shown nothing at that, though hesitating before saying, 'I'd heard nothing, and I've been told nothing. But it doesn't surprise me. One isn't silly enough to spread scandal about one's employer's son.'

'Of course not,' Lingard agreed, though dissenting in his mind. 'Between our two selves, Miss Coppin, could you give an inspired guess as to the identity of the woman involved?

142

Dead though Daniel might be, identification could point to his earlier credibility.'

'Could it?' she said as if deeply puzzled, then shaking her head vigorously, 'No. I could only guess that it might have been one of the students, which is unlikely. None sleeps here, and they would be equally unlikely to visit the school after lessons.'

'An awkward question,' Lingard smiled. 'Before you and Daniel became, so to speak, fond of each other, had you known or suspected that he and Mrs Horsbrugh were closer together than possibly they should have been?'

She had glanced at him sharply. 'I'm surprised that you've heard about that.' She appeared to have forgotten that she should be grieving, at least somewhat, for the dead Skinner.

So probably, Lingard judged, he really had been only the vehicle, *sans* affection, for the satisfying of her lusts. Lucky fella, the basement of his mind added to it, though it did seem to be a little cold-blooded.

'We do hear lots of things we perhaps oughtn't,' he said ambiguously. From her response it was plain that he had struck investigator's gold. 'Was that before or after her marriage to the colonel?'

'It was never a subject of discussion between us,' she said scathingly, 'and I can only presume that it was after Colonel Horsbrugh moved to a bedroom of his own. That, of course, was common knowledge among us.'

'And did Daniel sort of move in?'

'Nothing so obvious. However the affair was being managed, nothing showed of it. What we knew – or thought we knew – was by feminine intuition alone. You've heard of it, I imagine?'

And that's twice as copper-bottomed as a male's certainty, Lingard murmured to himself. Aloud, he said, 'Which means that you're reasonably sure?'

'I am sure.'

'Who makes the "we" you mentioned?' he asked casually.

Her mouth curved in a mocking smile, a brief showing of her beautifully white teeth. 'I'm afraid that is something you'll have to find out without my help.'

There seemed a measure of female obduracy beneath the

pleasant helpfulness and Lingard wasn't intending to push hard at it. He was guessing that the probable third party was the missing Mrs Traill, yet to be seen. He smiled at her, finding it easy to do. 'You weren't jealous, were you? Nothing so uncivilized as that?'

'Don't be silly.' She was schoolmistressy with him. 'I've already told you how the situation was between Daniel and myself. Naturally, after he had detached himself from whatever it was between them.'

Before he could put his next question to her – it wasn't much of one anyway – she said with a marked accusation in her voice, 'Daniel was killed, wasn't he? I mean, by somebody who wanted him dead. I'm sure the police don't make enquiries about people's sexual preferences just because they're killed in car accidents.' She was staring him out of countenance.

Ods blood, Lingard muttered beneath his breath. She's going to have me display some unearned ignorance over this. 'Well,' he said cautiously, 'assuming that to be possible – and mind, being only a sort of dogsbody, I'm not all that privy to exactly what happened – would you know of any reason, any motive, for his killing?'

Colour stained her throat and, for a moment, her mouth thinned and she looked decidedly unpleasant. 'When it comes to poor, poor Daniel having been killed, I don't feel that I should hold back, though I do want your promise of confidentiality.'

'As before,' Lingard told her, 'though there is a proviso that we exclude from it anything that may qualify as evidence against anybody. Including yourself,' he added with a quick grin.

'Thank you,' she said, leaving him wondering whether she had understood his last couple of words or not. She was silent for a short while, creases in her forehead suggesting a turmoil of thought. 'It's improbable that it's the motive you're looking for, but whatever there was between Daniel and Mrs Horsbrugh seemed to have left some serious scars on her, though I'm certain not on Daniel. I overheard them quarrelling once; bitter words from her and poor Daniel standing there trying to calm her down. There has since been hostility from her, an obvious

144

dislike for him, and she treated him with a coldness perhaps only another woman would recognize. He never referred to it, for so far as he was concerned I knew nothing of it. Why she let him stay on was a mystery for, clearly to me, there was nothing but enmity for him on her part.' She bit at her mouth. 'You will keep this to yourself, won't you?'

'You're really saying that all this resulted from the ending of their sexual relationship?' Lingard couldn't quite associate a woman's jealousy or resentment with the driving of the object of it over an extremely high cliff.

'I thought so, but I can't be sure of it, can I? I shouldn't have mentioned it,' she said glumly. 'It can't mean anything as serious as killing Daniel. Of course it can't.'

Lingard wished that he knew more about women; about what might make them cold and distant and perhaps revengeful to past lovers. 'What about the colonel?' he asked. 'Presumably he wasn't living in a happy ignorance of all that was going on under his nose between his wife and Daniel. He certainly seems to have been despatched to a separate bedroom for some reason.'

She was thoughtful, looking down at her hands now resting relaxed on her thighs. 'I don't know. I certainly don't think so, though even had he known I'm sure he would have concealed it from everybody outside the two of them like the perfectly mannered gentleman he was.'

'Not a touch of ill-feeling between him and Daniel? Or him and his wife? A cuckolded husband isn't necessarily oblivious, unaware of some other man fouling his nest, you know.'

She shook her head impatiently. 'There was nothing that I noticed and Daniel always said how much he liked and admired him.'

'Did you? Admire him, I mean?'

'I think everybody did. Well . . .' She bit at her mouth again. 'Everybody, that is, other than Willie. But that would be natural, wouldn't it? Being what the relationship is with another man supplanting his father.'

'Your colleague Mrs Traill,' Lingard said, changing tack. 'Is she likely to be back this afternoon?'

'Not, I understand. She ordered a taxi and took the travelling bag she had brought here this morning with her. I rather gathered that she had no wish to wait around a place where people were being shot at.'

Lingard had taken snuff while she talked and he flapped away grains from his nose with his silk handkerchief. 'Do you know where she's gone?'

'No, she didn't say and I didn't ask her. But wouldn't she go home?'

'I imagine so. What kind of a lady is she? I mean, would it be of any use for me to speak to her as I've spoken to you?'

'You mean might she have had an affair with Daniel, or Willie if it comes to that?' She was teasing him, her expression solemn, in what Lingard hoped was a friendly way.

''Pon my soul,' he murmured, 'you find me somewhat transparent. Had she?'

She slid her legs from the bed and stood, then fetched a flat blue packet from the drawer of a small writing-desk. Returning, she stood by him and shuffled through a thin deck of coloured photographs, finally handing him one. So close to him, her hip was an unsettling nearness to his face, the discreet fragrance of her scent putting unwanted eroticism in his thinking.

'Mrs Traill,' she said, something in her voice suggesting that she was less than a bosom friend of hers. 'I took it at her asking, but she didn't like it.'

The photograph she had given him was a close-up portrait taken in harsh revealing sunlight. Having obviously to make his own judgement of Mrs Traill from it, he guessed her age to be about fifty years. She was an unattractive woman with drab woolly hair framing a face with pale skin that looked damp, a sharp nose and a thin vinegarish mouth below the dark shadow of a burgeoning moustache, all suggestive of a sourness of spirit. While she might, for all he knew, have a magnificent body, there was little in what he saw that was seducible. He felt himself to be unkind in thinking that it would be a very deprived man who wanted to feed his hunger on her.

'Mrs Traill has no husband,' Constance Coppin said when Lingard returned the photograph to her, 'and she is a rather unpleasant woman who makes no secret that she disapproves of me and how I lead my own life. She says often that she has

146

no time for men as such. Other, I must admit, than the abominable Willie for whom she seems to have a soft spot.'

'A motherly one, I hope?'

'It couldn't be anything else at her age, could it?' she said, almost derisively.

With his narrow features showing only amiability, though thinking that there had been some unworthy bitchiness in her comments, he lifted himself from his chair, not finding it possible to speak to a woman while he was sitting and she standing. 'If I may say so,' he said, trying to read what was going on behind the spectacled green eyes, 'Benjamin Franklin once wrote in his *Advice to a Young Man on Matters Carnal* something about older women being so accommodating and so grateful.'

'If he wrote that, then Mr Franklin knew nothing about older women,' she told him crisply. She held out her hand which he took, manifestly having had enough and dismissing him. It was well done. 'I really am terribly sad about Daniel,' she said, 'but tears won't bring him back, will they?'

'True, they won't,' he said tritely, releasing his hand from hers. 'I'm grateful for the information you've given me.' Somewhere, he thought, he must have said the wrong thing though, irrespective, had he been in the unlikely frame of mind to be lusting after this undeniably sexually attractive woman with the voluptuous thighs, her quite limp and lukewarm handshake would have thoroughly damped it down. Whatever it was that the similarly blond and blue-eyed Daniel Skinner had in him capable of lighting a fire in her body, Lingard felt it was something that he, himself, must certainly lack.

On the way downstairs he tried to rationalize Constance Coppin's short-term grief over her dead lover and her unusual willingness to denigrate her classroom colleague; and, because he knew so little about women anyway, he was getting nowhere with it.

147

21

With the dying day's sun a crimson globe silhouetting the roofs
and chimney stacks visible from his office windows, Rogers sat
working at his desk, reactivated in part though definitely not to
his normal degree of consciousness. He had, in a sort of
desperation, taken a hurried cold shower and drunk hot black
coffee in his apartment, the latter together with three capsules
of *Eleutherococcus*, reputed – though not guranteed – to keep
him awake for an hour or two and standing upright in his size
10½ Oxford shoes.

As a by-product of his present irritation with life, he nursed a
malevolent hatred for his metal and imitation leather-topped
desk, representing as it innocently did the hours he was
required to spend at it in the writing up of his working notes,
the reading of too many crime files that were sometimes so
prolix as to defy a proper understanding of them, or staring at
one of the office walls and wondering why in hell the commis-
sion of a violent crime was so often impossible of a critical
examination. As in the investigation in which he was at present
engaged; an investigation in which he had had a bellyful of
lying flapping tongues and the fragments of part conversations
that insisted on bobbing to the surface of his tired thinking.

He wasn't his usual self and would admit to it if anyone
dared to push him hard enough concerning it. A belated
interview with a testy Chief Constable who was complaining
with some justification at not being kept fully in the picture,
and taking it seriously amiss, hadn't helped much either.

Before considering the possible motives, probable and
improbable, for the crimes he was investigating, and open to
whatever his limping brain could fancifully imagine, he cleared
figuratively his desk of the accumulation of exhibits and reports
relevant to his needs.

Prior to his entering his office he had been intercepted by
Lingard who was going off duty and had insisted on relating to

Rogers the stuff of his interview with Constance Coppin. Confirming Skinner's sexual interest in Mrs Horsbrugh and also his later role as a teacher's comforter, it could, he thought, be significant where it might concern the missing Colonel Horsbrugh. Even then, he couldn't think into it enough passion for either man to allow himself an indulgence towards a fatal violence.

Lingard had also confirmed that he and a policewoman had broken the news of Skinner's death to an already thinking-the-worse Angela Annetts and her hysterical reaction to it had shaken him rather more severely than he had thought it would. One of life's little kicks in the crotch, Rogers had told him, knowing exactly how he felt from his own experiences.

The most obvious article for Rogers's attention was a poly-thene-wrapped calf-leather wallet and two .22 cartridge cases accompanied by a report from Sergeant 1018 John Knox Lauder detailing their finding in an unlocked fascia compartment of Skinner's sunken Ford car, still to be hoisted surfaceward. The report had ended with his stating that the car was found to be in the neutral gear with the ignition key in the off position.

Unfolding the wallet, Rogers extracted carefully the plastic cards and the still damp and fragile documents from it. The plastic items were green and red cashpoint cards, one signed Henry F. Horsbrugh. The documents related to a Rover car, all issued and prepared for Horsbrugh. The two cartridge cases were, he considered, almost certainly those missing from the scene of the shooting at Mrs Horsbrugh's chair and television set. With the pistol still missing, he was only impressed with what he saw as the seemingly misapplied incongruity of what was there.

Earlier, between notes, Rogers had telephoned and asked the director of the Forensic Science Laboratory himself for an urgent analysis of the varnish-like stains he had recovered from the hard-standing where Skinner had parked his car. The serologist, disturbed by the director from his evening meal, had returned not too happily to the laboratory, taken possession of the material from a DC – whose short report Rogers now read – and quite quickly identified part of the staining as made by human blood, the grouping of which, he firmly insisted, should be done the following morning.

Also in between writing up his notes, Rogers had telephoned Dr Wilfred Twite, his friend and the local Home Office appointed pathologist, notorious for his cavalier and bloody wielding of a dissecting scalpel, cozening him into agreeing to do an early, almost immediate post-mortem examination on Skinner's body. To this he agreed, with Rogers promising to attend when Twite notified him that he was about to start.

A report from Detective Inspector Coltart, detailed to dig into the life style and recent movements of Primrose Booker's remarkably complaisant veterinarian husband, seemed effectively to remove him as a likely suspect in any killing off of Colonel Horsbrugh for doing whatever it was that a sixty-odd-year-old man could do for a wife separated from her husband. Gerald Booker had been reported attending unaccompanied a meeting of the Canine Veterinary Advisory Board at Coleport, some one hundred and twenty miles distant, for the past two days and had not yet returned. Coltart was furthering his enquiries at Coleport, but was reasonably certain that Booker was where his informant had said him to be. Rogers, holding back a yawn between clenched teeth, was not disappointed, for Booker had never been to him anything other than an unlikely suspect; almost certain to be a man too indifferent to his wife's lechery to bloody his hands over it.

Finishing his notes and recapping his pen, Rogers leaned back in his executive-style chair that squeaked under his restless weight like a bucketful of hungry mice and started to refill his still-hot pipe; something which, he had heard, could be potentially unkind to his lungs. Life, he told himself, might be all about living dangerously. While waiting his call from Wilfred Twite he proposed examining motives, even fancifully dreaming them up, for both the disappearance of the allegedly gentlemanly Horsbrugh and the killing of Skinner. This he did while unconsciously and continually inhaling more puffs of tobacco smoke than could possibly be good for his trachea and bronchi, apart from his lungs.

One motive, entering unsought into his imagery, caused him to wish that it had not. It was a theory – an unsubstantiated dirtying theory and nothing more – in which his reluctant mind told him that everything – well, nearly everything – slotted neatly into place. It was, he had to accept, emanating from a policeman's highly suspicious mind which could even lay mortal sins against a bishop or two. As with the man who, being but a few minutes from being hanged, was told by his executioner to think about something else, Rogers told himself that he should try to do the same as a distraction from dwelling on that particular theory. Because it's steamy, he complained to himself. It's so bloody steamy.

The theory was still persisting among others which were more realistic when his telephone bell rang. His caller was Twite's mortuary attendant – the chap who did all the stitching up afterwards – advising Rogers that the doctor had already started on his examination of the deceased Mr Skinner.

Rogers chose to walk to the nearby hospital mortuary in the early night's darkness on the fallacious assumption that the night air would invigorate his brain, his nose failing to detect the miasmal petrol fumes from passing traffic or the possibly toxic exhalations from the streets' still-warm asphalt.

Entering the brilliant shadowless light in the mortuary, his nose aware of the odour of raw flesh, he saw that Twite was finishing his cutting into the naked body of Skinner from beneath the bearded chin down to the crotch and was preparing to decant it. He had already stripped the head of its scalp and its blond hair and had laid it flesh side up over the face. A black hosepipe, hanging from the ceiling, dribbled water on to the stainless steel necropsy table.

Wilfred Twite, dressed in his surgeon's green overalls, shapeless cap and red rubber apron, was a fat and ebullient man with tightly waved black hair and a Mexican-style moustache. He had a gourmand's appetite for gulping at good food and at other men's wives, in between those activities being flashily adept at finding the hole in a body through which death had entered. He smoked imported scented cigarettes, one of which was now held in his mouth, its ash dropping on to the table.

'Sorry, old son,' he said to Rogers without turning his head from what he was doing. 'High-level conference at ten and I had to make a start.' He could white-lie happily with amazing conviction, though not always fooling the detective.

Rogers joined him, nearer to the smell of raw flesh than he wished. He indicated the head with its stripped scalp. 'I thought a comminuted fracture, Wilfred?'

Twite grunted around his cigarette. He was doing revolting things in cutting out a pair of unmottled pale pink lungs. 'See what you'd have if you didn't smoke that filthy pipe of yours, George,' he said, ignoring his own smoking. He pointed a bloodied scalpel at the naked skull. 'Right rear of parietal bone. Your guess not too bad, though there are both comminuted and depressed fractures. The first one killed him. Hit from behind by right-handed assailant. Thump, thump, thump certainly. That many times.' He coughed, then spat away his cigarette butt to fall to the wet floor and ground it to extinction with his shoe. 'And hard hit, too. I don't expect to find much water in his lungs, for I'm certain he was dead long before he was put into it.'

Rogers, pulling at his pipe against the rankness of Skinner's decanting, nodded his agreement. That was his own opinion and it fitted into the theory his mind seemed determined to hang on to, more from the hell of it than from any deep conviction. 'I believe he was a nice enough chap,' he said. 'I wouldn't like to think that he was conscious when he went over the cliff.'

Twite now had the lungs resting flabbily on the table at the side of the body. Seizing a dissecting knife laid ready, he sectioned rapidly through one of them, then expressed a small quantity of a pinkish liquid from a thick slab of it by the pressure of his rubber-gloved hand. 'An expected seepage,' he said. 'Water can be taken in through a dead person's mouth and nostrils. The quantity we have here by no means indicates death by drowning.'

'Would the time of death be somewhere around late evening?' Rogers asked. He had moved away from Twite and the table; his eyes – already bloodshot, he was sure – were determined to avoid further looking at the emptying of the gruesomely dissected body. 'He was definitely on his two feet yesterday

152

afternoon and I can't reasonably see him being banged on the head and run over a cliff in daylight.'

'Having been in the water at all doesn't help,' Twite said as he stripped his right glove off to light himself another cigarette, 'but I'd say offhand between twenty and twenty-four hours. I may be able to let you know more precisely tomorrow after I've worked at my figures.'

It was enough for Rogers and he said so, for he now felt what he guessed to be a large purple-coloured worm gnawing at the left side of his temple. Leaving the mortuary to collect his car from the Headquarters' hard-standing, he felt he was staggeringly on his last legs. He would, he thought, be surprised should he reach his apartment without suffering what had been the ill-fated Skinner's lot this time around the mortal coil.

He was never to remember entering the apartment and having enough nous to remove the receiver from his sitting-room telephone before somehow getting out of his clothing and dropping naked and insensible on the sheets of his still-unmade bed.

What he was later to remember – and to remember when he wished to forget – was his dreaming nightmarishly of being hunted across a plain wreathed in a moonless night's blackness by daemon dogs he couldn't see, but whose eerie baying he could hear closing on him. Superimposed on the dogs' baying, and coming from the unseen and distant horizon, the shrill ringing of a bell intruded upon his growing awareness of being himself. Stumbling naked and as if drunken from his bed to the sitting-room in the blackness of his waking stupor, he found the telephone receiver hanging loose and giving out a disengaged signal. The ringing noise now resolved itself into the sound of his door bell and its maddening persistence irritated him into a furious outburst. 'For God Almighty's sake!' he yelled at whoever it was as he staggered back to his bedroom. 'Wait a moment and give me a bloody chance!'

Finding the wall switch and giving himself blinding light, he grabbed his discarded shirt from the floor and wrapped it around his loins. Still not wholly awake, he returned to the sitting-room and opened the door to the outside hall.

The uniformed inspector standing there was blonde and

female, looking as astonished as Rogers was, his jaw dropping while he stared dumbstricken at her with dismay. W/Inspector Millier, some months earlier a detective sergeant in his department, was the last woman officer in the force to whom he would wish to display his unshaven, unbathed and half-naked self. At least, not on those occasions when he should be upholding the *gravitas* of his rank.

'I'm sorry, Miss Millier,' he said at last, trying to reassemble whatever remnants of his dignity were left to him and not daring to look, but hoping that his parts were decently covered. 'Both for my shouting at you and for my present appearance. I didn't know,' he finished lamely. 'What is the time?'

Inspector Millier, who as a sergeant equipped with blonde hair and a beautiful mouth, had been an innocently disruptive element in the department, said expressionlessly, 'It's nearly half-past four, sir. I'm sorry I disturbed you, but your telephone's been off the hook and there's an urgent message for you from Mr Lingard.' She had avoided looking at anything below Rogers's chin, though she must already have seen her very senior officer's version of what he could deem to be proper to wear in bed. And what she did not show, and probably never would, was that she thought herself to be in love with Rogers. Her unhappiness at the lack of any sexual interest in her by the unaware Rogers had pushed her into asking for a transfer back to uniform duties where future contact with him would be minimal and which had, adventitiously, led to her promotion. 'He wants you to know that he's been called out to Tower House for a suicide. A Mrs Rachel Horsbrugh has been found dead in her bedroom by her son who's now gone missing.'

Rogers stood there, behind the mask of *gravitas* he was assuming wanting to yell out something like 'God! God! Why are you doing this to me!' while Inspector Millier added, 'Mr Lingard also said that I was to drive you there should you wish for transport.'

Some vast distance away from being the calm and unflappable executive in command of events, Rogers struggled to manage a smile. 'Thank you, Miss Millier, I'd be grateful. Perhaps you'd wait in the car while I get dressed.'

With Millier gone and him back inside scrabbling into his clothes, Rogers wasn't quite sure which of the two events had been the more traumatic for him. He knew only that he would never be able to face the inspector ever again without reliving his dumbstricken embarrassment and the loss of his *savoir-faire*. Against that, until he viewed Mrs Horsbrugh as a dead body and found out what her bloody-minded son was up to, it had yet to make any proper impact on him.

22

As Rogers was driven through the darkness of sleeping streets in what he thought to be a godforsaken and uncivilized early morning after his five hours' sleep, his mood was less than ebullient. It would, he knew as he pushed tobacco into his pipe with impatient fingers, stay so until he had anaesthetized it with an adequacy of nicotine and strong coffee. Now properly dressed, he sat unspeaking in the passenger seat next to Inspector Millier who seemed offended into silence by her earlier sight of his near nakedness. She must have seen worse, he supposed to himself, holding a lighted match to his pipe and exhaling smoke through the side window in deference to her no doubt attractively unblemished lungs. He suspected he was making of his unthinking exposure a fuss more suitable to an octogenarian of refined upbringing.

Deposited at the door of Tower House, Rogers hesitated at smiling a 'Thank you' to Millier in case she took it to be the equivalent of a conspiratorial wink. Instead, he asked her to wait with the car as he had no wish later to walk to wherever else he might have to go.

Lingard's Alfa Romeo stood on the gravel drive in front of a communications patrol car manned by a PC whose face was tinted a livid green by the on-light from the inboard console. A police motor cycle stood propped further along the drive. There were shaded lights showing from the curtained windows of the house and a lack of human movement anywhere.

155

Pushing the door open, Rogers felt the heavy silence inside; sensing, he thought, the brooding presence of death there as much as he could in the hospital mortuary.

Lingard, alone in the sitting-room, pushed himself up from one of the high-backed chairs and stood as Rogers entered. 'They called me out again, George,' he said, a little too light-heartedly for five in the morning and for Rogers's present mood. Though his face showed signs of tiredness and strain, he still managed to look as if freshly bathed and recently shaved. 'Your phone's apparently on the blink.'

'I rather expected a buzz of activity, David,' Rogers growled, pointedly looking around him at the room empty of anyone else. 'I can see we've bought some trouble, so tell me what; and what we've so far done.'

Lingard regarded his senior quizzically. 'Stap me,' he said. 'I haven't been here for much more than an hour and the buzz of activity happens to have passed by. Do you want it in brief first, or as it happened in full?'

'Sloane first, David.' Rogers accepted that he was being a trifle bloody-minded and tried hard to put some amiability in his words. 'Inspector Millier says says that he's gone missing.'

'He's not wanted for anything, but I believe that he's slipped a cog or two over the death of his mother,' Lingard said carefully. It hadn't been difficult for him to see that his senior was in a decidedly finicky mood. 'I don't so far suspect him of having any connection with that, though I have circulated his and his car's description and sent out some bods to look for him. How all this comes about needs explaining from scratch. Scratch being a dog whining and a sleeping Miss Coppin hearing bumps and cries of anguish in the night.'

'I think I'd like to see Mrs Horsbrugh first,' Rogers said, holding back on his testiness, in no mood for his second-in-command's ambiguities. 'Let's start from there. She's still in her bedroom?'

'As I found her,' Lingard told him. 'Ready for you to give me the word.' He added with emphasis, 'It *is* suicide, George, and not anything else.'

'But still something likely to screw up our enquiries.' Turning and making impatiently for the door with Lingard in his wake,

Rogers relit his pipe while mounting the stairs to Mrs Horsbrugh's bedroom.

A uniformed PC, wearing motor-cycling leathers made garish with luminescent yellow and a shiny plastic helmet, stood outside the closed bedroom door with a stern expression on his face. He stiffened to rigidity as the two men approached, then opened the door for them to enter.

The lights, already on, showed the pervading pinkness of furnishings that Rogers had seen before. The room was no longer a sweet-scented boudoir, but one redolent of dead flesh. One door of the built-in wardrobe was open, the interior softly shaded. With a silent Lingard standing behind him, he took in the woman who had, a short few hours ago, been the attractive Rachel Horsbrugh. A woman hanged was, to him, a sickening sight; an outrage against her gentle femininity. She was clothed in white satin pyjamas and lying on her back on the floor of the wardrobe, her legs unnaturally folded beneath her. The emptiness of death was written in her distorted features, underlining her transition to a now unoccupied corpse. Her dulled eyes stared sightlessly at the row of clothes suspended above her, the tip of her dried tongue protruding from between her lips. A purplish ligature mark followed the line of her jaw exposed to the detective's sombre gaze. A twisted blue and jade shoulder scarf was looped and knotted around the clothes bar immediately above her. He felt it, finding it to be made of the fine silk cloth that could be drawn easily through a woman's finger ring, and in the feeling of it he discovered a small damp area of staining. Putting the back of a reluctant finger on the exposed throat, he felt it mildly warm. That close to the body, he smelled stale brandy.

'Who took her down, David?' he asked.

'Young Willie, poor fella, as you may hear.' Lingard was thinking that at the moment the less he said about that the better. 'There is a note she left. Well, you could call it a note, I suppose.' He stepped over to the dressing table at which Rogers – it now seemed to him to have been days ago – had seen Mrs Horsbrugh in all the desirability of her warm and living body.

'This,' Lingard said, indicating a green-glass brandy bottle, visibly less than half-full, resting on the dressing table. A crystal tumbler with a residue of brandy-coloured liquid in it stood close by it. 'You smelt it in the wardrobe?'

Rogers nodded. 'I thought brandy.'

'Then there's this,' Lingard said of the opened pages of a slim silk-bound diary, partially concealed by tubes, small jars and containers of cosmetics, with a tiny gold-coloured ballpen lying between them.

Peering at the diary without touching it, Rogers saw written in it the solitary word *Contrition*, in no way suggesting by jaggedness or by hesitation in the formation of it any agitation at the prospect of what she was apparently to do.

'You've checked the writing?' he asked.

Lingard nodded. 'Be assured, and done without handling it. There're appointments noted at a hairdressing salon and so forth earlier in the diary, though it'll need a laboratory examination to make it a legal certainty. I am, though,' he asserted confidently, 'sure of it myself.'

Using the butt-end of an unused match, Rogers delicately turned pages in the diary, familiarizing himself with the writing in it and satisfying himself that the word *Contrition* had been written by the same hand. His and Lingard's opinions would be meaningless in a court, but they were valid enough conclusions for him to act on.

Unseeing of the momentary sardonic expression in Lingard's face, he returned the match to its box. 'You've called Photographic and Fingerprints?' he asked.

'Sergeant Magnus,' Lingard said, poker-faced now, still a little touchy with Rogers. 'He should be here by now.'

Rogers had noticed a handsome leather handbag at the side of the dressing-table stool and he picked it up, opening it on the presumption that anything concerning the violently dead woman was open for his investigation. A cursory glance inside showed him make-up, credit and bank cards, car keys, a few £20 and £10 notes, a small number of coins and a long envelope addressed to her in a typescript with a bank's title and logo on its reverse. The envelope had been slit open and a brief look inside revealed official-looking documents which he decided to examine later.

Then, directing his attention to the bed, he saw that without question it had been slept in or lain on by the sufferer of a particularly disturbed mind. The rose-pink satin sheets and single blanket were twisted and rumpled with one of the two pillows and a featherweight white bedcover lying on the carpet. The dog basket he had seen before had part of the bedcover thrown over it.

'You mentioned the dog,' he said to Lingard. 'Where is she?'

'With Miss Coppin.' He was uncharacteristically terse.

'I see.' Then, unreasonably, 'Am I supposed to guess why?'

'A pox on it, George,' Lingard expostulated, trying hard to contain his own irritation. 'You're being a mite difficult this morning, aren't you? Why don't we plant our honourable backsides in chairs for ten minutes or more so that you can listen to what I've been trying to tell you since you arrived?'

Rogers's brown eyes darkened, staring under scowling eyebrows at his second-in-command for long seconds. Then his face cleared and he relaxed. 'All right, David,' he said. 'Point taken and I apologize. I started off on the wrong foot this morning, though that's no excuse for my being a miserable bugger.'

'Enough said, George,' Lingard murmured, though with a warning in his voice. 'Just so that you aren't doubting my competence.' It was the nearest he had got to ticking off his senior.

Leaving the room to the imagined brooding of the dead woman and in the care of the guardian PC, the two men returned to the sitting-room. Rogers sat in one of the tall-back chairs; Lingard, of his own choice, remained standing while he charged his nose – it gave Rogers, as always, the impression that it was too aristocratically narrow for that purpose – with generous amounts of Attar of Roses that perfumed the air around him.

'Information room had me out of bed at something before four this morning,' he started, 'on the grounds that they couldn't contact you by telephone. A female not giving her name before ringing off – she turned out to have been Miss Coppin – had been through on the emergency line in a fair old tizzy. The duty bod wasn't altogether up to taking it all in, but did get from the recording that she was at the English Language

159

School in Kingfisher Road and that a Mrs Horse-something had been hanged in a wardrobe.'

'Definitely hanged?' Rogers interposed. 'And not found hanging?'

'So it was said, and it did turn out that Miss Coppin thought initially that she had. Anyway, back to my being hauled out of bed. I left instructions for you to be found and told what was what, and also for our night duty sergeant – who happens to be Duffield who never gets anywhere on time – to be found and sent here with a couple of chaps to be on hand. When I arrived at the school the lights were on and I was let in by Miss Coppin,' – a smile creased his eyes – 'who was rather engagingly dressed in pyjamas and nightrobe with her hair very fetchingly undone from the ponytail she presumably wears as a teacher. I mention that in case we might wish to draw conclusions from it, though I do admit she looked suitably tear-stained and shocked enough to suit the occasion.'

He tapped the sides of his nostrils with his forefinger to dislodge any grains of snuff inside, then sniffed them into his sinuses. 'She said that she thanked God I'd come because she couldn't handle the situation and poor dear Willie – that's what she called him – was throwing something of a wingdinger over his mother being dead in her wardrobe. That,' he mused, 'managed to bother her a little more than having a dead woman virtually on her hands. I hung on to her while we were still in the hall, talking like a couple of conspirators because of Willie being somewhere, and coaxed her into giving me a picture of what had happened while it was still fresh in her mind.'

Rogers, his weight making his chair groan in its joints each time he moved, said, 'Before we go on, had she reported earlier that Mrs Horsbrugh's body had been hanged or had been found hanging from what she had seen, or from what she'd been told?'

'She'd seen it, though after what Willie told her. I don't think there's anything in it for us in pursuing a distinction.'

'I suppose not.' Rogers was looking through one of the windows at the early morning's darkness – an unusually warm and woolly darkness with double-sized stars in it, he thought –

as he stuffed tobacco absently into his fractious pipe. He grinned at Lingard. 'Don't let me interrupt you again.'

'As I've been given it,' Lingard said patiently, 'Willie was in bed when things happened, the time being well after three o'clock. That must be only a guess, for understandably nobody was checking the time in the resulting hoo-hah.' He gave a small self-deprecatory cough. 'The rather delectable Miss Coppin, innocently asleep in her far from virginal bed, says she was awakened by what she first thought to be the howling of someone in dreadful distress in the main part of the building. That, together with the sounds of banging. A brave lass because she was alone in the tower, she got up, put on her nightrobe thingy and came down the stairs and through the door into the house to see what it was all about.'

Lingard paused, shooting his shirt cuffs until they came half-way over his hands, manifestly arranging his thoughts for Rogers's inspection. 'It was her so-said detested sex-orientated Willie who was doing the howling, except that she said she then felt only pity for him. He was on his knees, distraught and weeping like nobody's business, in the corridor outside his mother's door. Not that she knew why then, of course, but in between his blubbing – she said that she felt impelled to hold him in her arms – he told her, not always in sequence and sometimes incoherently, that his mother was dead in the wardrobe; that while sleeping in Colonel Horsbrugh's bedroom which is next to his mother's, he had been woken up by the whining and scratching of her dog outside in the corridor.

'The dog as you've seen from its basket sleeps in her room at night and it would never have been shut out. Getting up and opening her door for the dog to enter – he was in pyjama trousers only then – he saw by the nightlight his mother usually slept by that she wasn't in her bed and that the *en suite* bathroom where she might otherwise have been was in darkness. Miss Coppin told me that it had been very difficult to understand what he was trying to tell her, but the wardrobe was referred to and the words "Mother is dead". That several times while he was weeping, she says, together with some words about being hanged. She says she was terrified, but decided that she'd at least look at the wardrobe, which she did, then wishing that she had not for she sounded distressed about what she had seen and said that she couldn't bear to talk about it.'

Lingard paused again, then said ruminatively, 'Poor lass. I couldn't help feeling sorry for her.'

'Did she tell you what the banging was about?'

'Yes. He was thumping the floor with his fists, I suppose in his impotence to be able to do anything. In a lesser sense he did much the same thing with the settee he was sitting on down here.'

'Reasonable, I imagine, though we'll need to be sure he was actually suffering,' Rogers pointed out, not unsympathetically.

'Yes, caution understood,' Lingard agreed. 'I had a surplus of it so I think he was. When I'd pumped Miss Coppin fairly dry – she said she'd persuaded Willie to come here while she dialled the emergency number for a doctor and us – I went to the bedroom and had a look at what had caused all the trouble.' He nodded his yellow-thatched head in the direction of Mrs Horsbrugh's bedroom. 'Exactly as you've seen her,' he said. 'With her being on the floor, it was my first opinion that she had slipped from the loop after death; my second, that Willie had unnoosed her so to speak on finding her strung up. This was before I'd seen the note in her diary so I also had to bear in mind that she could have been hoisted by somebody in what could effectively have been a hangman's noose.'

'And you'd naturally start thinking in terms of its having been Sloane for God knows what reason, as I would. Yes?'

'A thought, George, no more. She would have needed to be drugged or otherwise made unconscious.'

'So she would. And also somehow made to write *Contrition* in her diary.' Rogers shook his head. 'Not likely at all, is it? And not the sort of thing a son would do to his mother?'

'God forbid,' Lingard agreed. 'Matricide's a bit of a rare bird to me.'

'You noticed she'd be low enough to kneel once hanging from the bar? Not dangling freely, obviously.'

'We've seen it before, haven't we? From doorknobs and similar and somehow peculiar to women, poor dears.' Lingard, feeling that that had been settled rather more than less, continued, 'You know, tonight – this morning, I mean – is the first time I've seen or spoken to Willie. Or seen his mother for that matter. Rather much against the grain I questioned him in between his blubbing and did get a few little somethings apart from what Miss Coppin had told me. He had by then put on a pyjama jacket and bathrobe and he managed to get out that he'd last seen his mother when he said good-night to her at about ten o'clock. At first, he rather dodged away from any mention of finding her dead this morning, but I did get out of him that he'd pulled the scarf from off her throat and laid her on her back. That he had accepted she'd killed herself was something, I suppose, and he reacted as we tend to do by shouting down the existence of a God and even if there should be one then it was obvious that he didn't give a bloody damn for anyone down here; that everybody, including the effing uncaring police who hadn't prevented his mother from dying, could get stuffed or drop dead as far as he was concerned and that it was all the fault of *him*; which I took to mean his stepfather.'

Lingard allowed himself a pained smile. 'That, I know, sounds what you might expect from that kind of a family loss, but it wasn't just that. In between it and a couple of stiff brandies which I thought would calm him down, he went into a sort of lion's cage, pacing up and down with what I thought to be a potential for going completely off his rocker, and not being very pleasant company. When I'd got him settled on the settee he would sit for a while staring holes in the carpet and gabbling away to his mother – at least, that's what it sounded like – as if she were there with him. Then he'd beat his fists like I said on to the arm of the settee and off he'd go on his damned pacing the room as if he wanted to take on anyone who stood in his way. It was genuine, George, I'll vouch for that. And a bit fright-making at times, too. Especially as neither Magnus nor Duffield and his troops were arriving.'

He took what looked like a lethal overdose of Attar of Roses from its tiny ivory box and inhaled it in a couple of snorts. 'While I was trying to convince myself that I should try to handcuff him to one of the radiators for his safety and mine, Dr McNiven arrived to deal with Mrs H. Not being able to be in two places at once, I hadn't any option but to leave Willie in the sitting-room to go on talking to his mother or whatever he was doing. Nor, in the event, could the doctor do much under the circumstances; just looked a little horrified, went through the motions and said he was prepared to certify her as being dead and buzzed off back to his bed again. A little disgruntled, I thought, but understandable. I'd like to have gone with him.'

'Was he her doctor?' Rogers asked.

'No, he'd never seen her before. He was the first doctor on the emergency rota out of the hat, I imagine.' Lingard rapped his knuckles against his forehead as though punishing his brain, though he wasn't looking too worried about it. 'The crunch bit,' he said. 'While I was making sure that the doctor didn't go beyond his brief and move the body about, I heard a car being started up at the front, then taking off with a fair acceleration and somebody not too happily or politely shouting about it. When I'd made the front door and was able to see something, I realized that Willie's Volkswagen was missing, that a constabulary motor cycle was upon its side at the entrance gate and that PC Hooker, who I later put at Mrs H's door, was brushing debris from himself where he'd apparently dived in the shrubbery to avoid being a death by reckless driving.' He grimaced. 'That, of course, was Willie taking off for parts unknown and, possibly, I should have anticipated it.'

Rogers made no comment, recognizing a walking lightly on eggshells situation when he saw it, and not prepared to sit in judgement.

'Hooker', Lingard continued, 'said that he'd only just arrived with his engine switched off to do the hourly check and had parked the machine near the gate just as the Volkswagen shot out of the drive with lights blazing and knocked it so to speak from under his nose. Hooker – I think the poor chap's since taken to religion – had to dive sideways to avoid being riven into small pieces. By perverse fate, Duffield and his couple of bods turned up while I was getting the facts from Hooker, so I sent them off to get more transport and to scour the town to see what they could uncover. Which, I presume, they're still doing. Magnus, as you were, was apparently unobtainable, he not being home in his lodgings.'

'As a bachelor,' Rogers said, knowing that Lingard was also

one, 'he's almost certainly not to be trusted to be where he should be, and particularly not where women are concerned.'

'Yes,' Lingard agreed placidly. 'This particular bachelor has put out a circulation for Willie to be traced and knocked off if found, on the grounds of his personal safety. I'd checked his bedroom by then and whatever he was wearing it wasn't his pyjamas and bathrobe, for they'd been thrown on to his bed. Which, incidentally, did appear to have been slept in.' Lingard smiled. 'And that, apart from your arriving with a whacking great chip on your shoulder, is that.' He added cautiously, 'I think,' just in case it wasn't.

'Has your vinegary Mrs Traill returned yet?'

Lingard shook his head. 'It does look as if she's ducking out, doesn't it? I'll do some chasing up on her.'

'Are you satisfied that Sloane wasn't putting it on? It's not unknown, is it?'

'He'd have to be a first-class actor to do it. On and off he was producing real tears.' Lingard was bland in his answer, though there was a warning mind-your-step undertone in his words.

'I don't dispute your opinion, David,' Rogers said quite amiably. 'In fact, I'm tending to agree with it. But I think that, despite the contrition bit, we should give Mrs Horsbrugh's part in the investigation the full treatment. I shall certainly want Wilfred up here to see her *in situ* and to give us a pronouncement; and Sergeant Magnus, when he's found, to do the photographing and fingerprint search before she's moved. And even before that, perhaps you could persuade your delectable Miss Coppin to cook us up some strong coffee.' He smiled benignly at the thought of it.

'I've the feeling you believe that God's back in your particular heaven and that the end is nigh,' Lingard said flippantly. 'Is it?'

Rogers stood from his chair, rubbing his hands together. His worries had largely been anaesthetized by sleep and nicotine and he felt full of confidence. 'It's been oozing up from the bowels of my brain as we've been chatting away,' he told him. 'Not the whole of it, but enough – Mrs Horsbrugh's death in particular – for me to understand something of the beginning of it all.'

'You'll share it with this non-understanding being?' Lingard thought that Rogers was being optimistically out of character.

'Not yet, David. I might be wrong. You do your own thinking – particularly about the possibility of *modus operandi* and the probable whereabouts of our missing colonel. We'll have a meeting of minds after Wilfred has confirmed or not our opinion as to how Mrs Horsbrugh died.'

23

Before a predictably complaining, baggy-eyed, dragged-from-bed Dr Twite would be arriving to view *in situ* the body of Mrs Horsbrugh, Rogers was on the telephone to the Thurnholme Bay sub-division ordering the police inflatable – the pigboat as he had heard it called by dissatisfied customers – with Sergeant Lauder and his staff of two frogmen, plus a body bag, to be at the town quay steps as near to first light as was possible. Only one PC was to be in his diving gear, the others to be in shirt-sleeve order and wearing heavy boots.

He was acting on what others would call a hunch, but which he preferred to believe was a leaning fairly lightly on intuition. Or guesswork, being never certain which it was, though buttressed somewhat by one of the few Latin phrases used as a crime investigational weapon: *modus operandi*. Translated into a formula, it indicated that a repeated crime tended to follow the same, often unthinking pattern as the first, frequently identifying two or more crimes as having been committed by the same person.

While Lingard was re-interviewing his delectable Miss Coppin in her room and taking a detailed statement from her – something he seemed quite anxious to be doing – Rogers had Inspector Millier, because of her former CID experience, brought into the house and established in Colonel Horsbrugh's study to keep an ear on the telephone there and to organize and record incoming information. He uncomfortably assured himself that he was imagining things when, on several occasions, he detected her regarding him with what appeared to be an un-inspector-like interest in her dark-blue eyes. He believed that he now knew exactly why he had suspected her of being an innocent – he hoped – disruption in the department; a woman who, without any conscious deployment of her sex, could metaphorically cause the clashing of male antlers, the scraping of rutting hooves. O God! he said in his mind. Lead me not into more temptation that I can already handle.

One of the first items she brought to him in the sitting-room he was using as his base was a message from Sergeant Duffield saying that Sloane's Volkswagen Beetle had been found, apparently abandoned, in a lane near the village of Mortefuot. It was unlocked, the ignition key in place and the radiator still warm. With the village lying in the shadow of looming Great Morte Moor, Rogers had no difficulty in deciding that Sloane might be somewhere on the moor. Or not, if the youth was exercising a modicum of cunning. He gave orders for the search to be switched to that area; more of an optimistic knee-jerk reaction to it than to any belief that Sloane would be fool enough to expose himself on an expanse of moorland. Following that, he drafted a Wanted for Questioning circulation giving Sloane's description in full though forced into stating 'dress unknown' which necessary uncertainty could prove a handicap in identifying him. Whichever way he looked at Sloane's running away, Rogers was convinced that the death of Mrs Horsbrugh was the crux of what went before and what came afterwards.

Remembering the handbag he had brought with him from her bedroom, he took from it the opened envelope and examined the contents. There were two certificates relating to Mrs Horsbrugh's marriages to her first and second husbands as had been reported by WDC Sadler, together with a Certified Copy of an Entry in the Adopted Children Register referring to William Rupert Sloane, a male child then of five years of age. Gregory and Rachel Isobel Sloane were recorded as the adopters, together with the date of the child's adoption. Enclosed with these documents was a slip of paper endorsed by the same hand which had written *Contrition* in the handbag diary: *Will at solicitors Kneebone, Kneebone and Tully. R.I.H.*

That Sloane had been an adopted child was significant in one sense to Rogers, though not affecting substantially the motive burgeoning in his thinking. But he accepted that the note supported strongly the suicide by the purpose and orderliness of her mind in preparing it.

Sergeant Magnus, the photographer of the unnaturally dead *in situ*, the finder and the developer of latent figerprints, and the searcher for the almost microscopic debris shed by the human body, was already keeping Mrs Horsbrugh's body active company in her bedroom. Treading impatiently at his heels, Twite had arrived in much the condition and frame of mind that Rogers had imagined he would, and he joined him in his preliminary contemplation of the body.

Twite's heavy-breathing bulk was clothed in a pale-blue linen suit which he had patently put on over his pyjamas, the jacket serving him as a navy-blue open-neck shirt. Grunting as he squatted on his fat haunches with the body of Mrs Horsbrugh before him, he took a cigarette from his black bag of tools and lit it, kept it between his lips and frowned his evaluation of what he was seeing. During it, he fingered and pressed at different areas of the face and throat, grunting audibly and clicking his tongue in between what he was saying.

'You've got a classic case of self-hanging here, old George,' he said, his cigarette jerking and dropping ash as he spoke. 'If you're anticipating murder, I think you're going to be disappointed. Here you've all the evidence and symptoms of a death by self-suspension; and that apart from the ligature mark' – he smiled at his coming friendly witticism – 'which even the generally retarded constabulary couldn't miss. Her face is pallid, her lips bluish in colour; there're petechial haemorrhages in and congestion of the conjunctivae – eyeballs and associated tissue to you – and some saliva from the mouth. This can be a slower death than one sought by a full body suspension.'

He shook his head, deploring it all. 'Poor lady. Any act of partial suspension shows a fine old determination to end one's life. If you are silly enough to do it, you enter a coma, or even a semicoma, effected by pressures on the blood vessels in the neck, resulting in the stoppage or partial stoppage of blood to the brain. When that happened to her' – he indicated the body by wagging his diminishing cigarette at it – 'it would allow asphyxiation to get on with its work of killing her.' He looked up at Rogers. 'You've smelled the booze on her?'

'Yes. There's a one-word note, too, which may or may not indicate suicide.'

'I thought you'd called me out for your usual problem in homicide, of course.' He put on an air of mock reproof.

'I never thought she'd been murdered, Wilfred,' Rogers corrected him, 'though not qualified to say so until receiving your august opinion that she was. Nevertheless, I'd be a damn sight happier if you'd consider a later analysis for something like an hypnotic drug. It'd be the only way, wouldn't it?'

Twite lifted himself from his crouching, the pained expression on his face showing it to be no easy movement. 'Is that what you think?' he queried.

Rogers shrugged. 'Who knows? It's been done before. I don't believe so in this case, but I've no wish to be proved wrong.'

'Nor do I, old George,' the pathologist muttered. 'I'll operate after I've had my bath and a breakfast. At a guess, by the way, she's been dead four or five hours. You know why she did it?'

'I imagine something to do with the Skinner chap you dealt with last evening.'

'The things some of my subjects suffer for a few minutes of transient sexual irritation,' Twite said, putting on what he thought to be a pi-face, being to Roger's knowledge an indefatigable fornicator.

'So they do,' the deadpan and equally pi detective said, knowing that Twite wouldn't believe him either. 'There surely must be other less squalid ways of trying to perpetuate our species.'

Lingard returned to the sitting-room from the tower and his second interview with Miss Coppin while Rogers was waiting impatiently for someone or whoever to do things about the apparently tardy appearance of daylight.

'A trawling of information I didn't get before,' Lingard told Rogers. 'Miss Coppin now recalls that when she first clasped young Willie to her comforting bosom, he said among the other things of which we know, "It's my fault, my fault, you know."

169

Well, so much as she remembers the sense of it. Certainly, she felt, a *mea culpa* outburst straight from the heart.'

Rogers looked thoughtful at that, manifestly fitting it in with what he already suspected. 'It could be, David,' he said. 'Though it's difficult to understand why she didn't tell you in the first place.'

Lingard flopped in a chair, much as if he'd exhausted himself in climbing up and down the tower's stairs. 'I regret to say that I'm now of the opinion that she's a very shallow woman. Further, she has, I'm sure, a touch of the doxy in her. It leaves me wondering whether, despite what she has said, she had already taken Willie into her bed. You think?'

'He's probably the type of pushy well-hung youth some women like to sharpen their teeth on,' Rogers observed. 'I don't at the moment attach too much importance to it and it'd have done neither of them much harm anyway.' He was staring out of one of the windows into the greyness of the coming daylight. 'Wilfred's been and done his pre-PM examination of Mrs Horsbrugh and he agrees for the moment that it's suicide.'

'Was there ever any doubt?' the elegant Lingard murmured, getting no answer from his deeply thinking senior.

Rogers, turning his attention back to Lingard whom he hadn't heard, said, 'That contrition business of hers throws a different light on how far she's likely to have been concerned in the disappearance of her husband and Skinner's death. And,' tentatively, 'probably as much sinning as being sinned against. You don't write down that word just before you put your dog out of the room and hang yourself in the wardrobe unless it's meant to be taken seriously.'

'So it needs an entirely fresh approach,' Lingard pointed out.

'It's been made, David. I think that any assumption that Colonel Horsbrugh is dead is a right one and, that being accepted, she's concerned in his death. Which means that she's almost certainly been lying to me. In fact, she told me that we all lie to a certain extent and that has to be accepted.' He frowned his sudden irritation. 'Which might mean also that the poor chap wasn't *non-compos* at all; nor need he have been the tree-worshipping, wife-threatening and homicidal husband she made him out to be. Which again, remembering that Sloane

170

made those accusations to me, could make him a liar, too. It's the how of it that I'm trying to fathom, for I think – only think, mind you – that I've come up with a likely motive, though perhaps we'll never know for sure.'

He chewed on the stem of his pipe-gone-cold, staring out of the window again at the now fish-silver cloudless sky. 'Accepting that the colonel *is* dead and has been murdered, what do you think of our applying the gospel of *modus operandi* to both the shootings and to him and your friend Skinner, and giving it a bash?'

'It's a thought and a trifle better than nothing,' Lingard answered him, 'though don't forget that the colonel's car is still in the safe-keeping of his garage.'

'I don't think that Skinner or his car were meant to be found,' Rogers said flatly. 'That they were had to be unexpected and certainly unwanted.'

Lingard stood from his chair. 'You want me to confirm it?' he asked. 'I'll sort out a search party.'

Rogers shook his head. 'I started it, David, and I'll finish it. I'd like you to stay here and finalize things, get Mrs Horsbrugh off to the mortuary and be my eyes and ears while Wilfred's chopping the poor lady up. I've also a feeling that Sloane could return here, though don't ask me why he should.'

'And the motive to which you dare not put a name?' Lingard asked flippantly, paraphrasing Oscar Wilde.

Rogers told him, including his examination of the contents of the handbag while realizing anyway that his second-in-command must have already guessed at it, as indeed he had. 'If you say it as we now know it to be, it doesn't sound so risibly perverse,' he finished. 'At least, it doesn't to me.'

'Though bad enough.' Lingard's face creased in a proper distaste.

'But not so repugnant an activity as I had at first thought. And not a provable criminal offence either.'

None of which meant, in the bodily absence from the investigation of Mrs Horsbrugh, that Rogers could prove any part of what he surely knew the truth to be.

24

With the now risen sun stabbing the brightness in his eyes, Rogers was being driven by the so damned attractive Millier over the hilly route that lay between Abbotsburn and Thurnholme Bay. Being in the passenger seat and in too near proximity to her for his peace of mind, Rogers was uneasily conscious of the heady scent she had only recently put on, of her growing warmth towards him, of a touch of familiarity, though nothing of this had been expressed in words. He knew it flattered him and he didn't want it. Nor had it been provoked by anything of his doing, his *savoir-faire* still bruised from his earlier performance as a sleep-sodden cretin hiding himself behind a crumpled shirt. Too, in the growing brilliance of the sunshine, he was becoming aware of his unshaven chin and jowls and generally much-used early morning appearance.

This display of unspoken affection, coming from a woman he was seeing now in profile from the corner of one eye, must, he thought, be fired only by his rank, as might an affair between a managing director and his personal secretary. Admittedly, it could do things to his breathing were he to let it; certainly a word or two, a relaxing of his *gravitas*, and he would be lost, recognizing well his weakness for very slim small-breasted women, preferably with a streak of proper feminine arrogance in them; which, he thought, Millier might not have.

Allowing for a later rush of blood through his system tempting a tasting of her professionally dangerous sexuality, he had, in between the few trite remarks about the day's coming heat and the criminal recklessness of other car drivers during the short journey, decided, subject to a change of mind, that he wanted an association with her as little as he wanted to suffer an attack of epizootic lymphangitis, the only animal disease he could recall from his training school days.

He put his admittedly pusillanimous thoughts into hold, switching to being back-on-the-job Detective Superintendent

Rogers as they descended the steep hill into Thurnholme, traversing its relatively unbusy streets smelling of frying bacon and of the fetid miasma given off by the estuary's mud recently exposed by an ebbing tide.

With the car being pulled up against the town quay, satisfactorily uncrowded of nothing-to-do holidaymakers, Rogers unloaded himself with what he hoped was a young male's litheness and not the lesser agility of a middle-aged man of forty-two. Metaphorically putting on a hair shirt, he thanked Millier and told her that driving him was no job for an officer of her rank and experience and that she could now return to Abbotsburn and arrange for a CID car and a DC driver to be put at his disposal. He would have been an insensitive fool not to recognize the puzzled hurt that showed on her face. It did, in fact, make him feel one nevertheless.

Sergeant Lauder and his two men – one of whom was the hissing, knuckle-cracking PC Potter – were waiting for him and he briefed them on the proposed search of Spye Head beach for the body of an elderly male who, if found, could be the missing Colonel Horsbrugh. 'A probably wild guess,' he finished cautiously, covering himself against failure.

The police inflatable was, on the ebbing tide, moored lower down the almost corroded-to-frailty ladder than it had been in Rogers's previous climb down to it. As the boat headed out along the coast, the choppy sea made it dip and sway in sick-making motions with Rogers grateful that he hadn't yet had his breakfast.

With the Spye Head cliff face towering monstrously above them, Rogers, Lauder and Potter had to jump from the capriciously heaving inflatable on to any chance adjacent rock flat enough and free enough of slippery algae to make the beach. Rogers just did, wondering as he scrambled with jarred ankles and scraped shoes to relative safety why in the hell he felt persuaded at so many different times to leave his soft-padded executive chair for such masochistically uncomfortable occasions as this.

The beach, narrow as a dual carriageway and not much longer than a couple of hundred yards, was a chaotic nightmare of fallen and embedded limestone boulders ranging from those of the size of a car to those which could be held in a man's two hands. The rocks within the watery reach of rising tides were green from the growth of algae and seaweeds, the naked others already beginning to give off ripples of reflected heat. In the canyons and craters formed by the larger rocks, and there were many of them, were small pools left by receding tides, tiny green worlds of bladdery seaweeds and anemones, populated by pea-sized crabs and fiercely clinging limpets.

Rogers, leaving the PC in the wet-suit to fend from the rocks the tethered but restlessly mobile inflatable, directed Lauder and Potter to each search separately a half of the beach while he supervised the operation from the nearly level top of the huge lump of limestone on which he chose to stand.

Standing so with the sun beating on his head and shoulders, watching the sergeant and PC scrambling over and through the jumble of boulders, he could appreciate that it was unlikely that there would be any landing on this beach other than as flotsam and jetsam, from dire necessity or – his mind harked back to the two Oxford brothers he would not now forget – for the smuggling in and concealment of narcotic drugs. Even in friendly sunlight it was starkly forbidding viewed from off shore; the water running deep and made dangerously turbulent up to its very edge by submerged rocks. Too, the monstrous cliff overhanging the beach looked, and was, ever ready to shed more boulders from its face. Rogers, his mind put back into idling, thought it the most unpleasant and uncomfortable piece of landscape he had yet seen, a suitable place to reflect on the impermanence of one's life. Or, more interestingly, to consider the same of others' lives.

Filling and lighting his fractious pipe – he had already decided on dumping it for another on some convenient occasion – he was realizing that the rock on which he perched was becoming painfully warm through the soles of his shoes when Sergeant Lauder, seventy yards or so distant, hailed him, waving an arm and indicating that whatever it was he had found was in front of him. Rogers, feeling uncharacteristically infallible, moved towards him, his ankles giving him hell.

Standing at Lauder's side, sharing the same slab of rock, he took in the broken body wedged between two boulders below the level of their feet. Rogers had no doubts that they had found the so-called Lieutenant-Colonel Henry Fraser Horsbrugh but, more truly, the late Captain Horsbrugh HF, of the Prince Nicholas's Own Gurkha Rifles. The poor old bugger, he said in his mind, giving him a policeman's benediction.

Having been dropped from a height of four hundred feet or more, the body had sustained such a demolition of bloodied and mangled tissue and bone that no normal man, even in his wildest nightmares, would wish to see it twice. It lay on what was possibly its back with one leg forced into the crevice formed by the juxtaposition of the two boulders between which it had fallen and to which the tides and fish had had obvious access. This horror of a body was held together only by a deeply stained blue check lightweight jacket, what had been a blue tropical shirt, a pair of once white trousers and the only grey leather shoe visible on a socked foot. With a pathetic sort of jauntiness, a turquoise-blue silk handkerchief had remained displayed in the breast pocket of the jacket.

What Rogers was looking at had been a man of sinewy build with grey hair and a darker bristling military moustache. He appeared at a guess to be from about sixty to sixty-five years of age. What flesh had not been scraped or eaten from his face, or was in the early stages of decomposition, was creased and strongly suntanned. In scrutinizing the head, he saw a thin black cord looped beneath the collar of the shirt and disappearing in the shirt's breast pocket. Hiding his revulsion from the touching of it and holding his breath against the sickly smell of putrefaction, he reached down, pulling on the cord and withdrawing a splintered monocle.

'Meet Colonel Horsbrugh, sergeant,' he said to Lauder. 'He's been blamed for a lot of things for which I'm quite certain he's not responsible.'

'But he's something to do with the man Skinner we fished out yesterday?' Lauder wanted to know.

'That's about it. I wouldn't be a bit surprised were they to be now arguing about how and why it happened to them.' He lifted a leg, balancing like a black-plumaged stork, and tapped his pipe against the heel of his shoe to empty it of ashes. 'Put

Potter – he's still searching up at the far end – on guarding the body,'he said, 'and you take me back to the quayside.'

He had decided with the confidence of somebody already proved right in one respect that Horsbrugh had been dead for at least three days, his disposal over the cliff certainly predating Skinner's. And, as certainly, he had been already dead when the shots had been fired at his wife and stepson. 'Silly man, Rogers,' he muttered to himself as he made his way back over the rocks, feeling half-way to being seven feet tall and fireproof with it, sure now that he was going to be, in this case at least, one of life's winners. 'You should have seen what was being waved in front of your idiot face right from day one.'

25

Returning from Thurnholme Bay and entering the Head-quarters' building, Rogers was intercepted by the duty chief inspector. Lingard had, it appeared, telephoned in only twenty minutes earlier, leaving a message for Rogers who had not then returned. The message was to the effect that Sloane had telephoned Tower House a few minutes before Lingard's own call and asked to speak to Rogers. On being told that Rogers was not then available, Sloane had said that he wanted a meeting with the superintendent later that day. Lingard, who had been disconnected by Sloane, said that he was going immediately to Thurnholme Bay to find Rogers and to return to Headquarters were he unsuccessful.

Rogers, being only slightly surprised at the unexpected turn of events, said that when it happened that his whereabouts were in doubt he would follow established custom by sitting unmoving on his backside somewhere – in this case, his office – until he was found.

At his desk and in his chair, grateful for once for its foam-stuffed comfort and for the electric fan that whirled a mixture of lukewarm air and his own exhaled tobacco smoke at him, he telephoned Twite at his bachelor flat where he was breakfasting, telling him of the finding of Colonel Horsbrugh's body. There was, he said with an intent to goad the pathologist into early action, no doubt at all that Horsburgh had been murdered, though in view of the broken condition and decomposition of the body he thought that the determining of how death was caused might prove almost impossible. Moreover, he, Rogers, would be eternally grateful were he to use his scalpels on the husband before – and that implied more or less straight away – starting on the examination of his wife.

He was writing up his notes on the finding of the colonel's body and reminding himself that he must have the intimidatingly breasted Primrose Booker told of it, preferably not by one of the younger impressionable male officers, when there was a token knock on his door and Lingard entered.

' 'Pon my word, George,' he said, 'you're a difficult man to keep up with. You've been given the message?'

'The bare bones of it, I imagine?' Rogers flapped his hand at the visitors' chair. 'Sit, you're beginning to look bushed. You know about Horsbrugh?'

Lingard folded himself elegantly on the hard-seated chair, trying not to look too bushed. 'Lauder told me. It was as we'd thought, wasn't it?' he said nonchalantly as if it wasn't anything much to scream about. 'And now I believe young Willie's offering to do some coughing.'

'I would hope so.' Rogers had been watching his second-in-command doing his elaborate snuff-taking routine as he talked, adding the scent of it to the air in the room. 'Tell me something that'll shoot a quart or two of adrenalin into my system.'

And in the doing thereof he shall deliver me up to be slain, Lingard misquoted, necessarily to himself. Aloud, he said, 'Luckily I had to answer this call myself after you'd whisked Inspector Millier away with you. Just after eight, so he was up on his feet and able to use a telephone kiosk or a payphone bright and early. He hadn't said who he was, just that he wanted to speak to you, though I recognized his voice of course. He sounded peculiar, as if he were still under stress, which I suppose he had to be. You know? The sort where the breathing chokes up the words which are anyway having difficulty in coming out. I told him that you weren't about and that it might be helpful if he said what it was he wanted. Nothing much there, I'm afraid. He said no, it was you he wanted to speak to about his mother, and only then to his mother to whom he seemed to want to explain something, but which he never did. You comprehend, George? He appeared to me to be slipping a cog or two and every time he mentioned his mother you could tell it was tearing strips from him. In between all this he was doing some quiet blubbing.' He grimaced. 'Most affecting, I felt.'

Lingard had put aside his flippancy in deference, it appeared, to Sloane's distress. 'Dammit, George, that was genuine, if nothing else. I said to him, message understood, old son, so where do we go from here? He said I should tell you to be where you'd met him before at ten tonight. You were to come alone and if you didn't there would be no meeting. Neither then nor ever. He kept repeating that there was to be nobody with you, and that he'd know if there was.'

He frowned. 'I was trying to keep him talking in the hope that some idle sod would come into the room and I could then think of a way of having the call traced, but nobody did and he disconnected from me in mid-drivel.' Lingard eyed Rogers enquiringly. 'He was meaning the Gibbet, wasn't he, when he said it was where you'd met him before?'

'It has to be,' Rogers agreed. 'You said he was calling from a kiosk or payphone. I'm sure there couldn't have been anything there that'd help.'

'There wasn't. I heard cars and suchlike passing, but nothing to identify where he was.' He noticed Rogers looking pleased with that. 'You're going, are you?'

'Well, naturally.' Rogers busied himself scraping carbon from the blackened bowl of his pipe.

'You'd want me to look after you, wouldn't you? He might have the gun with him and I'd hate the thought of you having your respected balls shot off in the heat of the moment.'

'I appreciate your concern, David,' Rogers said drily, 'but if he's got the gun I want him to bring it with him. Nor do I believe I'd be too likely a target. He did say I was to be on my own and I don't want to risk his shying off, for it's certain that he'll be watching my approach.' He shook his head. 'Think

178

about it. We've no evidence against him worth a damn, and I'll need him to do some talking to get any.' He looked straight at Lingard with his eyebrows down. 'Between the two of us and specifically forgetting the Chief Constable for a moment, I don't want too much of a search laid on. Sloane being found and arrested beforehand will only result in resentment because I didn't meet him, and a tight-shut mouth. At the moment he seems to want a shoulder to weep on, and who am I to deny it to him? If it involves him in making an admission, then so be it. If it doesn't, then I'll have to knock him off without it and do it keeping my fingers crossed.'

'He's no fool, George,' Lingard warned him.

'Neither am I,' Rogers growled, 'so leave it be. I want you to attend on Wilfred who'll be doing both post-mortems this morning. After I've seen the Chief Constable and made obeisances to keep him off my back, I hope to be eating a definitely unhealthy breakfast of bacon, sausages, kidney, eggs, fried potato cakes and anything else I can think of just before going to my billet and trying to get some sleep in. If you're back on your feet by eight-thirty this evening, call me and give me the results of both the examinations.'

With Lingard gone, Rogers picked up his internal telephone receiver and dialled the Chief Constable's secretary with a request to see him. Despite his having at the time dismissed them, he still had in his mind a niggling recall of Lingard's words of caution about Sloane's possible possession of the missing target pistol.

26

The moon, floating high over the Gibbet and painting the landscape a pallid blue, threw the darkness of concealing shadow over the figure of Rogers standing motionless against the thick trunk of a sleeping beech tree at the rear of the small clearing. He was, apart from the whites of his eyes in the dimness of his face and the points of his white shirt collar, an

179

amorphous blackness merging into invisibility. Arriving there by intent at nine o'clock and having searched like a black ghost the Gibbet's wooded area and the road below it, he took up station within the shadow of the largest and nearest tree to what must, he thought, be for ever blackly cursed ground.

In between the soft whisperings of leaves, he could hear the movements of small animals and roosting birds, the occasional creaking of what he hoped were moving branches. From the road below he was, at irregular intervals, briefly and fitfully illuminated by the headlights of cars passing where he had parked his own car.

Before leaving his apartment, he had put a miniaturized tape recorder in his jacket pocket, its matchhead-sized microphone poking its nose out from behind the lapel buttonhole. Earlier, he had been called by Lingard and told that Horsbrugh – who had been shudderingly identified by Miss Coppin – had undoubtedly been strangled from behind by his own necktie and had been dead for several hours before being thrown over Spye Head. Mrs Horsbrugh's death had been confirmed as from a self-inflicted hanging, with no grounds for suspecting her of having been drugged to insensibility beforehand.

In the waiting – he had wrongly expected that Sloane might have anticipated the meeting by arriving early and concealing himself there – he had seen for the first time a small rusted metal plate set on a low stone plinth. Using the narrow light from his pencil-shaped torch and feeling some of its indecipher-abilities with his fingertips, he read, *This Tablet marks the Site of the notorious Morte Hill Gibbet on which the Bodies of 114 Malefactors suffered the cruel ignominy of exposure after Execution; the last to Suffer such being Jas. Raggett, aet 20 yrs and 5 mnths, Counterfeiter, on a day in February 1713. Res judicata. A.C.C. 1893.*

It added little to lighten the tedium of Rogers's waiting, but did use up some of its time. Time, in comfortless fact, that was filled with an unusual sense of isolation in which he thought he could sense some of the past torments of long dead men and women pressing in on him.

By ten o'clock he was beginning to drop the notion that he was being shone on by a benign hunter's moon, his vertebrae suffering badly from his long standing, his nervous system from

180

its hour-long deprivation of nicotine. Ten minutes later, when he was convincing himself that he had been fooled, he heard the faint sounds of trodden-on leaves, moved not by the tiny nocturnal inhabitants of the thickets about him, but by the cautious placing of approaching human feet.

'I'm here,' he called out in an undertone, moving to the side of the tree-trunk away from the sound nearing him.

After a half-minute's waiting silence, the shadow that was Sloane emerged from the deeper shadow of the trees, looking apprehensively around the moonlit clearing. He was wearing a dark-striped jacket with grey trousers, his hair disordered and his face pale. His right hand was concealed beneath the skirt of his jacket, Rogers guessing that it held his stepfather's pistol. 'I can't see you,' he called out, his head swivelling from side to side.

'I'm alone and I'm coming out,' Rogers said, switching on the tape recorder in his pocket and stepping out into the moonlight with all fingers crossed and praying that he hadn't misjudged Sloane's potential for shooting at worried policemen. Even a dozen or so yards away from the youth he was able to see in his features the stress remarked on by Lingard. 'You wanted to speak to me,' he said, his voice neutral. 'I assume about the death of your mother?'

'Is there anybody with you?' There was a slurring in the words as his eyes traversed the shadowed area behind Rogers.

The obviously nerve-racked youth before him was not the same over-confident young bastard Rogers had known a few short hours ago. There was much about him that suggested a not too successful covering up of the extreme mental anguish and shock attendant on bereavement.

'I've been here since nine o'clock and you've probably been watching me.' Rogers was authoritative, needing to take the initiative. 'When I say that I'm on my own I expect you to believe it. And you'd feel a lot more comfortable if you took your hand out from under your jacket.' He didn't add, 'And so would I,' but that was what he meant.

Sloane slowly withdrew his hand, his eyes dark and unreadable in his colourless face and fixed on Rogers. The long-barrelled pistol he held pointing to the ground glimmered in the moonlight. 'I brought it with me in case you'd try to arrest me,' he said, having difficulty in controlling his mouth. 'I honestly won't use it unless I have to. I've nothing against you, but why should I trust you?' He wagged the pistol at the detective. 'Sit down where you are, please.'

Rogers lowered himself on to the rough grass, his gaze never leaving Sloane who was doing the same thing while laying the pistol to one side. Settled, though not too comfortably, and intending to ignore the menace of the pistol until its threat became a reality, Rogers said, 'To repeat. I understand from Chief Inspector Lingard that you wish to speak to me about your mother. In relation to yourself, naturally,' he added, making that a significance.

There was clearly an inner struggle going on behind the unhappy face with its deeply shadowed eye sockets and, though Rogers knew that pity for him could never be justified, it was in him to feel a mite of sorrow for his wretchedness. 'You know, don't you,' Sloane said. It was a statement of fact, not a question.

'Your having Colonel Horsbrugh's pistol with you says it all,' Rogers pointed out, deciding to plunge in at the deep end. 'Apart from a questionable sexual association to which we shall come, it does prove that you and your mother were together involved in the murder of your stepfather and Daniel Skinner. Which, I take it, is the reason for your being here.'

'Not murder . . . no. I want you to keep her out of it. I made her do what she did.' His voice choked. 'Her memory . . . you mustn't dirty it because she doesn't deserve that.' There were tears in his eyes that glittered in the moonlight. 'Will you?'

'I'll try, though I can make no promises.' Rogers knew he could be walking in a legal minefield. 'What you now feel you may say in answer to my questions is not contingent on any promise you might think I've made. You understand that?'

'Yes.'

'Good. Now, do you want to tell me about you and your mother? I do know, incidentally, that you were an adopted child.'

Sloane had crossed his legs, sitting Japanese fashion and not looking at the detective, but at the ground in front of him. There

182

had been a long silence before he spoke, then so quietly that the words only just reached Rogers. 'What we did was something I couldn't handle; something mother couldn't either. After my father's death, she had a nervous breakdown, a very bad time. I was sent home from school to be with her, which was the form on those occasions. I was still a boy of fifteen to her and one whom she hadn't seen all that often, so she treated me like one. We were a comfort to each other, for I'd loved my father too. One night I heard her crying in her bedroom and I went into her to comfort her. Into her bed that is and we slept together as we had done occasionally when I was much younger. What happened was nothing that she did or encouraged me to do, but I don't think she realized that I was nearly sixteen and had grown away from being a boy. We woke up clinging together and it happened then because we loved each other so much.'

Sloane paused, his breathing sounding harsh in the quiet of the clearing. 'It happened again before I returned to school . . . mother knew that I loved her and she couldn't bear to stop me, though she did try. I'm sorry now that I took advantage of her sadness and loneliness, for it wouldn't have happened but for that.'

Rogers, impelled to visualize her as he himself had first seen her, could imagine how a too close encounter with her sensuality might fever the new-found lusts of an adolescent. 'It didn't end there though, did it?' he asked, his voice an accusation, for Sloane seemed to have sunk deep into thought.

When he jerked himself to an awareness of what Rogers had said, he mumbled, 'No, it didn't. I'm sorry it didn't because now I know that she suffered for what I'd done to her. While I was at school I dreamed nightmares and worse about God's punishment and of going to hell for what we'd done, and about mother going with the men she knew and what I thought . . .' He shook his head violently. 'I only lived for between terms and being with her, though inside I knew it was wrong. I couldn't have done it had she been my proper mother; I'm sure I wouldn't have wanted to. And though in the beginning she did try and stop me, and treated me like the boy she thought I was, I really made her let me love her. That was how it was each time I came home.' He was silent for several moments, breathing deeply. 'Then she wrote to me at school . . . telling me that she was going to marry the man she called Colonel Horsbrugh.'

Emotion was moving Sloane to brimming tears and he beat at his thighs with his fists as he fought to take control of himself. 'The thought of her going with an old man like him was torture . . . that was something else I couldn't handle. Yet I still made her go with me when she didn't wish to, because I'd threaten – which I regret – to tell him honestly what the situation was and that we didn't want or need him either in the house or the business. I know she didn't like him, that she'd made a mistake in marrying him . . . I know that she married him to have a reason for not loving me. That didn't work ever, as I knew it wouldn't, for I was crazy enough to want her just the same, even though I tried not to by going out with girls.'

Rogers was watching him with unconcealed disgust. He was, he thought, a bloody distasteful wet and somebody who, in his book, had put himself beyond the familiarity of being addressed as Willie. 'You've made your point,' he said, 'so was it your jealousy that made you kill the colonel?'

It was evident from Sloane's reaction that he hadn't hit the mark, and he rethought his question. 'No?' he corrected himself. 'Then you killed him because he caught you making love to your mother, yes?'

Sloane reached to his side and picked up the pistol – Rogers had tightened his stomach muscles at that – then rested it with the long barrel across his thighs. As he squatted there, the moonlight and shadow gave him a seeming bulkiness and he appeared, despite the occasional weeping and emotional instability, adult and formidable in what Rogers feared to be a change of mood.

His voice was stronger, more wary, when he answered. 'He came back to the house early in the evening when he wasn't expected and looked for mother in the Lodge.' He seemed to be chewing on his teeth for long moments. 'That was an occasion when we were . . . well, together. I tried to explain to him that she wasn't properly my mother, but he wouldn't listen . . . he was angry . . . losing control of himself and shouting terrible things at me . . . calling mother filthy names . . . pushing me away and hitting her while she was on the bed. It was dreadful. I tried to stop him . . . catching hold of his shirt collar to pull him away from mother who was screaming and crying . . . not hitting him . . . not attempting to, and then he fell down. I thought he had fainted and while I was trying to bring him round from it, mother ran back to the house and shut herself in her bedroom.'

Rogers, judging him a liar in part, said, 'Even accepting from what you say that the colonel was unaware of your real relationship with your mother, it wouldn't have made much difference under the circumstances, would it? Though how he did see it, it was criminal incest of the worst kind.' While he had talked his right hand resting at his side had found and held on to a small rock. It was something, he thought, though not so bloody much since he hadn't thrown a stone or some such at anyone since he'd been a whey-faced fourth-former with mega-acne.

'He didn't know. Why should he? It wasn't any concern of his or anybody else's.' Sloane's voice suggested an annoyance at the question.

'Why indeed,' Rogers said, trying to keep sarcasm out of his words. 'It would be only a question of degree anyway. You say you thought the colonel had fainted?'

'I did. I really did. I'd no reason to think otherwise, though when I thought of his coming round I was frightened, knowing that he would probably kill me and mother. So I left him on the floor and after locking the door went over to the house and joined mother. We talked about it and agreed that we'd go away from there for a while until perhaps he would go back to Thurnholme where he belonged. Mother had already started to pack her suitcases and when we hadn't heard anything of him I crept down to the Lodge and looked through the bedroom window. He was still on the floor where I'd left him to recover, but with his face a quite awful colour and I guessed that he had died from heart failure in the struggle we'd had.'

He paused, chewing on his teeth again. 'It was the most horrifying thing I'd ever done, but I went back in . . . touched him and felt his pulse . . . knowing for certain then that he was

dead. I hadn't meant to do anything that would mean his death
. . . it really was a pure accident.'

Rogers had labelled much of it as lies again, fixing him firmly
with his eyes and bearing down on him. He said coldly, 'I'm
telling you now that we recovered his body from below Spye
Head this morning. He'd apparently been strangled from
behind by using his tie as a ligature.' He paused. 'If you thought
his death had been from natural causes, why the pressing need
to throw his body over a cliff?'

Sloane had winced at that, briefly holding a hand over his
eyes, holding back on answering. When he did his voice was
broken. 'I didn't know,' he groaned. 'I honestly didn't know. It
was like I said . . . pulling on his shirt collar to stop him hitting
mother. I hadn't expected him to be dead and I couldn't think
of what to do with him. So I took him up there and let him fall
over. It seemed at the time to be the only thing I could do.'

'And the following day when we met here, when he was
already dead, you told me he was trying to kill your mother;
had tried to on a couple of occasions. That had to be with her
connivance, hadn't it? I mean, she knew what you'd done and
was a party to your lying about it.'

'No! Sloane's head had jerked as if in direct confrontation. 'I
made her. I really did make her. She didn't know how to refuse
me. I told her that if anything about it became known I would
be in terrible trouble; expelled from school, sent to prison . . .'

'There was active co-operation,' Rogers said sternly. 'She
used her husband's pistol to fake an attack on herself while you
were with me in order that he should be suspected of attempting to murder her and was, by inference, still alive.'

While Sloane shook his head blindly and remained unprom-
isingly silent, the detective said, 'As you wish. You aren't in
any case obliged to answer my questions, though if you do
they'll be taken down, on this occasion on tape, and may be
given in evidence.' Dammit, he cursed to himself. He had
deferred cautioning him for as long as he could, now having
probably shot his bolt when he'd little enough in his bag to
justify it.

Waiting in vain for some acknowledgement, he recalled an
incident that had almost escaped his reckoning. He said, 'By

bringing Colonel Horsbrugh's pistol with you tonight, you've made it obvious that it was you who went through the charade of firing three shots into your own bed. That, of course, was to divert any suspicion from yourself to either the colonel or to Skinner when it became known that he was missing. Are you accepting that?' His necessary mention of the weapon had presented him with a frisson of unwonted foreboding.

After glancing briefly at the pistol as if reminded of it, Sloane clamped shut his mouth.

Rogers shrugged. 'So be it,' he growled. 'Let's come to Skinner's killing, shall we? Are you saying that was an accident, too?' He could see from the corner of his eye the saffron street lights of Abbotsburn. A long two miles away downhill from the dark pit of revealed human cruelty and suffering, they had lost much of their aura of civilized safety.

'I don't know what you mean.'

'I think you should reconsider that answer. I know how and where he died and that it's an odds-on certainty that your mother brought you back from Spye Head after you'd driven Skinner's car over the cliff. Am I to be left with that? To have it proved against you both?'

With a now uncommunicative and hostile-seeming Sloane who had patently withdrawn his co-operation, Rogers was left only with Sloane's need to protect his mother. To use her he had, to some extent, to denigrate her in his questioning, and that was little to his taste.

'The motive for Skinner's killing involved your mother even before she drove you back from Spye Head,' Rogers said, hazarding his theory of what had happened. 'I'm going to draw you a picture of what happened on a late evening some three months back. You and your mother were in the bedroom of the Lodge, probably before the colonel had become suspicious of what had been going on in there, and what appeared to be going on in there then.' Sloane had stiffened at that, a wary look in his face. 'Skinner, coming through the house gate and passing the Lodge, heard a woman's voice in there and thought mistakenly that you were making love to his girlfriend Angela. I needn't remind you of the unpleasantness with Skinner which arose from that and of your protests to him that what he had

187

heard had been a radio play you were listening to. He had, let's face it,' Rogers said, deliberately brutal, 'heard a mother fornicating with her son. I'm sure, as you apparently were, that there was an ever-present danger that Skinner would eventually realize that it was she he had heard, instead of his wrongly suspected Angela.'

Rogers left his words hanging for Sloane to think about, a dark cloud in the night air. He had seen his hand edging with a snail's slowness towards the pistol and thought that his suddenly fast-beating heart must surely be echoing its thudding around the clearing. 'I'm going to smoke my pipe,' he said from a dryish mouth, risking that any unexpected movement on his part might be the catalyst to having – as Lingard had crudely put it – his respected balls shot off. Releasing his grip on the rock, he filled and lit his pipe, doing it carefully and slowly with Sloane watching him closely, his hand now held motionless within reaching distance of the pistol.

While his pipe was making up its mind whether to live or die and with his rock back in his hand, Rogers said through the puffs of smoke, 'When you realized that Skinner had been interviewed by us and might later be led into being talkative, you would inevitably begin to worry that he could remark on what he might now think to be the true identity of the woman he had heard in your bedroom. Even a wild guess by Skinner would have been pretty damning for your mother, wouldn't it? That's something I'd like you to think over seriously for a few moments before I tell you more.'

He waited, his backside numbed from sitting on the hard ground, tapping his teeth with the stem of his pipe while he leaned on Sloane with the hardness of his will. When he saw that it was having no discernible effect on what he saw as a continued agonizing over a dead mother, he said, 'From the bloodstains I found on your hard-standing and the findings of the post-mortem examination on Skinner's body, it's evident that you banged him on the head there, killing him to stop him from ever realizing that it was his employer he'd heard in that discreditable situation with her son.' Speak no ill of the dead, he told himself, unless you're a not-all-that-certain detective superintendent trying to bring a cold-blooded murderer to book.

Sloane had appeared to be looking fixedly at the trees on the opposite side of the clearing and was manifestly talking to himself. It irritated Rogers and, when he wasn't answered, he rasped at him, 'Are you listening? Aren't you going to say something about that?'

Closing his mouth, Sloane gave a quick shake of his head, his eyes now on Rogers and showing an aroused hostility.

Rogers, not in the business of extending friendly words towards murderers, particularly armed murderers, knew from Sloane's demeanour, his response to the accusations, that his theorizing of what had happened was not too far from the truth. 'I assume now,'he continued, his voice cold and forbidding, 'that in the hour between the security visits by the PC looking after you, you drove Skinner in his own car to Spye Head, planted Colonel Horsbrugh's wallet and two cartridge cases in the car to throw suspicion on him should he ever be found, and then ran him and his car over the cliff. Before this, there had been the problem of your travelling the twelve miles back to the house, once having disposed of Skinner and the car. So, to your mother. She followed you in her car, which she used in returning you. That, of course, made her an accomplice to a particularly contemptible murder.' He thought it might be a bit over the top if he added that it had been even more contemptible because the yellow-haired good-looking Skinner had almost certainly once been her lover.

When Sloane finally spoke, it was Rogers's opinion that he had grown considerably in maturity, if not for the better or quite enough, in the past forty-five minutes. 'You don't have to bring mother in for this or for anything else,' he said. 'It's the truth that I walked back part of the way and hitched a lift for the rest. Mother didn't even know I'd left the house.'

'Some would say that's reasonable,' Rogers told him, though he neither thought so nor believed what he had said. As it stood, it was a disappointingly ambiguous admission. 'It leaves you having killed Skinner and disposed of his body on your own, does it?'

The silence attending on his waiting for the answer was

broken by the sound of a car passing below them, its sweeping headlight beams momentarily illuminating Sloane in hard-edged relief. 'Yes,' he finally said. 'It makes no difference to me now. My mother was in no way concerned, nor did she know anything about it. Is that what you wanted?' His voice broke again as though he were losing control of it and his hand moved closer to the pistol at his side. 'You don't understand what I'm doing here, do you?' His voice rose. 'I'd always promised mother . . . there isn't any other way.'

'No other way?' Rogers echoed blankly, wondering what the hell he was getting at and why he was staring at him with unsettling wildness in his eyes.

With his attention fixed hypnotically on Sloane, who was clearly losing touch with reality, Rogers guessed that he could be showing symptoms of paranoia. His mother's last words to the detective had warned him in his investigation to consider a degree of mental instability and he had assumed she had been referring to her husband. Now he thought not, and this added to his uneasiness.

Admitting to a degree of apprehension, though impassively faced about it and clutching hard at the rock he held in his fist, he had seen that the hand in too close a proximity to the threat of a violent death was shaking. He felt a tightness in his throat, his mind telling him that he'd been the mother and father of bloody fools to have come here alone. Or at all.

'I agreed that what you said about your mother would probably be judged reasonable,' Rogers reminded him, watching unblinking the shaking hand now even nearer to the pistol.

Sloane's words were difficult to follow, now almost inaudible even in the silence of the clearing. 'I want your promise . . . you'll leave mother out of this . . . you have to. She never did anything . . . and I love her . . .' He wept soundlessly, staring through his tears at Rogers in his torment.

'For God's sake!' Next to a woman unburdening her tears on him, Rogers feared those of a man. Driven to it and exasperated, he said, 'I promised you I'd do what I could, but I'm not the bloody Director of Public Prosecutions or even his . . .'

His words died in him, for the pistol was already in the suddenly upstanding Sloane's hand, its muzzle aimed at Rog-

190

ers's face. Though it was held unsteadily, the uncertainty that it would ever be aimed accurately was never going to be enough for Rogers to convince himself that a bullet from it wasn't going to hit him between his eyebrows. In the two or three seconds he supposed he had left to live, he considered and then abandoned the throwing of the rock he held in his hand, told himself again that he was a bloody fool not to have listened to Lingard and, incongruously, sadly regretted that he hadn't had the resolution to have taken an obviously willing Inspector Millier back to his apartment for what would have been his last sexual fling.

Breaking into his momentary paralysis, coming to him with the clarity of what he thought were to be the last words he would listen to, he heard Sloane cry out, 'You promised! I shall know . . . mother will, too!' Then, with what seemed an inexorable creeping motion to his staring eyes, the muzzle of the pistol moved around towards Sloane's own distorted face and was, after a glimpse of glistening tongue and teeth, pushed into the darkness of his gaping mouth. As Rogers turned sideways to lift himself upright, shouting his instinctive need to prevent it, he heard the crack of the discharged cartridge, its echoes swallowed to silence by the encircling trees, and followed by the solid thump of the slowly falling body. Then there came with the quietness his own hard breathing and the thrashing of wings as a large bird took flight into the darkness.

Heaving himself upright and dropping the rock he still held, Rogers moved slowly towards the fallen body, fishing into his pocket with unsteady fingers for his tobacco pouch. Filling his stubbornly uncooperative pipe and lighting it, he gazed sombrely at the youth lying motionless on his back who had apparently gone to join the mother he had loved too much; a near incestuous love which had been so unwisely returned.

The .22 bullet, a tiny morsel of lead and lethal to the brain while causing little visible damage to tissue and bone, had successfully and neatly separated Sloane's persona from its fleshly envelope. Blood was still oozing from the mouth, from one of the nostrils and from behind the head now pillowed by the coarse grass. The eyes were still open, gazing sightlessly at a cold and indifferent moon. He had died at once and, strangely to Rogers, his face had in it an expression of undeserved tranquillity.

It wasn't in him to condemn the dead youth for loving his mother as he had, for he recognized that adolescent lust could be vividly disturbing and lead to an uncontrollable emotional turbulence. For his merciless killing of the grossly maligned Colonel Horsbrugh and the well-favoured Skinner he felt that an adequate justice had been meted out by Sloane on himself and that there need be no pity for him. His mind shied away from any contemplation of Mrs Horsbrugh, for he had learned never to sit in judgement on women, a very different species from the men they provoked with their femininity. She had been a woman whose sexual attraction had initially affected him and he, honest enough in his weaknesses, recognized that he could have stumbled headlong had she chosen to lift one of her slim fingers to indicate an interest in him.

He decided that after he had kept as much of her quasi-incestuous proclivities as he decently could from the press, tried to forget that Liz Gallagher and Inspector Millier had ever engaged his mind with thoughts of carnality, and handed over the tidying-up of the case to Lingard, he would spend a week or two at his golf club belting hell out of a quite inoffensive small white ball to get whatever it was that haunted him out of his system.